Rose and Spindle

Hayden Thorne

Published by Hayden Thorne, 2018.

Also by Hayden Thorne

Arcana Europa
Guardian Angel
The Flowers of St. Aloysius
Hell-Knights
Children of Hyacinth
The Amaranth Maze
A Murder of Crows

Curiosities
Dollhouse
Automata
Eidolon

Dolores
Ambrose
Echoes in the Glass
A Dirge for St. Monica

Ghosts and Tea
The Ghosts of St. Grimald Priory
Agnes of Haywood Hall

A Most Unearthly Rival
The Haunted Inkwell
The House of Creeping Dolls

Grotesqueries
A Castle for Rowena
The Rusted Lily
Primavera

Masks
Masks: The Original Trilogy
Curse of Arachnaman
Mimi Attacks!
Dr. Morbid's Castle of Blood
The Porcelain Carnival

Standalone
Renfred's Masquerade
Rose and Spindle
Gold in the Clouds
Helleville
Icarus in Flight
Arabesque
Banshee
Wollstone
The Glass Minstrel
Henning
The Twilight Gods
The Book of Lost Princes
The Winter Garden and Other Stories

Desmond and Garrick
The Cecilian Blue-Collar Chronicles

Watch for more at https://haydenthorne.com.

Table of Contents

"What remarkable lungs that child has!" the flame-haired Duchess observed, looking quite impressed. "He'll make a very effective commander someday."

Bawling and wailing, Hamlin was half-dragged, half-carried by his flustered and embarrassed mother up to the dais.

"Hamlin, hush! Behave yourself, or you'll give poor Roderika nightmares!"

No! No! Not the frog baby! Surely his own mother wouldn't be so cruel as to subject him to the sight of a cursed infant—much less make him pay his respects or—oh, horrors—*kiss* the repulsive creature where she lay—in the same manner that other guests had been showering her with gurgling attention. No! He wouldn't do it! He'd sooner die than be made to kiss wart-causing slime!

"No! No, no, no, no! Papa!" he cried, desperately believing that some invisible magical creature of the air would carry his pleas to his father.

"I'm warning you! Be quiet!"

Cold—his mother was so cold and cruel. Hamlin managed to kick himself off his mother's arms and fall, landing on his backside with a tight shriek, which was immediately followed by a fresh round of hysterical wailing as he felt one of his arms grabbed and his body lifted up in the most ungenteel way possible.

"That's enough! I'm ashamed of you!"

The world around him spun so quickly that Hamlin didn't feel himself stumble to a sudden halt. The angry slap against his backside barely even made him gasp and momentarily pause in his hysterics. In fact, he only wailed more loudly—or, rather, screamed more tearfully—till his throat withered dry and cracked, and his voice faded to a feeble guttural croak.

Croak. *Croak?* As in frog voice?

Frog voice!

Hamlin's horror deepened at the realization. Surely he wasn't being cursed as well! After all, his harassed mother had just complained that he was being excessively truculent and stubborn (her words, whatever those might mean), violent in his protestations against public displays of affection for the newborn princess (again, her words). And as the mortified young queen picked him up and carried him toward their hosts—indulgently smiling their welcome as kings and queens were trained to do—Hamlin clung desperately to her and peered through tear-dimmed eyes at his limbs. He held his breath.

Ah, no scales! No slime! No pond scum and muddy filth!

He wriggled his toes in his velvet shoes.

And no webbed appendages!

A surge of joy wracked Hamlin's body, though he remained paralyzed with fear at the thought of having to kiss the frog princess. He'd lost his voice now—and no less his breaths, which had been reduced to exhausting, shuddering hiccoughs. Adults also outnumbered him by far. A mad dash to the nearest door simply wouldn't do. No, not even with the advantage of his small size.

He could imagine a gaggle of satin-and-velvet vultures swooping down on him, mouths open wide to batter him with incomprehensible chatter. He could imagine the feel of bejeweled hands all clamping down on his arms before lifting him bodily up and flying him back to the accursed crib. There he'd be held down, his head fixed between genteel talons and made to bend closer to the green, bug-eyed face that stared up at him. And, oh, help, what if that loathsome beast decided to strike out at him with her insect-snatching tongue?

He felt faint. He was barely holding on to his mother now, his heart beating more and more weakly with every step closer to the dais.

His eyes swept helplessly over the sea of faces around him. He wished his father were there, but it certainly didn't help that he was the son of a king, and that king happened to be off somewhere on some ridiculous, trifling affair involving war. No, indeed—had his father been there, he'd be plucked out of this torturous situation and whisked off to safety.

Oh, no, no, no, indeed! Prince Hamlin was—ideally—not to be humiliated like this! He was not to be subjected to anything upsetting! No, unless one were hoping to feel sure, swift retribution from the king! The king *his* father, that is, for there were several kings in attendance.

"Your Majesties," the poor young queen finally said, and Hamlin felt her stop and curtsy with exquisite grace and fluidity in spite of her wriggling burden. His tense, clinging body dipped lightly with her, and he knew that he was doomed, for the frog princess's crib stood only a few steps away.

"Hamlin doesn't feel well today, I see."

"Do forgive him, Friedrich. The boy's tired from our traveling."

"There's nothing to forgive. It's all perfectly understandable, of course. Perhaps, Elfriede, it might be best to let the child forego the blessing if he's so tired."

Hamlin heard the royal hostess pipe up, "Yes, I can have one of the servants prepare a room for the poor thing. He can sleep there for as long as he wishes."

But the visiting queen thanked them profusely and insisted that her son ought not to run away from his obligations to his new friend. "Some food will bring his humor back," she added with a sheepish laugh.

"He'll have plenty, I assure you. And he's so beautiful! How old is he now?"

"Four, though I'm afraid temperamentally, he's yet to leave the crib."

Hamlin wept anew while those preposterous adults continued to exchange pleasantries. How could they? How *dare* they? Cursed princesses shouldn't deserve this much reverence from anyone. This was cruelty in its lowest, its worst form.

He wailed again, this time flinging his arms out in a desperate effort at reaching for someone—a kind, charitable soul who'd finally—*finally*—take pity on him and remove him from this dreadful situation. But the nearest onlooker stood at least fifty feet away, and he was covered from head to foot in cold metal, his large, gloved hands holding a spear, all in all looking rather doubtful as a sympathizer.

And all Hamlin could manage to glimpse through his tears were endless faces that regarded him with what appeared to be smiles of amusement—of the kind that could only be expected from terrible, heartless adults. There were also the bewildered stares from children of high birth, who clung to their parents' hands as they watched the tortured prince get forced into paying respects to a pond-beast.

"Hamlin, will you *please* stop your fussing?" his mother hissed wearily once they reached the crib. "You're embarrassing me!"

He would, if he could, voice his protests in more dignified terms than a dribbling "Nonono! Nononononono!" But desperation afforded him not much room for a more rational dialogue with his intractable parent.

"Perhaps, Elfriede, if you were to turn him over so he can see Roderika—that might help his mood," their hostess suggested.

Hamlin was pulled away from his mother's drenched shoulder and was turned, still bawling, to face the crib. He felt himself dipped toward the horrid piece of furniture, felt himself forced to look down on the tiny figure that was being startled out of its sleep by his horrific noise.

"See now, darling," Queen Elfriede half-whispered in his ear. "Princess Roderika."

He cracked a wet eye open and found a baby. A *human* baby. And it lay comfortably protected under layers of blankets, pinkish and soft and rounded and utterly helpless. He stared at the little figure in stunned silence, unable to believe his eyes.

"She's lovely, isn't she?" his mother prodded, relief evident in her voice. She lowered him further when he reached tentatively out and gently poked a finger against Roderika's cheek, earning himself a tiny whimper and a restless shifting under the blankets.

How could this be? He'd heard of her cursed past. For as long as he could remember in all his four years of life, tongues had wagged over the circumstances of her birth—of how Queen Franziska had happened upon a frog while she bathed—a frog that reassured her with prophetic words involving the birth of a daughter. And was it not true that such prophesies were really curses? His nurse had told him so.

Hamlin blinked through his tears, and he scowled blackly at the sleeping infant.

Lies! He'd been fed lies!

Hamlin grimaced, opened his mouth, and, oh, hell hath no fury, indeed. Gales of raging screeches from Hamlin tore through the entire court now. Wild, shrieking wails of betrayal and poured out in one smooth, endless, passionate flow. If Hamlin were king, he'd wreak vengeance on any and all who'd misled him with their tales of curses.

By the time he'd taken his place among the revelers once again, he was dismally exhausted, utterly short of breath, soaked in sweat and tears, and in absolute pain, the last round of frustrated spanking from his mother finally fulfilling its purpose in silencing him into submission.

And perhaps it was to his benefit that the rest of the guests seemed to find his hysterical fits quite charming, though his mother looked as if she were on the verge of dying from mortification. Red-faced and barely able to hold her head high, she expressed her apologies wherever she turned, to be soothed with low murmurs and smiles from other nobles who clearly understood her pain.

"Oh, Hamlin," she murmured as she dropped to her knees before everyone, pulling out a handkerchief to wipe his face. "I don't know what's gotten into you, but the way you behaved was appalling. Do you hear me? You're here to represent your father and your kingdom." She sighed, looking stricken. "I wish you weren't so temperamental. Honestly, I don't know where you get that from."

"I'm hungry, Mama," he replied, his voice hoarse, but his mother merely frowned at him and stood up, pulling him close to her while dabbing away at her wet shoulders with the handkerchief.

Perhaps Hamlin ought to appeal to her once she showed signs of boredom toward the proceedings, for the heavens knew how many more guests needed to present themselves to Roderika's parents. His mother was always easy to distract when bored.

More nobles and their children stepped forward in turn and paid respects to the infant princess, the tedium of the process finally soothing him till he stood beside Queen Elfriede in a state of exquisite blasé disinterest: reddened eyes swollen and idly scanning the crowd, nose stuffed and forcing him to breathe through his mouth, renewed mind now feeding itself with thoughts of expected relief coming his way in the form of toys that would be showered on him in compensation for his agony. He stuck a thumb in his mouth and sucked, awash in tired contentment.

Yes, it was good to be the prince.

His mind now fixing itself completely on the hoped-for toys, he almost missed the tall boy walking by. Wide, dark eyes flashed irritably at him as the young prince (he carried himself like a prince, anyway) marched past—pale and haughty and seemingly too old for his age. He spoke in a murmur—three simple words that could still be heard amid the jubilant celebration.

"Spoiled, soggy brat."

Chapter 2

At seven years of age, Prince Edouard felt himself a bit out of place in a celebration such as this. There were far too many adults for him to feel completely at ease, yet the object of the festivities was too infantile—literally and otherwise—for him to give it serious consideration, though he meant no offense to his new cousin.

He sauntered up to the crib while his parents conversed happily with King Friedrich and Queen Franziska, sighing as he peered inside. He regarded the sleeping princess blandly and took note of the tiny, pinched face and the wisps of gold curls that looked so weightless around her head.

"Tsk," he muttered as he reached inside and gingerly felt the silky strands between his fingers. "Yellow? Why do *all* princesses have to have yellow hair—yellow, *curly* hair?"

"Oh, isn't that lovely, Rikard?" he heard his mother say. "Edouard's such an attentive boy. And he doesn't need to be told twice to do something." Indulgent pride dripped from her words, while his father grunted his agreement, and their hosts echoed Queen Clarimond's praise with glowing terms that he couldn't comprehend (though he was quite sure that they were excessively flattering—he recognized the tone they used anywhere).

Edouard felt all admiring eyes on him, and his boredom lifted for the moment. They seemed to be very pleased with the fact that he'd gone to see his cousin without waiting for another urging from them, so he thought to indulge them and played it up. What did he have to lose, after all? Besides, it was a profitable enough way of spending the next few tedious minutes.

He gurgled and made faces at Roderika in spite of the fact that she slept throughout his performance. He toyed with her hair, shook her tiny hands, murmured all sorts of flattering nonsense while the infant periodically flailed in her sleep as though she were desperately shooing him away.

"Oh, the boy's simply enchanting!"

"He always takes initiative in his obligations, you know. I can think of no other child his age who'll do that."

"I can tell that he'll be very close to Roderika."

Edouard rolled his eyes as he continued to perform, his cooing having now settled into a dull, murmured repetition of "You'd better not turn out a shrill brat like my sister," which, he figured, sounded like an endless stream of infant talk in others' ears.

Roderika's pinched features contorted further as she shifted in her crib, turning her face away from her dour cousin with an emphatic "Kaka!" which seemed to mark the end of their conversation. Edouard merely shrugged and stood up, straightened his magnificent blue-and-gold suit and turned to face his parents, who looked very, *very* proud.

After another brief exchange of pleasantries, they left the dais and melted back into the crowd, where Edouard's father was immediately caught up in diplomatic conversation with foreign dignitaries, and his mother, likewise, was cornered by a group of noble friends. Edouard was left to fend for himself, but it was something he wished, for he disliked mummery in spite of his burgeoning talent at it, and preferred to be left alone with his favorite pony.

He wove his way through the colorful crowd, looking this way and that and finding nothing of any interest to fill his time before the food was served. He paused only once, when a sudden burst of terrified wailing from the front of the crowd sliced through the revelry, and he shrugged and made a face in the direction of the miscreant before moving on.

Toward the rear of the massive hall, a group of old women huddled together, immersed in a very solemn conversation. They looked out of place, Edouard couldn't help but note, given their humbler trappings, and he wondered if they were petitioners who managed to convince the sentries to allow them inside despite the obviously exclusive celebration.

The rest of the guests seemed to both ignore and keep their distance from the women, who had a corner all to themselves. All the same, since they were so far removed from the rest of the aristocratic crowd, they were interesting enough to engage his attention, and he walked nearer them for a more thorough observation. Edouard was even bored enough to resort to counting them, finding their number to be a nice, round twelve. Perhaps there was something significant about that point, but he didn't care.

"Well, what do you think?" the one in a dull gray dress asked her companions.

"The king and queen are a very handsome pair," another replied quickly, earning herself a round of emphatic nods. "And it only stands to reason that the princess will grow up to be a very beautiful young lady."

"Does anyone know what she looks like?" a third broke in, looking quite domestic in her faded brown costume.

"I daresay she's red-haired, like the king."

"The queen's got very light hair—not quite yellow, but not quite white."

Another pressed her mouth into a firm line and said, "I say gold hair—something darker than her mother's but most certainly lighter than her father's."

"What about her eyes?"

"We can't say anything definite, seeing as how we're not even certain about her hair."

The gray woman wrung her hands, her weathered features flushing. "I have to have something to say to their Majesties!" she cried. "I can't just go to them and gift the child her future appearance without specifics!"

"Unless you have another set of eyes floating above the crib, my dear, you really can't do much of anything until you're actually standing beside the princess," one of her compatriots said with some impatience. "And why are you complaining? You've got the easier job, with all this hocus-pocus about beauty and all that, whereas I have to say something about her talents, and how do I do that with only a baby who's no more than a few days old?"

"Hush, hush, before someone hears! You know how witches are treated hereabouts!"

The little group fell into an argument, which Edouard, for a moment, watched bemusedly. But he was a very gallant young man, and when it looked as though nothing close to a compromise was going to be reached, he stepped closer and gave one of the women's skirts a sharp tug.

"I've seen the princess, and she's got yellow, curly hair," he said with so much authority that the whole group stood in silence before him, eyeing him in amazement.

"See?" the one who predicted gold hair crowed.

"And what of her complexion, my dear?" the gray woman prodded, her eyes lighting up. She moved toward Edouard and knelt before him.

"Light, I suppose, but her crib's quite dark, and it was a bit hard thinking about her skin when she was making all sorts of faces at me."

His interrogator refused to give up. "Does she look like anyone you know?"

"My sister, who's a princess with yellow, curly hair," he replied simply, shrugging.

"What's your sister's eye color, my dear?"

"Blue." Edouard paused and frowned as his mind slowly caught up with the moment. He immediately brightened and spoke quickly. "She's got yellow, curly hair, blue eyes, fair skin, and red lips—like a rose, some people say. Does that help?"

"It does, you marvelous creature, you!" the gray woman cried, giving him a kiss on the cheek, and she stood up, turning to face her companions while Edouard grimaced and wiped his face with his sleeve. "Has anyone anything sweet for our young friend here?"

"Agatha, you're teaching him bad habits. You know very well that food's going to be served soon."

"Oh, yes, of course."

The woman in brown now stepped up to Edouard and asked him if his sister had any special talents.

"No," he said after some thought. "She annoys me, though. Doesn't that take some talent?"

"Does she sing? Dance? Play a musical instrument?"

Edouard sighed and scratched his head. These women were a bit too demanding, he thought. "I suppose she sings, but I can't rightly say if she sings well because I always run away when she does."

"That's enough, my dear, that's enough. All princesses sing, and that's all I need." He was given another wet kiss, and at this point Edouard was half-afraid of ruining his clothes from all the face-cleaning he was forced to do with ten more old women eyeing him hopefully, so he excused himself from their company, citing a pair of missing monarchs he needed to find.

He moved through the crowd back in the direction where he believed he had left his parents, and he realized that the horrific shrieking from earlier on had shifted to something else entirely. Whoever the source, he seemed to have changed extreme moods from terror to fury, for the outbursts this time sounded almost war-like.

Edouard shuddered reflexively as he endured the torturous noise, which eventually ended—almost abruptly, at that. He searched for his parents, momentarily weaving through the front of the colorful crowd. And there his gaze fell on the figure of another boy, whose red, tear-stained, and disheveled features betrayed his identity.

The Wailer (as Edouard now called him) was dressed in green and white finery, and he stood beside a tired, blushing young woman who was likely his mother. She was busily dabbing one of her shoulders with a handkerchief. And it didn't come as a surprise to the contemptuous prince that this hysterical child was golden-haired, for he sounded too much like his sister when she didn't get her way, and from the way the boy pinched his face as he knuckled residual tears from his eyes, he looked no differently from the baby Roderika.

Around the pair, a number of people turned and whispered among themselves, gazes shifting to the flustered young queen, their smiles turning to sneers behind her back. Some stifled laughter, some made faces, and it was very clear that they were mocking her and her overly dramatic son.

Edouard's curiosity was piqued, and he idly wove through the crowd, listening. Being bored out of his wits required nothing less, after all.

"Lord, she's bold to show herself here," someone noted.

"Indeed. I didn't realize the princess's blessing day was open to strumpets."

"Oh, just *look* at her! She's so *common!*"

"I don't know what Reinhard was thinking, taking on a merchant's daughter for a queen," another huffed, outrage dripping from every word. "I mean, really? He could've had any well-bred and gorgeous noblewoman! I heard that every eligible princess's family was practically throwing themselves at his feet, begging him to choose her for his wife!"

"So tawdry. Just look at the way she's strutting around, showing off that brat of hers."

"The boy looks so adorable, but good grief, that temper! Absolutely no discipline whatsoever! I'll never let my children go around behaving like that!"

"Definitely a commoner's spawn. Humph."

Apparently this young queen, who stood alone and apart from everyone else, still blushing and mortified with her eyes now downcast, wasn't well-liked by many. She was a commoner who got lucky in marriage?

Edouard grimaced. No small wonder that sniffling brat of hers made such an appalling spectacle of himself. No quality, indeed. That the queen resorted to spanking and lectures in front of everyone like an ordinary mother—why, that was unheard of in a noblewoman! No aristocrat would stoop to—the heavens help him or her—such low domestic displays! That was what nurses were for!

Edouard marched past the two, taking care to catch the other boy's gaze and meet it with one of pure disdain. He made a face, muttered a couple of choice words about spoilage and sogginess at the other child, and turned away with his nose in the air.

Chapter 3

There were so many kings and queens—in addition to dukes and counts, barons, and margraves, lords and knights with their wives and children—that Hamlin's head spun. Queen Elfriede, having (rather reluctantly) earned herself some attention from other royal guests, was now spending her time talking and introducing her son, much to Hamlin's chagrin. She should have remained alone. The two of them stood apart from everyone else for some time, which proved to be a nice, relaxing moment for Hamlin, but apparently his mother decided to reach out to other guests and be friendly with them. A terrible idea, to be sure.

Surely she wouldn't expect him to remember every person, his or her corresponding rank, and the land over which he or she ruled. It was too much to ask, after suffering such a terrible shock earlier involving Roderika's frog-curse. He'd already told her about being hungry, and yet she chose socialization over her own child's starvation.

Hamlin took to ducking behind his mother's skirts, at times using them to wipe his mouth whenever his thumb-sucking turned a little too wet and messy. His mother never noticed, and neither did anyone else, so he left the growing damp spot on her skirts alone, not bothering to tell his mother.

"The twelve wise women, Your Majesties," a voice announced, and much of the humming conversations from one end of the throne room to the other died to whispers.

Hamlin ran from behind his mother's skirts, pushing his way past the crowds for a better view. He'd heard of wise women before, but he'd yet to see any, much less listen to them perform some wise magic.

To his surprise, a group of old peasant women shuffled forward, curtseying before King Friedrich and Queen Franziska and hissing incoherent words through their wrinkled mouths. Then one by one they approached the crib, bending over it and reaching in, alternately whispering and giggling as the little princess squealed and burped in their faces.

"Oh, what a darling creature she is!" one of them declared, bending closer to the cradle and tearing a sudden shriek from the princess. The wise woman quickly straightened up, blinking, and then murmured her blessing to the now wailing baby, waving her skeletal hands about in nervous, fluttering movements.

"Now you've done it!" another wise woman complained as they changed places. She stared down at the crying princess, her furrowed brows darkening further. When Roderika refused to calm down, the old woman sighed and looked in the queen's direction, for King Friedrich's attention was currently fixed on a quiet conversation with a distinguished-looking, elderly fellow, who appeared grim as he whispered continuously in the monarch's ear. "I think she just soiled herself, Your Majesty." The woman's voice echoed throughout the court.

"Oh, she's just tired," Queen Franziska replied with a small laugh. "She's been lying out here on display for hours now."

The wise woman scowled and began fanning her face. "No, Your Majesty, I'm quite sure the princess just soiled herself."

"Dear me," the queen said, sighing. She looked up and swept her gaze over the glittering crowd that surrounded them. "So many people still need to pay their respects, too."

"I'm sure they can wait." The fanning increased in its ferocity. "They *must*."

Queen Franziska sighed again and looked around, worry creasing her porcelain features. "Where's the nurse?" she demanded.

The wise women moved around, chattering and gesticulating. The princess cried more loudly, and this time the distinctive sounds of farting and something wetter mingled with her wails. The queen's anxiety increased, and she raised her voice in order to be heard. The king bent closer to his whispering companion—very likely a counselor—in order to hear as much as he could amid the din. The nobility lost interest in the silly little nursery moment that was unfolding before them, and they returned to their conversations. The throne room now throbbed with voices and all sorts of noise, with Roderika's pitiful wailing being drowned out.

Hamlin shrugged and moved back into the dense throng to find his mother.

He found her lost in conversation with a trio of nobles, and he immediately took one of her hands and waited out the time in abject boredom, yawning loudly several times in the course of infinity.

The world spun as fatigue overtook him. Voices raised in laughter, debate, and easy conversation swelled and coalesced in an endless human hum. Hamlin yawned again and leaned heavily against his mother, and he felt himself picked up and held against a familiar warm body. His eyes slipped closed the moment he rested his head against his mother's shoulder.

At the very moment sleep finally claimed him, he barely took note of the cries of horror and dismay that suddenly rose up and then melted into a sea of confusion. Perhaps Roderika had vomited in someone's face the way all babies did, unless she'd completely shat all over her crib and made the nearest guests double over and retch. He thought he heard his mother say something in shock, but it mattered little. She felt quite nice and warm under his weight, and, sighing in contentment, Hamlin faded off into sleep.

· · · ·

HAMLIN AWAKENED IN a strange room and on a massive, exquisite bed. He blinked away the remnants of sleep, rubbing his eyes with his knuckles and yawning a few times. When the haze cleared, he found himself staring at a luxurious canopy above him, dark blue velvet fabric that tumbled to the floor in a thick, rich curtain.

"Mama?" he called out.

"She's not here," a voice replied.

Hamlin struggled to sit up and looked around him. He was in a bedroom of considerable size, stone walls nearly hidden behind many pieces of furniture of dark, polished wood and rich fabric.

"If you're hungry, you'll have to wait—like everyone else," the voice continued.

Hamlin turned in the direction of the window, where a boy stood, peering out. "I'm not hungry," he replied. Not anymore, anyway.

The other boy merely stared at him for a moment and then turned his attention back outside. He shrugged and let the conversation die away.

Hamlin crawled off the side of the bed and slid down. A minor surge of panic at the idea that his mother wasn't anywhere near immediately dissipated, to be replaced by growing curiosity toward the other boy. He recognized him as the dark-haired snob who'd sneered at him in the throne room, but

Hamlin, urged on more by simple interest than by resentment at being called a name, walked up to the other boy. Wide-eyed, he stared at the other, unabashed and even slightly amused.

"What?" the irritable creature retorted, turning to glare at him. "What are you staring at?"

"You. Do you live here?"

"I do, yes. I'm Roderika's cousin, and this is my room—well, not my real room, but the one I'm given whenever I come to visit."

Hamlin looked around him vaguely. "Oh."

"Yes, 'oh.' You're a guest, and I have to let you rest here while everyone takes care of the princess."

"What's your name?"

"Edouard. You don't need to give me yours. I'm not interested."

"I'm Hamlin."

Edouard sighed and shook his head, muttering something under his breath as he looked back outside. He seemed both bored and irritated—as though being kept in his room while the rest of the castle carried on with activity ate away at him. Hamlin watched him lean against the window, crossing his arms on his chest the way adults did. He watched Edouard scowl and look impressively thoughtful at whatever it was he was observing from his bedroom.

Hamlin also saw how tall Edouard was compared to him. The other boy cleared the window ledge without any help from smaller pieces of furniture (though he had to crane his neck in order to see whatever he was looking at outside). Hamlin hopped until he was dizzy trying to see out the window, and even then, he could only catch bits of the outside sky.

"What's happening out there?" he asked, panting.

"A bonfire," Edouard replied, and he went no further.

Hamlin pursed his lips as he regarded the other boy. It was proving to be quite the chore, tearing answers out of this proud statue. "What bonfire?" he demanded.

At this, Edouard sighed heavily and turned to glare at Hamlin. "Where on earth were you when that cranky witch came?" he snapped. "Everyone saw what happened! Were you off crying in the corner or something?"

"What bonfire?" Hamlin repeated with greater emphasis. He hated it when people answered questions with questions.

"A curse, you idiot! A stupid witch showed up, called everyone names, and put a curse on Roderika! Now all the spindles in the kingdom are being burned outside, and that's what the bonfire's all about," Edouard said, stamping his foot.

Hamlin blinked. Then he frowned. That didn't make any sense. What did a spindle have to do with a princess who stank up her crib? He'd heard about spindles before—yes, from that same nurse who'd lied to him about frog princesses, curse her. Unless she'd lied to him again, how would people make yarn for clothes if spindles were now forbidden?

"What did the witch say?"

"We're all trying to prevent a curse from coming true, though it's stupid because curses aren't real," Edouard replied, and he spoke slowly, enunciating clearly as though talking to a dribbling idiot or perhaps someone who was hard of hearing. "If you were paying attention to what happened earlier, you'd know. But you didn't, and I'm not about to tell you the story from start to finish. You figure that one out on your own." With another contemptuous sniff, Edouard turned and looked back outside, leaving Hamlin to stare at him, baffled as ever.

He couldn't understand why the other boy didn't like him. He'd never met him before, and if anything, it was Edouard who behaved badly toward him first, walking past him in the throne room and calling him a name. That would be a dreadful breach of etiquette in Hamlin's father's kingdom.

For his part, Hamlin didn't know what else to do or say, but he recognized insufferable pride when he saw it and, as a prince, he wasn't going to stand for it. Narrowing his eyes at Edouard, who continued to ignore him, Hamlin moved closer to the other boy and stomped on Edouard's foot, earning a loud yelp of pain.

"You're rude and ugly," he retorted, watching Edouard hop around and howl, holding up his injured foot.

Hamlin was going to turn his nose up at his antagonist and exit the room with dignity, but all plans were immediately and effectively thwarted when Edouard pounced on him, yelling and pushing him to the floor, defending his slighted honor with wildly flying hands that punched and tore at Hamlin's clothes.

It wasn't until later, after being pried apart by a couple of frightened servants who'd been drawn to the room by their furious shouts and the sounds of upended chairs and stools, that Hamlin understood just how infuriating and petty Edouard was, and that the other boy wasn't going to be his friend no matter what.

Chapter 4

Edouard scowled as he watched his mother berate Hamlin's, making a very strange picture of noble domesticity. He'd never seen two queens argue before, let alone one queen passionately scold another. Judging from the way Queen Clarimond seemed to tower over a drooping, humble Queen Elfriede, it was quite clear who was in the wrong.

Hamlin was not in the room with them, for he'd been dragged away and shut up somewhere, awaiting punishment from his mother. Edouard expected nothing less after this savage attack on him, and his mother seemed to make that clear from the way she stared down her nose at the bowed head of blonde hair before her. Edouard, though smarting all over and gingerly rubbing his face, which felt swollen given the way Hamlin showered it with his little fist a dozen or so times over, couldn't help but feel inordinately proud of his mother and the way she asserted her status as the victim.

Head held high, contemptuous sneer curling her mouth, chest out, pale finger raised in warning, while Queen Elfriede stared at the floor and wrung her hands in a very unqueenly display of guilt—oh, yes, Queen Clarimond was definitely the brutalized victim here.

Edouard's thoughts flew back to the mocking exchanges he'd heard earlier in the throne room. If any of those nobles were present to witness Queen Elfriede's utter humiliation, they'd likely remark on the way she carried herself without a shred of dignity. Like a sad little commoner, of course.

"Humph," he snorted, frowning and turning away to appease himself by noting the quality of his bedroom furniture and how fine the room looked.

The sound of soft footsteps hurrying off and the door slamming broke his concentration, and he turned to find his mother staring daggers at the door before looking back at him.

"You behaved very admirably, Edouard," she said. "Just like your father, you reacted quickly and defended your honor. Remember that. No one ever crosses our family and gets away with it."

"Yes, Mama."

"That savage little creature left his mark on you, but you'll survive. You're strong, aren't you, my pet?"

"Yes, Mama."

"Good. Never be ashamed of what you did. You make me terribly proud, you know." She paused to smile at him, lifting her chin and looking down on him when she did. Standing in a way so that she could look down on people was a habit of hers, being queen. She clasped her hands over her stomach as she drew herself up to her full height, and she was a tall woman. Edouard had to crane his neck in order to meet her gaze.

"Thank you, Mama."

"I'll have the physician come up and look at you," she said with a firm nod. "He won't be long."

"I hope he doesn't bring his leeches again."

"He won't. You don't need them, though I'm sure that surly little wretch will."

Without waiting for a word from him, she turned around and swept grandly out of his bedroom in a swish of skirts. Edouard sighed and walked toward the window to look out into the courtyard below. The bonfire still raged, with swarms of people—peasants, mostly, standing around it and watching the conflagration in awe. There was an uneven stream of people walking through the gawkers and tossing their spindles into the fire. From where he stood, Edouard managed to catch a few despairing looks from some of those gathered. Were they destroying the only source of livelihood they had?

Edouard rolled his eyes. Peasants! They were always so pitifully needy when it came to money. If they found their livelihood threatened by a stupid witch's curse, the least they could do was to be less selfish and think about the fate of poor Roderika instead. What did their families matter when the life of their future queen was at stake?

"They can always find new work, anyway," he said as he moved away from the window and waved a hand dismissively.

Since the physician had yet to arrive, Edouard thought to while away his time by playing up and down the corridor where his bedroom was located. Most of the activity happened below, anyway, so there were no servants wandering about who were in any danger of being run over or pretend-stabbed.

The throbbing ache in his face bothered him, so Edouard distracted himself with an imaginary sword-fight with a dragon. He tried to remember the basics of sword-handling he'd learned from his Beginning-Soldiering-for-Noble-Children weapons master, so he practiced while pretending to defend his land from scaly, fire-breathing monsters. Huffing and whispering threats as he played, he raced forward, stabbing and slicing, until he reached the end of the corridor, where it turned a corner and stretched to the right.

Two figures in the middle of that next corridor brought Edouard's play to a halt, and he quickly jumped back and hid behind the corner. Assured that he wasn't seen, he slowly peered out.

Hamlin stood before an open door, which Edouard guessed to be the room where the other boy had been sequestered after their fight. Hamlin's head was bowed, and he was crying softly. Queen Elfriede, in the meantime, knelt before her son, whispering earnestly to him. Once in a while, she reached up and wiped Hamlin's face with the same handkerchief she'd used earlier. It would have to be soaked by now, given its abuse, but the young queen kept at it. Hamlin nodded sometimes, shook his head sometimes, and stuttered a response sometimes.

In the end, however, Queen Elfriede pulled her son close to her, holding him tightly and stroking his hair as he continued to cry on her shoulder.

It was a very brief moment that Edouard witnessed, and he withdrew in silence before he was caught spying. He tiptoed back to his room, now in a strange mood. Frowning, he closed the door behind him and then went to his bed, where he sat and brooded.

Something in his chest tightened as he relived that scene over and over again in his mind—a peculiar pang that came from nowhere, and it made him feel the need to rub his chest as he felt his confusion spiral. Little by little, the truth dawned on him, and confusion turned into shock and then resentment.

Hamlin was clearly loved and adored by his mother. Commoner or no, Queen Elfriede was surprisingly open in her expressions of affection toward her son. Edouard's mind lingered on the way she alternately scolded and then soothed Hamlin, even ending their conversation with something Edouard himself had never once enjoyed in his mother's company: a hug.

With a grunt, he fell back on his bed and stared at the lengthening shadows in his room as the minutes ticked by.

• • • •

DURING THE EVENING festivities—for Roderika's special day lasted, literally, twenty-four hours, so only heaven knew what the rest of the kingdom would be up to through the wee hours of the morning—Edouard only saw Hamlin and Queen Elfriede for a very brief moment, and it was while the two were taking their leave of Queen Franziska, who appeared a touch put out because King Friedrich was once again absent. Kings were most likely to skip baby-themed occasions in favor of war or diplomatic meetings or perhaps a gentlemen-only drinking binge. Edouard's mother told him so, anyway, and she did look a bit put out when she spoke about it, just like Queen Franziska at that moment.

While nobles gathered in the great banquet room to raise genteel holy hell and servants in their finest livery bustled in and out of rooms and through large and massive corridors, Edouard peered out of a window to watch the two guests say goodbye.

For her part, Queen Franziska appeared to be very sympathetic and friendly toward Queen Elfriede, who, after all she and her son had been through, looked positively pale, exhausted, and very, very sad.

Edouard watched her closely. Ignoring her elevated commoner status, she seemed to be a sweet woman, who appeared to be quite lost in her new place. She might have attempted to reach out and befriend other nobles that day, but Edouard still had to see her being flanked by new acquaintances who'd cheerfully converse with her. As it was, even standing outside, she remained alone, with no one else for company but her child.

Queen Franziska spoke to her earnestly, behaving almost like an older sister. That thought touched Edouard, for he knew that, despite his independence, he still looked to his siblings for conversation and company. Then his aunt turned her attention to Hamlin, who watched her with his usual look of wide-eyed amazement. He didn't shrink from her when she bent down, smiled, and talked to him.

Hamlin clung to his mother's skirts but he listened, nodding. The bruise on his face wasn't as severe as the one that Edouard sported—a fact that rankled a bit because Edouard was not only bigger than Hamlin but also older, which meant that he should've had the upper hand in the battle, but Hamlin had proven to be a very agile and squirmy little bugger of a fighter.

After talking to him, Queen Franziska turned and beckoned to someone, and from somewhere in the gathering shadows a liveried servant appeared, bowed to both monarchs, and produced a toy—a wooden horse, it appeared. He gave the toy to Hamlin, who took it with a bright grin that nearly split his face in two.

Queen Elfriede smiled as well, and she talked—mercy, how she talked! The moment she opened her mouth, she didn't seem to run out of words to say, but it was clear that she was flustered and pleased and quite grateful. Queen Franziska merely laughed and shrugged, a very unqueenly thing to do, Edouard thought, but her casualness and apparent friendliness toward the unwanted queen and Hamlin impressed him.

Before long, Queen Elfriede and Hamlin boarded a waiting coach that was escorted by six armed guards, and they left the castle. Queen Franziska stood in the early evening dimness, watching them go, which was again a bit of an unqueenly thing, but Edouard somehow thought that it was quite fitting for her. Then she turned and walked back into the castle.

Edouard scrambled down from his perch and hurried along, intent on meeting his aunt somewhere in one of the corridors as she made her way to the banquet room. He did, eventually, and panting, he ran up to her and greeted her with a breathless, "Are Queen Elfriede and Hamlin going home, Auntie?"

She glanced down at him, looking bemused. "My, my, you and Hamlin certainly got off on the wrong foot. And, yes, they're gone, dear. I didn't want them to leave, but perhaps it was for the best."

"No one likes Queen Elfriede around here."

"You didn't exactly show much of a friendly welcome to Hamlin, either," she replied, cocking a brow at Edouard, who instantly blushed. When he failed to say anything in return, she sighed and took his hand and led him to the banquet room.

For the next two hours, Edouard managed to forget about their unlucky guests, for he was once again the center of attention among noble children, who gathered around him and gaped at his bruises. Words of admiration and vows of eternal friendship were showered on him from all sides, and whatever pangs of vague guilt he felt earlier were immediately replaced by immense pleasure and pride, and he was once again strutting about with his head held high and his chest out. No, he shouldn't regret anything; he was a prince, after all, and he'd defend his honor to the death.

Chapter 5

Hamlin's parents spent the morning hours catching up on each other's adventures from the previous day, and his half-brothers were off with their tutors. He was left all alone, which he didn't mind at all, and he spent the greater part of the morning hiding from his nurse—whom he'd yet to forgive for lying to him about Roderika—and playing with his new wooden horse in his mother's private little courtyard garden.

Their arrival the previous evening was met with a great deal of fussing, though his mother downplayed the horrors of Roderika's special day. When Hamlin's father asked after him, his mother merely glanced over in his direction with a strained look on her face and diplomatically steered the king away with a hand looped around his arm and some whispered words. In the meantime, Hamlin was handed over to a servant for cleaning and changing in preparation for bed. His nurse would have looked after him, of course, but he'd insisted on someone else, for his mood had remained pretty sour toward her.

Nothing more was said of their visit, and the following morning found Hamlin quite refreshed, energized, and eager to flee his she-demon of a nurse. The most effective way of doing so was to sequester himself in his mother's private courtyard garden, for it was off-limits to everyone but the royal family.

In theory, anyway.

"Ah, and who's this sweet-looking child?" a familiar voice cawed from somewhere above. "Is that a foundling I see? Then no one will miss him if I had him for lunch, yes? I'll peck away at his eyes first and then gobble up his brains, yum!"

Hamlin beamed as he looked up to watch the raven circle above him, black wings beating in the calm, warm air.

"May I have a feather, please?" Hamlin asked, scrambling to his feet and reaching up with both hands.

The raven sighed, though he didn't stop in his flight. He circled around Hamlin a few more times before he paused in mid-air and shook one wing, sending a couple of feathers loose and floating down. Hamlin laughed as he chased after them, taking delight in running and stumbling and rolling on the thick, soft grass before jumping back up to his feet and waving the feathers above his head.

"I got them!" he cried, hurrying back to his toy.

"I do wish you'd ask for something other than feathers, Your Highness," the raven said, sighing again, as he sailed downward and settled himself on a small rock resting on the grass nearby. "I don't grow those things quickly enough, you know. I've got too many bald patches all over me now, and I've no idea how many of my feathers you've collected."

"I don't know," Hamlin replied as he admired the magnificent black feathers he held, awed by their size and the way they gleamed in the sun's light. "I just like them."

The bird snorted. "I'm sure you've gathered enough to create a raven of your own."

"I don't know magic," Hamlin said, looking up and shrugging. "I wish I did."

"I'm heartily glad you don't. Heaven knows what you'd be using it for."

Hamlin grinned and pointed at the bird. "Turn you into a wild boar, and we can hunt you down with arrows!"

"Charming."

"Can you tell me a story, Master Audwin?"

Audwin looked left and right. "Why ask me for a story, Your Highness? Where's that dreadful nurse of yours? I'm sure she's got quite a few more wicked tales to frighten you with in that dark, dark mind of hers."

Hamlin made a face and waved a hand dismissively. "She lied to me about Princess Roderika," he said. "I don't want to listen to her anymore. I like your stories better."

Audwin snorted again. "My stories?" he echoed. "My stories are all filled with doom, violence, despair, and endless suffering! They're all nursery tales, Your Highness."

"I like them. Tell me one, please." Before Audwin could say anything more, Hamlin rolled over and lay on his back, breathing in deeply and closing his eyes and enjoying the gentle blanketing warmth of the bright, cloudless sky above. "Go on. I'm ready."

"Tsk. Children. Very well, very well." A pause followed, along with the rustling of feathers, as Audwin most likely shook himself in preparation. "Well, seeing as how I can't tell you stories without giving you nightmares and then condemning myself to being chased and threatened by your nurse, as she always does, I suppose I should listen to what the wind says and then relay her story to you."

Hamlin huffed, shaking his head in the grass, though he kept his eyes closed against the sky. "I'm listening," he said as he clasped his hands on his stomach, lacing his fingers together.

"So, once upon a time, a young boy was born into a royal household. He was, unfortunately, looked after by this cretinous woman whom he called a nurse."

Hamlin frowned, his eyes still closed. This sounded awfully familiar, he thought, but he decided against mentioning it and listened.

"Now this young boy thought that he was to go through life quite comfortably, growing up spoiled by his family and tutors and servants. He thought that he was all set to grow up and fulfill his duties as only a good prince would, with no roadblocks ahead. Seeing as how he was the youngest in a family of four boys as well as the only half-brother, he expected to be able to live quietly and unmolested by the usual pressures that came with being the next in line to the throne, et cetera, et cetera."

Hamlin opened his eyes and scowled at Audwin, who remained on his rock perch and had paused to peck under his wing with his beak. "That story doesn't sound like a story," he complained. "It's stupid."

"Tell that to the wind, Your Highness. She's the one who's feeding me this nonsense."

As though in answer, a sudden wind blew, picking up stray debris including the two feathers that Hamlin had claimed and tossing them around.

"Now you've done it," Audwin said after the wind stopped. "She's upset. Perhaps if I were to simply tell you the story in whole, you can decide afterward if it was worth your time. Then you can take it up with the wind and leave me out of it."

Hamlin grunted and closed his eyes again, a touch annoyed. He'd just lost his feathers, and he was getting bored. "Very well."

"So this young prince creature met another young prince creature, who turned out to be a right ass, and the two didn't quite get along at first. But down the line, things happened that turned their worlds upside down, and the first young prince creature found himself faced with choices he'd never before expected, and he realized that whatever ending awaited him depended on those choices, and he sat down to think things over."

Hamlin waited for Audwin to continue, but silence fell on the little courtyard garden, and he opened his eyes to find his magical friend pecking at his feathered armpits again. "What, that's it?" Hamlin demanded, scowling.

Audwin looked up, shaking himself till his feathers plumped up, and he looked as though he'd just been frightened half to death by a murderous cat. "That's all I got from the wind, Your Highness. The story hasn't ended yet because much of it has yet to happen, and nothing ruins a good story more than the ending being revealed before it even takes place."

"Huh?"

"Oh, never mind. It's an ongoing story, she tells me. We'll have to be satisfied with that." Audwin went back to pecking at his armpits.

Hamlin grimaced. "Don't listen to the wind anymore," he said. "She's awful."

"How about if you were to tell *me* a story, Your Highness? After all, you were able to travel to the kingdom past our eastern borders, and from what I heard, things got a bit exciting over there. What happened?"

Hamlin thought for a bit. "It wasn't that good. I didn't like it there."

Audwin, for a bird, looked quite grave and—smart. He nodded as he listened. "I see. Did you meet people while you were there?"

"I did. I don't like them, either. One of them hit me. See? His name was Edouard." Hamlin turned to his friend and pointed at his face. The bruises were still there, but since Edouard had proven to be a rather ineffectual fighter, they were fading quite quickly. Unfortunately, his father's ire would take a little while longer to dissipate, and nothing Hamlin said could convince the king that it was that other demon boy's fault and not his.

Audwin actually stuck his head out and narrowed his little bead-like eyes. "Huh," he muttered. "I see. Well, I can't pretend to understand human nature, so I'll just say that it's probably best to avoid crossing the eastern borders again and risk getting assaulted by that Edouard person."

Hamlin sighed as he rolled over onto his stomach, resting his chin on one folded arm and idly moving his wooden horse forward and backward over the grass. "I'm bored, Master Audwin," he said after a moment's pause.

"I am, too. I was hoping that you'd be able to amuse me for a bit, but it looks like it's all in vain. Not that it surprises me, of course, but it really does dampen one's morning hours."

With a sudden flutter of his black wings, Audwin hopped from where he'd perched himself and landed softly on the grass next to Hamlin's new toy. He stared at the horse, blinking his little black eyes at it.

"I hope I get to do great things someday," Hamlin said. "All princes are supposed to, you know."

"Oh, I'm sure you will, Your Highness. You're too young to worry about that now, but I do understand if you can't help it. Youngest child and all—I've seen it happen countless times before. Oldest sons don't have to worry, seeing as how their futures are already set in stone, and their lives are dictated to them. All they need to do is what's expected of them. That's the reason why none of them have personalities."

Audwin paused and shook his feathers again.

"As for younger princes, they're always in a bind. Happiness or obligation? Happiness, obligation, happiness, obligation, happiness, obligation—wise birds can be driven mad from all that back-and-forthing that goes on again and again. But don't expect all that to happen till your adolescence—not that I want to ruin your development or anything, but you know what I mean." Audwin made a bit of a rude sound that seemed to be halfway between a snort and a fart, and he began to peck at the wooden horse with his beak.

No, Hamlin didn't really know what his friend meant, but he simply let it go. It was all he could to watch Audwin entertain himself in such a pointless, idle way. A sudden wave of restlessness surged through him. Hamlin was definitely bored out of his wits and, at the same time, he felt a pang of loneliness.

He'd seen how well the other noble children were able to mingle with each other the previous day, behaving as though they'd known each other their entire lives, while Hamlin could only look on. He remembered most of what happened in the throne room after he'd paid his respects to Roderika, and he wondered if it was because he was so frightened at first that the other children didn't bother to make friends with him.

Not that his mother had any better luck, anyway, in reaching out to fellow noblemen and women. Politeness aside, no one seemed to want to have anything to do with his mother or him, though he didn't know why, for neither of them had done anything wrong. Now Hamlin regretted being so tired that he'd fallen asleep in his mother's arms, for he was quite sure that he'd missed some of the more enjoyable things besides the strange witch creature showing up and making a mess of things in the end.

He let out an irritated little sound as he rolled over on his back again to stare at the sky. It was a vivid blue, but not as brilliant and rich a shade as the clothes that that awful Edouard had worn. What a pity that they had that dreadful quarrel. Hamlin was convinced that they'd have become the best of friends if they hadn't argued like that.

"Your Highness, forgive me, but the wind won't shut up," Audwin said, breaking up Hamlin's thoughts. "She wishes me to tell you that you're meant to do something very special someday."

Hamlin nodded, yawning. The wind, he realized, was simply full of strange ideas, though perhaps that was why the wind was the wind—airy, vague, and not quite there.

Chapter 6

There'd been quite a bit of grumbling among the queens and princesses regarding Roderika's special treatment by the wise women of the kingdom. But all complaints were always tempered by badly suppressed sniggering at the reminder that, yes, the princess was doomed to prick her finger on a spindle and sleep for a hundred years. Edouard, being a very practical young man, would choose to hear none of the usual moaning and groaning within noble ranks, especially if those complaints interfered with his scholarly pursuits.

"The boy should be out shooting animals, flaunting his looks, and riding his horse for the pleasure of young princesses," his father, King Rikard, said as he scowled at Edouard.

"Now, now, my dear," Queen Clarimond cut in. "You've already got two older boys doing exactly that. You can't expect all your sons to turn out like each other. Besides, we need an intellectual in this family. I had hopes for Aloysia, but the girl's determined to thwart my expectations."

Edouard's younger and only sister had developed an unusual interest in basket-weaving, which she'd supplemented with an even greater interest in magical arts. As the years passed, their mother fretted over Aloysia's marriage prospects, given the young princess's strange propensities. Worse, no one dared curb her, lest she turn them into toads, lizards, or mold. Edouard, for his part, didn't care what his sister did as long as she didn't interfere with his passion, which was books and undisturbed solitude.

"Mama, Papa, would you mind not arguing so loudly?" Edouard finally asked, sighing as he slumped back in his chair. He looked up to frown at his parents, both of whom stood nearby and were now regarding him with looks of amazement. "I'm in the middle of reading about eastern civilization, and I can't retain anything with all the noise you're both making over there."

"My goodness," his father said, his expression a study in extreme shock. "The boy has some nerve!"

"Yes, isn't that simply wonderful? Imagine what an aggressive, intelligent diplomat he'd make!" Edouard's mother replied as she drew herself up to her full height, beaming with great pride at the scowling prince.

"And you're spoiling him, Clarimond."

"Nonsense. I'm simply doing what any good mother would do for her child—give him room to pursue his passion. He's only thirteen, anyway, and terribly deserving of everything we can give him." She directed her smile at her husband, while taking his arm and steering him toward the library door. "Now come along. You heard our little scholar. We need to give him some peace and quiet so he can learn about eastern civilization. Think about it, darling—what better way to learn about a kingdom's weaknesses so that we can conquer it? Our little boy's a genius!"

Edouard's father continued to argue against her excessive indulgence, and the debate carried on after the library door was shut behind his parents, their voices fading gradually as they made their way down the corridor. Once silence fell in the library, Edouard sighed his relief and yawned, stretching his arms above his head before cracking his knuckles. Adults were always such a bother, he thought, as he went back to reading the precious tome that lay spread out on the table before him.

Within seconds he was once again absorbed in history, tradition, war, plagues, and other calamities that tended to define early civilizations. Thank heaven for modern times, indeed. The castle library remained silent for what felt like an infinity, with no other sounds but Edouard's soft breathing and occasional murmurs as he reread passages aloud to emphasize key points to himself.

"Psst."

Edouard frowned at the yellowed but colorful pages before him. Damn those pesky flies, especially when they managed to find their way into people's royal libraries.

"Psst!"

He groaned and rubbed his eyes, blinking away the bubbling irritation of being disrupted yet again. Edouard sat back and looked around him, straining his eyes to catch sight of a fly. He saw nothing, however, but the old shelves surrounding him and the older books that crammed them. The windows above the tall bookcases yawned into the outside world, and sunlight streamed through their narrow, arched openings.

Edouard didn't know what time it was, but judging from the angle of the sun's light, it must be mid-morning. The pennants hanging down from the ceiling captured some of these golden rays, which brightened their colors even more, and Edouard couldn't help but stare at them in admiration and wonder.

"Psst! Good grief, Edouard!"

Oh. Edouard's sigh came out as a snort this time as he glared in the direction of the voice. "Aloysia!" he hissed, narrowing his eyes at a particularly vile-looking spiny toad grinning at him from the War History section of the library. "I'm busy! Go somewhere else if you want to practice your magic!"

"I'm trying to practice spells for Roderika's birthday," Aloysia said with abnormal cheerfulness. Edouard grimaced as he stared at his sister. She certainly made for a particularly ugly toad, and the heavens help her husband if any unlucky sod were to fall in love with her someday. "What do you think?"

"Ugly. Very, very ugly. Now go away till you get things right."

"Perfect!"

"Repulsive."

Aloysia didn't seem to care what her brother thought of her clever disguise because she not only didn't change back to her human self but hopped over to the large table, much to Edouard's dismay. She also proved to be very strong, and it only took her one powerful push of her hind legs to catapult her preposterously horrid body through the air and into Edouard's collection of illuminated manuscripts.

How had she been able to leap like that, without her discolored and bloated body being punctured by any of the long, fierce-looking spines that poked out of her in every possible direction? Edouard was forced to admit feeling rather impressed by that, but he still couldn't help but suppress a most violent urge to vomit.

"What color is your skin supposed to be?" he demanded.

Aloysia rolled her eyes, and with her being a toad, it was quite a sight for such a simple act. "I don't think of specifics. You need a sense of humor and a little bit of imagination, brother."

"And what do you hope to accomplish looking like something a demon just shat out? And for a princess's birthday, too?"

"Entertainment, of course. I plan to dazzle everyone with a dozen new tricks I've perfected. Anyway, it's not easy being a princess, you know. I refuse to grow up boring and stupid and vacant and pretty. I daresay Roderika's well on her way to being a stupid, vacant, and pretty queen."

Edouard leaned over his book to glare at his sister. "You can't be around her with spikes or spines on your body, you oaf. You know she can't be around sharp objects."

Aloysia burst out laughing, her spiky toad form jiggling like an overstuffed bladder. Edouard was forced to press a hand against his mouth to keep himself from heaving. In fact, it was all he could do to turn away and pinch his eyes shut, forcing the nightmarish sight of his transformed sister out of his mind.

"She can't be around spindles, which isn't a very hard thing to do, seeing as how spindles have been banned in her kingdom since she was born," Aloysia said amid snorts and giggles. "Good grief, you take things far too seriously and literally."

"Sharp objects on the whole, not just spindles. Go ask Uncle and Auntie."

"Bah. That's neither here nor there."

"Anyway, you know very well that everything our uncle's done means absolutely nothing because she'll still end up getting pricked someday," Edouard said, and then he stopped, blinking. Something in what he'd just said felt wrong. In fact, it sounded rather naughty. He felt himself blush, which Aloysia didn't seem to notice, or if she did, she didn't particularly care.

"And one can say that Fate is Fate, and she's also bound to wake up after a hundred years' worth of sleep. The wheels are turning, brother, and there's nothing we can do about it but make the best of each day till the moment comes."

"You're very philosophical for an ugly toad."

"Why, thank you! I work hard at it, you know, though Papa and especially Mama don't understand."

Edouard took a deep, soothing breath, relieved at feeling his stomach settle down into a nice calm. He leaned forward again, scanning the open pages before him to find where he'd left off before his sister so unceremoniously interrupted him.

"Then perhaps you can work hard at disappearing," he said as he carefully marked the passage—no, the actual line—that he'd been reading before

Aloysia's appearance. That is, he pressed a finger on it and kept it there. "Come on, Aloysia," he added, frowning in impatience. "You're wasting my time. I've got a lot more pages to read. Go frighten some of the servants if you're bored."

Aloysia snorted. "I'd love to have some witch read your future," she said with a very unladylike croak. "Then I'll cast a sympathy spell on your sweetheart and comfort her for a lifetime of grief."

"Humph. That's the problem with girls, I find. You're always consumed by all things romantic, and then you complain about not being taken seriously."

"I don't understand how falling in love can be considered frivolous." Aloysia snickered when Edouard blinked. "Yes, yes, I read non-magical books, too, and my vocabulary's improving. You ass. But that's not my point, and I think you're trying to change the subject by looking confused at my eloquence. Yes, I just learned that word, too! Stop it!"

Edouard shook his head. "Get out of the library, Aloysia," he growled, "or I'll swat you with my atlas. I don't care if you've got those horrible spines on your body. I'll still come after you."

"And they say chivalry's dead. Fine, fine, I'm going." The toad croaked again as she turned, hopped across the table, and then flew off—literally. In the midst of jumping off the table, Aloysia changed herself into a swallow and flew around the library for a few seconds before sailing out of the room through one of the windows.

Edouard rolled his eyes as he watched his sister vanish, finally. "What a braggart," he muttered. Yawning and stretching his arms again, he turned his attention back to his book and then fell back against his chair with a yelp.

Apparently his sister thought very little of his education because in the course of flying about, she'd actually left a messy present on the page that Edouard had been reading. And if Edouard weren't so horrified, disgusted, and outraged by his insane sister's rudeness, he'd have conceded that the gigantic bird splat gracing his illuminated history manuscript looked suspiciously like a map of their kingdom.

Chapter 7

"Come along, quit fighting us! Baldrick, hold him!" Otto snarled.

"I'm trying, you idiot! He's too slippery!"

"It's the dress. I told you it was a bad idea," Mallory, ever the one for dry commentaries and a knack for avoiding blame, said as he sauntered beside his brothers, dead branch in hand, and whacked away at the thorny weeds and colorful wildflowers that practically buried the footpath the four princes took.

Mallory had been sent on ahead to clear the way, but the overgrowth proved too thick and unresponsive to thin under a bored young prince's methodical swinging of a dead branch. With so many hazards hidden in the dense underbrush, it was a good thing that children of the nobility went around in leather boots. Or at least the older ones did.

"I don't want to play! I want to go home!" Hamlin cried, kicking and squirming in his brothers' arms.

"Shut up! How can we practice being proper princes if you won't cooperate?" Baldrick snapped.

He was the one who held Hamlin under his arms, while Otto struggled with Hamlin's legs. Like a captured wild beast being carried off to the slaughter, Hamlin—dressed in a princess's gown, at that—cried and wailed and kicked and writhed, making it as difficult as he could for his half-brothers to keep their hold on him.

Unfortunately, numbers and age trumped size and agility, for Otto, Baldrick, and Mallory—at sixteen, fourteen, and thirteen respectively—had long advanced down the path of physical development, with all three showing impressive musculature and strength after hours spent in weapons classes. It was just too bad that there wasn't more mental development—they'd all grown into bullies who picked on Hamlin for their sport.

Then again, such behavior was never questioned in that day and age, for stepchildren—or in Hamlin's case, half-brothers—were always suspect and considered to be outsiders deserving of every possible insult without breaking the skin.

For that day's entertainment, Hamlin had been dressed in a gown after the older princes had decided to practice chivalry or other some such nonsense, and when he fought against it, they resorted to physically carrying him out beyond the castle walls.

"Just drop him somewhere," Mallory said, glancing back over his shoulder. "I'm tired of his wailing."

"He's worse than a girl, I swear," Otto said, following that with a string of the most un-royal-sounding curses. "Quit your whining, you little brat, or so help me, I'll break your legs!"

"Over there. Just leave him there." Mallory indicated a spot somewhere in the middle of the meadow.

"All right, fine, fine," Otto snapped. "Come on, Baldrick, hurry up!"

"You and your stupid ideas," Baldrick panted as they all picked up the pace while Hamlin's energy began to flag. "We could've just made him lose his way in one of the closed-off areas in the castle, but no..."

Hamlin could only resort to panic and tears once the realization dawned that his older half-brothers meant to leave him out in a meadow. They'd fooled him into believing their desire to work on being "proper princes," but then again, he also should have known that they were up to something more sinister. How many times, after all, had they demonstrated their dislike of him and his mother? He'd been called a "snot-dripping bastard" and his mother a "social-climbing trollop," but with their own mother long dead, how was Hamlin's mother at fault for being chosen for the king's new wife?

Hamlin was only ten years old, and there were several issues that were too nuanced for him to grapple with and walk away from with a clearer mind.

He was finally dropped, literally, on a spot picked by Mallory. As Otto, Baldrick, and Mallory stepped away in a widening circle around him, Hamlin yelped as thorny plants dug into his hands and pierced his arms. The gown's layered skirts managed to save his legs, though he did wear his usual hose and velvet shoes under them. He scrambled to his feet, crying and tearing away at thistles that had clung to his clothes and hair.

"A bit vocal for a princess, aren't you?" Baldrick said, smirking and crossing his arms over his chest. He turned to Otto, the default ringleader. "You want *this* to be a practice princess? You could've just paid some milkmaid for the part."

Otto rolled his eyes. "Don't be stupid. Little Helene here does the part pretty well. Look, see? Golden hair, rosy cheeks, eyes bigger than his head—all that's needed is a dress."

"He cries too much, too. Definitely suited for a girl's part," Mallory added, snorting.

"I want to go home," Hamlin stammered, not daring to wipe his nose on the gown's sleeve, though he could feel it running. Not that it mattered, anyway, considering his dreadful state. "May I please go home? I won't tell, I swear."

"What's to tell?" Baldrick asked. "What're you thinking of?" He glanced at the others. "What're we doing that's worth telling someone? That we let you join a game? Is that it? In case you haven't noticed, Little Mouse, we all went through worse in our schoolfellows' company. Were you ever beaten up? No. Were you ever humiliated in front of a big group of boys your age? No. So what would be worth talking about in the first place, eh?" He leaned forward, sneering. "Not that it'd matter, would it? It's not as though you've got much of a say in the family, *Half*-brother."

Hamlin shook his head, suppressing another wave of frightened tears. "Nothing. I'll be quiet. I won't tell Mama anything."

"Because there's nothing to tell her. Say it!" Baldrick retorted, pointing a threatening finger at him.

"There's nothing to tell her," Hamlin said, wincing. "May I go home now?"

His brothers exchanged looks, and almost in unison, they shrugged. "You may if you want," Otto said. "Wait till after we go, though. You know the rules—real nobility first. And stop your sniveling, for heaven's sake! You call yourself a prince? What utter shit."

With that, the three older boys turned around and marched off, leaving Hamlin crying in the middle of wildflowers and thorny weeds. From some-where in the near distance, Otto yelled, "Five-minute rule! Remember that!"

Five-minute rule—how could Hamlin forget? It was one of those insane rules that his older brothers had made up for him, which required him wait-ing a full five minutes before following their steps. It was an arbitrary and cruel rule, and Hamlin dared to break it a few times because they'd left him terrified and alone in dark and dangerous places, and he couldn't bear to wait five minutes before fleeing them.

But he paid dearly for these "betrayals," which meant being dragged back to the same spot and threatened, his older brothers taking a random path back to the castle and making it an utter misery for Hamlin to follow them after five minutes had gone. No, ten minutes. Doubling the wait had been part of the punishment.

As he wandered about, lost and confused, he had to be rescued by random strangers—a very dangerous thing, to be sure—who, mercifully, turned out to be kind folks who escorted him to the castle.

Once safely home, he was forced to stay quiet about his adventures, not saying a word about it to his nurse and his mother, and he'd learned early how to be a good actor, though his heart was crushed, and his spirits were depressed.

So Hamlin was forced to stand there, those parts of him that had been pricked by thorns and thistles throbbing dully as his distress faded into a familiar suffocating loneliness. The dress he was forced to wear would be difficult to explain away should anyone catch him sneaking into the castle in it, but he was practically naked under the costume, with no shirt and just a hose and shoes.

"You do realize, Your Highness, that your brothers just lied through their teeth about school," a voice broke through the breeze and the general calm of the area.

Hamlin wiped his eyes and looked up to find Audwin flying down toward him. He smiled tiredly as he watched his old friend swoop down and land on the ground.

"I wouldn't know," he said. "I've never been to school."

"Neither have those lying royal bastards," Audwin said. "They all had tutors and weapons masters. That's all. Schoolmates? Oh, don't make me *laugh!*"

Hamlin looked down at his hands, which were now sporting scratches and welts.

"Why do they keep picking on you, anyway?"

Hamlin shrugged. "I don't know. I didn't do anything to them. Mallory said that all royal princes have to be tested somehow. Prove their mettle, he told me."

"Prince Mallory's just as full of shit as his brothers," Audwin retorted. "I've no patience for bullies and overgrown babies who're desperately trying to prove something to the world. You, however, don't need to stoop to their level. Clearly they're harassing you to feel better about themselves, and the fact that you're smaller, younger, and weaker than they only goes to show that they're spineless idiots."

"They pick on me because Mama's married to Papa, I guess."

"That just lowered them from the level of idiots to slobbering, underdeveloped imbeciles."

Hamlin looked at Audwin, shocked. "You can't talk about the crown prince like that."

"Ha! I can't? And what would Prince Otto do to me? Roast me on a spit? I don't have enough meat on me to satisfy a cat for half a day! You can't tell me to stop being critical of fools, noble or otherwise, Your Highness. Trappings aside, an idiot is an idiot is an idiot."

Hamlin blinked and then broke into a little smile. "I hope I'm not stupid enough to make you want to dislike me."

Audwin sighed, shaking his black, feathered head. "Your Highness, I'm the most misanthropic old bird you'll ever know, but I can also differentiate between what's deserving of scorn and what isn't. Good grief, how do you think I've become such a cantankerous old bastard? Why, by watching humanity through the years, that's how! And you, young man, are one of the least deserving of my venom—though perhaps you do try my patience at times, but I'll have to excuse you for being a ten-year-old."

"I might test your patience more at sixteen, I'm sure," Hamlin said, now smiling brightly.

"You might, but I'll be ready for you, regardless."

Hamlin sighed, his spirits rising as calm finally took over. He tugged at his skirts. "I don't know what to tell Mama if she sees me like this."

"My dear boy, give Her Majesty some credit. I'll bet you that she'll understand things better than you expect her to." Audwin paused, mumbling.

It was a bit strange to watch such an opinionated and confident bird hesitate. "It's—mothers are more receptive than their children think. Trust me."

Hamlin nodded. "All right, then. I'll tell her if she asks. But I'll still try to avoid getting caught by anyone."

"Then follow me, Your Highness, and I'll lead you back to the castle through safe and secret paths." Audwin cawed as he flapped his wings and flew up, and he kept low as he led Hamlin back home to ensure that Hamlin was able to keep him in his line of vision.

Later on, after he cleaned up and dressed, taking care to hide the gown from prying eyes, Hamlin joined his family as they gathered for their afternoon repast. He said nothing of his adventures as usual. He greeted everyone cheerfully as usual, took his seat as usual. He could feel his mother's questioning gaze on him, pressing and probing, though he took care to flash her a careless little smile, which she didn't return. When the king and the older princes conversed about war and other princely subjects, Hamlin kept silent and avoided everyone's gaze, eating his food without complaint and without an expression of gratitude. As usual.

Chapter 8

A grand celebration was planned for Roderika's tenth birthday, and considering the fact that the last big party thrown in her honor was just after her birth, Queen Franziska and King Friedrich decided that a decade was surely nothing to sneeze at and agreed to spoil their little princess one more time.

And since their last grand celebration had resulted in a curse and a destiny that poor little Roderika couldn't get out of, they were forced to send out notes to all the wise women throughout the land, apologizing for not inviting any of them this time around but ensuring that they were still highly regarded in court.

To soften the blow, the king and queen also sent small gifts to them along with their notes of apology and, from what had been gossiped all around, the wise women dealt with the snub with a great deal of sportsmanship and good will. Indeed, it was all dealt with very democratically.

Even the cantankerous old witch who'd cast the spell on Roderika was loath to burn the monarchs in effigy, and she was reported to have snarled and cursed till she'd exhausted herself into a string of unintelligible grumblings. Reluctant acceptance of the peace offering followed, and she simply distracted herself with other schemes involving the downfall of preposterous aristocratic snots outside the court.

For Edouard, now seventeen, it was yet one more thorn on his side. Aloysia, at fifteen being the princess closest to the child's age, was charged with looking after Roderika. Edouard was obliged to look after Aloysia's nerves because of that. Aloysia simply couldn't get along with Roderika, cousin or no. Having the two in the same room meant the ever-present danger of Aloysia turning the little one into something like that four-headed gargoyle from last year, when Roderika had refused to behave despite Aloysia's scolding and threats.

"I really don't understand how you can be so affected by a ten-year-old," Edouard said, scowling at his sister. "And I thought you enjoyed doing tricks for her."

"I mistook her for an adorable babe, but she made me eat my words. My opinion now is that she's a horrid little demonling."

"She's practically a baby. You're fifteen. There's something off in the scales."

Aloysia marched up to her brother, her face red and her eyes shining with malevolence. She held up an arrow. "See this? I found the little monster playing with it. How many sharp objects has she collected since she woke up this morning?"

"She can't help herself, you know that."

"That stupid old cow did this," Aloysia snarled as she broke the arrow against her thigh. "She was the one who cursed Roderika and made her obsessed with sharp, pointy things. And don't tell me it's only a phase!"

Edouard snorted. "I know it isn't a phase. She can't help herself because her future's already laid out for her. Heaven knows what else awaits us when she grows older. Singing? Dancing? A sweet, sparkling personality? An easy communing with nature, especially charming little forest animals?"

He grimaced. Nothing spelled disaster like a young, pretty, golden-haired princess who was blessed with every imaginable talent just because a gaggle of wise women decided to ingratiate themselves with their king and queen by heaping all sorts of perfect attributes on her.

"I can stab you with one half of this arrow if you keep saying that, brother, and you know I won't think twice."

"At least we have a consensus on the 'perfect princess' bit." Edouard paused, sighing heavily as he glanced around, taking in the sight of a gorgeous, sprawling meadow generously peppered with wildflowers of every variety.

About twenty feet away stood Roderika, visible only from the shoulders up. She was busy putting together a garland of flowers, which she apparently seemed to be having quite a bit of trouble with. She soon asked Aloysia to help, but she was even worse with them than Roderika. Aloysia took her frustrations out on the mangled flowers by turning them into rabbit droppings. Then she discovered yet another sharp "toy" that Roderika had managed to spirit away from somewhere.

Brother and sister had only been watching their little cousin for an hour, and their patience was already next to nothing.

"You know, I wish that Mama and Papa treated us to big birthday cele-brations the way Auntie and Uncle treat Roderika," Aloysia said after a sullen moment's pause.

She continued to watch the little princess, who'd now given up on flower garlands and had decided to dance and sing among the thorny weeds and flowers, yelping every so often whenever her dress caught or her hands were scratched. Neither deterred her, and she continued to sing with great energy and passion.

Edouard winced. "I don't know about that," he said after wiggling his fin-gers in his ears and shuddering. "It doesn't look as though being spoiled rot-ten ensures a graceful process toward maturity. Oh, good grief, she won't stop singing."

"I suppose I'll have to agree with your theory, Edouard," his sister said. She shook her head, her features a study in utter disbelief as she watched Roderika cavort about, flinging her arms out and throwing her head back, song after song pouring from her. "Being blessed with perfect attributes by wise women does nothing to confer natural talent. You're either born with it, or you're not. Poor Roderika."

"The storehouse appears to be rather empty, for all the pretty blessings they gave her."

"And yet here she is, compelled to sing and dance as though she were born with those talents." Aloysia paused, shaking her head and clucking. "I must admit that I feel rather sorry for her. If it weren't for those wise women and that grumpy hag, she'd be an ordinary princess, happy with whatever nat-ural talents she was born with."

Edouard nodded vaguely as he watched Roderika leap up, throwing her arms out, while letting out a high screech that was, most likely, supposed to be a part of a song. "I'm feeling rather sorry for us, too."

With a delighted whoop, Roderika suddenly threw herself into the wild-flowers, her little body vanishing in an explosion of color as flowers, leaves, twigs, and possibly frightened spiders that had taken up residence among the blooms flew all over. Her skirts and velvet-clad feet momentarily popped out and then vanished as well. Where she used to stand, a group of wildflowers shook in every direction as she probably rolled around or flailed or did what ten-year-old princesses did when given a momentary break from the stifling rigors of court life.

"She's going to be a mess," Aloysia noted blandly.

Edouard was going to say something about stating the obvious when Roderika let out a little shriek.

"Cousin Aloysia!" she cried from where she lay. "I found something!"

"Oh, I can't wait, I'm sure!" Aloysia said, her tone still a dry monotone.

Roderika's head and shoulders suddenly popped up amid the flowers. To say that she was a sight would be an understatement. Hair disheveled and tangled, crown missing, gown sporting all kinds of debris everywhere, Roderika turned to her cousins with a triumphant grin. Edouard wasn't quite sure, but her left cheek looked scratched.

"Look what I found!" the little girl crowed, and she held up an object that glinted in the sun. It was a narrow cone, about a foot long. Though crusted with soil from sitting outdoors for only the heavens knew how long, its sharp point seemed to gleam as the sun shone on it. "Can I play with it? I want to play with it!"

Beside Edouard, Aloysia gasped—a sharp, rattling inhalation that reminded Edouard of the last breaths of a dying, disease-riddled beast. He rested a hand on his sister's tense shoulder and gave it a comforting pat.

"Relax, it's only a spike," he said. "Easy enough to get rid of. There's nothing to worry about. Take a deep breath and exhale slowly."

. . . .

"A THOROUGH SCRUBBING is in order," Edouard said as he handed his little cousin over to the nurse, who stared at the soiled and rumpled princess with her jaw hanging low. "Oh, and search her dress for hidden sharp objects. We've confiscated what we could, but little cousin here's proving to be a sly thing, and I wouldn't be surprised if she managed to sneak a few weapons in her gown."

"Oh, Your Highness," the nurse said, glancing at Edouard with the most pathetically helpless look in her eyes.

"We all must ensure that Princess Roderika remains free from the hazards of pointy things."

Well—not that confiscating weapons from the sharp-object-obsessed princess would do much to prevent the predestined catastrophe that loomed in the distance, but it was certainly better to at least try to keep the girl safe till her fifteenth birthday, when everything was set to fall apart.

Edouard walked off, carrying the broken arrow, the spike, and the tree branch that was shaped like a spear. He walked past the busy swarms of servants and courtiers who hurried to and fro, all caught up in the frantic preparations for a spoiled little girl's tenth birthday celebration.

He dared not check up on Aloysia, whom he'd excused and sent off to her assigned room. The random discovery of the spike in the meadow proved to be the final straw for the irritable princess, and she retired to her room with a major case of the headache, coupled with a stomachache and a generous dollop of hate directed at the world. Edouard wasn't sure, but he thought he saw his sister transform into a raging squirrel the moment she stepped across the threshold of her room.

She was, of course, in the middle of a very colorful rant about curses and their after-effects when she suddenly vanished in a puff of gray smoke, and in her place, a wildly squeaking squirrel stood, its fur standing on end, its tail straight and stiff and puffed up, flailing its little arms and hopping around in a tizzy. Edouard was obliged to close the bedroom door on it and left it to cool down in private.

He went to the nursery, which was a massive room adjoining the queen's suite. He sighed his relief when he entered and closed the door against the noisy bustle of the castle, and he leaned against the door, frowning as he realized how tired and bored he was.

"I really would rather be studying," he said, massaging the sudden knot in the nape of his neck. He grimaced as he pushed himself away from the door and walked over to the gigantic wooden chest that sat in one corner of the nursery. Around him, all kinds of toys lay scattered, and he could only frown at them in disapproval. Why, if he were Roderika's father, he'd ensure that his daughter would pick up after herself—or at least ensure that the nurse did a much more thorough job of cleaning up after an overly energetic child. No, indeed—a cluttered room was completely unacceptable in Edouard's extremely uncluttered and tidy mind.

He knelt down before the large chest, fiddled around with the lock, and lifted the lid.

"Good grief, Roderika," he muttered, shaking his head.

The chest was the little princess's "forbidden corner" in that it housed all of the sharp, pointy objects that Roderika had stumbled across in one way or another and taken back to play with. The princess was only ten years old, and the chest was already half-full. Broken arrows, spears, knives, spikes, nails, and every other imaginable object that resembled a spindle was hidden in that chest.

For that day's booty, Edouard tossed in the arrow, the spike, and the oddly shaped tree branch. He really didn't know why his aunt and uncle insisted on collecting those things because burning them the way those spindles were burned once upon a time would've been a great deal more effective in protecting the cursed princess.

Was this collection something akin to relics? What a disturbing thought that was.

After locking the chest, Edouard sat on it and scowled at the floor. Roderika's birthday celebration was set to begin at around noon. Already the castle was being swarmed by guests from neighboring kingdoms, and courtiers took care to welcome everyone. Edouard had been wracking his brain for ways to avoid the party, but knowing his fawning mother, his presence was going to be demanded, and disobliging her meant being subjected to her nagging for at least a week.

"Bugger," he grumbled, rubbing his face with a hand.

Chapter 9

Hamlin glanced up and watched his mother, who sat across the coach from him. Queen Elfriede looked absolutely resplendent and beautiful, the years not taking too much of a toll on her physically, though she'd always had about her an overwhelming sadness. She'd dressed herself in a very fashionable cotehardie and surcoat, both of which were in muted colors that ran contrary to popular trends in court, her hair completely hidden by an embroidered caul and padded roll.

She looked every bit the queen of their kingdom, but she watched the passing countryside with a palpable air of wistfulness, the faraway look in her eyes making Hamlin wonder what memories she was now immersing herself in. He found that she did that quite often, for she was very much an introvert and was terribly shy despite her position. Perhaps the wistfulness was really a product of a role that had been forced onto her, one that she didn't want despite the fact that she had not been forced to marry King Reinhard; that finally, Hamlin's father married for love and not for obligatory reasons.

"Mama, are you sure we have to attend this birthday party?" Hamlin asked after another moment of silence.

His mother looked at him and smiled. "What are you going to complain about now, darling? Too long a ride?"

"No. I just don't like it there. I didn't enjoy it the last time I was, you know, in attendance."

The queen laughed, looking like an adolescent dressed up in an older woman's clothes. Hamlin couldn't help but grin in delight. "True—I remember you playing fisticuffs with Clarimond's son, and I'm afraid to say that you'll likely see him again now. I mean, he's Princess Roderika's cousin, you know."

Hamlin sighed, grimacing, as he slumped in his seat. "He was a real ass. Hopefully my half-brothers will get along with him and keep him away from me."

"Maybe. Then again, it's been ten years since you two last saw each other. Maybe he's improved with age."

"I doubt it." Hamlin scowled and folded his arms over his chest, turning his attention to the brilliant day outside. "An ass is an ass is an ass, I say."

Queen Elfriede clucked, and Hamlin felt one of his legs kicked. "Watch your language, young man," she said, though amusement continued to tinge her words. "I don't know why young people nowadays are so enamored of cursing."

Hamlin rolled his eyes. "Oh, come on, Mama. You were my age once upon a time. I'm sure that even ladies get to spew a vile handful when everyone's backs are turned."

"Emphasis on 'when everyone's backs are turned', Hamlin. Do you see my back turned?"

They both laughed, with Hamlin's face burning. Heavens, but he hated being caught out by his mother. "Well, Otto and the others curse all the time, and I don't see anyone saying anything about it."

"But you're most certainly not any of them."

Hamlin paused, regarding his mother earnestly. She met his gaze with a faint smile, the melancholy immediately back. "No, I'm not," he said in a near whisper, feeling himself blush again.

"And between you and me? I'm very glad."

Hamlin wasn't sure, but he thought there was a glint of moisture around his mother's eyes, but Queen Elfriede quickly blinked and turned her attention away from him, fixing her gaze back on the countryside. The conversation was over—or at least that subject was, anyway.

Hamlin was grateful that his half-brothers had gone on ahead of them, leaving his father's castle about an hour prior, all of them dressed for travel and mounted on their best steeds. It would be another adventure for them in addition to another way of passing the time. The three older princes had been going about their days bored out of their wits (the downside to peacetime), and Roderika's birthday surely offered them some much-needed diversion—without declaring war on a kingdom just to keep them entertained.

Now that Hamlin was fourteen years old, they didn't think it worth their while to bully and humiliate him the way they did when he was younger. For better or worse, they had taken to simply ignoring him, as though he'd never been born. Not that Hamlin minded, for he'd rather be ignored than taunted, locked away, or left behind and forced to find his way back home, all because he wasn't their "full" brother, and the older princes disliked his mother so much.

Riding to the kingdom to the east of theirs in his mother's company proved to be enjoyable overall, though his mother's melancholy subtly ate away at him. Then again, it was also a pretty effective distraction from the possibility of crossing paths with that odious Edouard.

With any luck, Edouard would be too busy strutting around and puffing out his snobby chest to recognize Hamlin. Even better if the older boy were no different from his half-brothers, and he'd be flaunting himself before every eligible young princess. If he were bedding a dozen or so girls, even better; he wouldn't have the strength or mental capacity to recognize Hamlin or to pick up where he'd left off ten years ago.

"I hope, I hope, I hope," Hamlin murmured.

• • • •

LIVERIED SERVANTS GREETED them on their arrival, and they were escorted indoors amid a great deal of activity. Nobility from all over filled King Friedrich and Queen Franziska's castle, not the least of which being an endless swarm of children running, yelping, playing, crying, laughing.

Hamlin grimaced as he followed his mother through the corridors, deftly sidestepping people of all ages as they hurried past. His ears were already ringing, and they'd just arrived. Heaven knew what awaited him in an hour or even half an hour.

The throne room looked just as huge and imposing as before, though Hamlin admitted that he could barely remember much otherwise, being far too busy being in a panic and then falling asleep in his mother's arms the last time he was there. He wondered how his half-brothers fared, for they had not attended Roderika's first grand celebration. They were most likely spending time with new friends who were equally obnoxious as they.

Hamlin and his mother wove their way through the glittering assembly, which was surprisingly less formal than before. Perhaps it was because Roderika was already grown up, and this gathering in the throne room was more for the adults. In the meantime, the birthday girl was very likely out somewhere, busy playing with friends and guests' children.

"Elfriede! How wonderful to see you again!"

Hamlin glanced up and found Queen Franziska squeezing past a gaggle of gossiping duchesses, her arms outstretched. She grinned broadly, and Hamlin saw no falseness in her manner. In fact, her cheerful greeting only made him remember his and his mother's final moment with Queen Franziska a decade ago, and a lovely warmth swept over him at the assurance that, at least in their hostess, his mother had found an ally and friend.

Queen Elfriede stepped forward and curtsied, but their royal hostess merely waved the formality with a happy "Pish!" before taking his mother's hands in hers and giving the blushing queen a sisterly kiss on the cheek.

"It's been a long time!" Queen Franziska said, laughing. "Look at you! I'm so glad you're here! Is this little Hamlin with you?"

"I'm not that little, am I?" Hamlin blurted out, unable to stop himself.

"No, you're not, but I'll always remember you as that fiery little boy who was frightened of a baby. You became quite a legend among the children back then."

It was now Hamlin's turn for a kiss and friendly squeeze of his hands. Queen Franziska pulled away and looked him over from head to toe. "My goodness," she said. "It's simply amazing how much you've grown, Hamlin. I wouldn't be surprised if your old nemesis didn't recognize you now."

She spoke with a mischievous twinkle in her eyes, and Hamlin's mother laughed along with her.

"I suppose I'd be glad if he didn't," Hamlin stammered, embarrassed. "I'm sure I wouldn't recognize him, either."

"Well, you won't have to worry about crossing paths with him anytime soon. I think he went off with some other boys, and heaven knows what they're up to now. Maybe putting on a show to impress young ladies?" Queen Franziska rolled her eyes.

"I'm sure he won't have a hard time finding someone," Hamlin said. If his memory served him well, Prince Edouard was a handsome boy. Ill-tempered and a right snot, but handsome.

Here Queen Franziska led Hamlin and his mother away, linking arms with Queen Elfriede like they were young girls, while Hamlin walked alongside them.

"I don't know," she said. She sounded a bit thoughtful but still in high spirits. "The running joke hereabouts is that Prince Edouard's betrothed to his books. No one—and I mean no one—could tear him away from his parents' library, or if they did, it would be short-lived. My nephew's known for breaking ranks and vanishing, sneaking back to his room or library or wherever he finds some privacy, and there he'll stay for hours, his nose buried in his books."

"It'll take a very special young lady to win his attention, it seems," Queen Elfriede said, sounding equally delighted.

"I feel rather sorry for her," Hamlin muttered.

Before long the three of them were out in Queen Franziska's private garden, which seemed to be located several leagues away. But it was a pretty, quiet little patch of land within castle walls, and only a few people wandered through the lush vegetation, their privacy assured by thick flowering shrubbery that rose to about shoulder height.

"I come here to clear my head," Queen Franziska said with a pleased sigh. "I wish I had showed you this the last time you were here, Elfriede. I wager Hamlin would have diverted himself immensely here, and perhaps the trouble with Edouard would've been avoided."

Hamlin found himself surreptitiously eyeing a couple of young lords, quickly turning his gaze away when they glanced in his direction. Was he blushing? It sure felt like it. Still, he couldn't help himself, and as his mother and Queen Franziska chatted on and on like giddy adolescent girls, Hamlin absorbed the serene beauty of the garden and alternated his admiration of his surroundings with wide-eyed stares at an occasional handsome young man who happened to wander within his field of vision.

There was one youth, in particular, who not only caught his eye but also managed to haunt him enough to steal several more glances. It was a fortunate thing, indeed, that the two queens suddenly stopped walking and were now engaged in a pleasant conversation about dull, queenly things. The young man who'd caught Hamlin's eye stood a few shrubs away, visible from the chest up, looking rather put out as he stared at something just off to his right. Hamlin followed the young man's line of vision and saw nothing but a flowering tree, whose leaves shook and shivered, perhaps because of a bird or two or more that had just taken refuge within its colorful branches.

The youth was tall, had short, neat, mousy brown hair and dark eyes, his pale complexion slightly flushed from the sun, perhaps, unless it was because of his mood. He wore clothes in a rich, black velvet, with only the barest hint of white adding embroidered definition here and there. He was quite stunning in Hamlin's humble opinion.

"Aloysia!" the young man cried, still glaring at the tree. "Don't you dare leave!"

From among the flowering branches came the wild chirping of a bird.

"Ha! Don't even think about it! I'm not leaving Auntie's garden if that's the case!"

The bird chirped again. Hamlin wasn't sure, but the little creature sounded rather saucy, taunting the young man, in fact. Did birds taunt humans in bird language? He might have to ask Audwin about that.

"Oh, you're a fine one to talk!"

Hamlin blinked and then grimaced. Oh, dear. What a cruel joke it was for the fellow to be so dreadfully attractive and yet tragically insane. He hoped it wasn't a sign of things to come where Hamlin's romantic attachments were concerned. Pursing his lips and sighing in defeat, he was forced to turn his attention back to his companions.

Chapter 10

Edouard had never realized till that moment how indescribably difficult girls could be. Sure, he'd been witness to their unaccountable fits in the past, but perhaps because the current situation stretched everyone's nerves past the breaking point, he was dismayed at being subjected to a desperate sister's shapeshifting antics.

Considering the fact that Aloysia wouldn't think twice about abandoning him to a fate worse than death—that is, leaving him to play the Perfect Princely Son for their proud mother to show off and parade around—Edouard was quite close to falling into an apoplectic fit.

• • • •

THE TWO OF THEM HAD fled into their aunt's sanctuary, believing that they'd be safe there from Queen Clarimond's demands for an appearance. Unfortunately, the first person they ran across was their mother busily gossiping with a couple of other noblewomen, and Edouard's days were immediately numbered.

"Oh, there you are!" she'd cried, while Edouard nearly jumped out of his skin at the sight of his mother and her friends suddenly appearing from behind a particularly tall and thick shrub. With a big, brilliant grin (a very rare sight), she reached out and grasped her son's arm and immediately said, "My dear Edouard, since you haven't been visible since you returned Roderika to her nurse, I expect you to make the effort to show yourself during the celebration and let everyone know that you're alive, and you're here."

"Indeed, young man, you've no idea how many beautiful young ladies you can meet!" one of queen's friends piped up, her grin mirroring Queen Clarimond's.

For a quick, panicked moment, Edouard thought that she was going to lunge forward and grab hold of his free arm, and from there, he'd be dragged out and then tossed unceremoniously into the midst of the revelry.

"How old are you now? Seventeen, I heard? Why, that's just the perfect age for a handsome young man like yourself to do justice to chivalry and go searching for that special girl," the other woman said, her voice a deep, gravelly sound that made Edouard want to cough and clear his throat.

"Now that you two have mentioned it, I can think of just the perfect young woman for my beautiful boy," Queen Clarimond said. Her eyes widened, then sparkled with pleasure and realization, though her grip on Edouard's arm remained firm, even painful. She looked at him, this time pride radiating from every pore of her body. "This is simply wonderful! Oh, I really must introduce the two of you—"

"See, Mama, that's exactly what I've been telling Edouard," Aloysia, who'd been completely ignored the whole time, suddenly said.

Edouard looked at her, horrified. What in the world was his sister up to now? She didn't even bother to glance at him, moving closer to the older women and holding their attention with slightly exaggerated gestures and a tone that was conspiratorial and gossipy.

"You know how withdrawn and aloof my brother is. Well, I was just trying to pull him away from the celebration, so we could have a quiet talk here in Aunt Franziska's garden. I need to remind him—as a princess and his sister—the importance of keeping up his role and fulfilling his obligations to you and Papa."

She smiled as she straightened, pulling her shoulders back and clasping her hands over her skirts. Demure and level-headed—it was a remarkable façade she'd taken on. "I'm so glad that we met you here and that you're discussing his marriage prospects. That's just the support I need to talk with him."

Then she turned to face Edouard, still smiling. "See, brother? I'm not the only one who thinks highly enough of you to consider attaching you as soon as possible to a girl whom you surely deserve."

"That's rather low, actually," Edouard muttered between clenched teeth, and he sighed in relief when his mother released him.

"I'm very pleased to hear that, Aloysia," Queen Clarimond said, nodding her head and looking unspeakably happy now.

She leaned forward and gave Aloysia a quick kiss on the cheek before pushing past them both and leading her friends away, making Edouard's jaw drop. Their mother, whom they'd grown up to regard as the "ice queen," was behaving uncharacteristically. Where was the stiff solemnity? The raised chin? The condescending half-smile?

"You're using your head. Go ahead and advise your brother, but don't linger too long. We need both of you—especially you, Edouard—to be out where everyone can see you."

"Of course, Mama. You don't have to worry about anything. I'll look after him."

The three women left, and Edouard kept a wary eye on them until they vanished around a corner. Then he turned to scowl blackly at Aloysia, who was scratching her nose.

"Thank you, you lying little spore, for trapping me in a situation that I hate," he said, his voice coming out in a growl.

"I got rid of them, didn't I? Who says that you have to follow along with what they tell you?" Aloysia paused and scanned the area. Then she beckoned to Edouard and led him farther into the garden. "The celebration's too big, anyway, for anyone to be seen by everyone. You can always pretend later that you were out and about as ordered, but no one will know if you're lying or not. In the meantime, you get to stay here, in Auntie's garden, safe from the affectations of husband-hungry girls and their mamas."

"And how, exactly, does that solve Mama's newest obsession of match-making?" Edouard asked, feeling the ground open up under his feet. "Even if I hid in Auntie's garden all day long, she'd still be thinking about introducing me to Princess Whoever tomorrow and the day after. She won't rest until she's assured that I'm engaged."

"Listen, ingrate, we'll deal with Mama one day at a time. For now, if you're so worried about your royal icy bum, you'd do best to stay here and avoid being seen by her anywhere."

They'd found a little open space that was bordered by shrubbery and some pretty flowering trees, with an elegantly carved stone bench.

"I might have a royal icy bum, but at least it remains human twenty-four hours a day, seven days a week," Edouard retorted. "And since we're on the subject of avoidance, I suppose I should ask you about your not-so-subtle efforts at avoiding your responsibilities. Clovis has a great deal more patience than you give him credit for. You can turn yourself into a garden snail and find a way to stay that way forever, but that'll never turn him off the chase."

• • • •

AND SO BROTHER AND sister argued over responsibilities, each going nowhere, for both were saddled with the same burdens, now that they were at the prime age for matrimony—or at least endless, soul-eating hours of dull courtship. In fact, the conversation shifted in subject so many times that by the time Aloysia had a tantrum that resulted in her shapeshifting into the ugliest bird Edouard had ever seen, Edouard had forgotten what they were quarreling about.

Ignoring his sister, he glanced at the stone bench and slapped a hand to his forehead. "Oh, damn me, I didn't bring anything to read," he hissed. "If I'm going to be trapped here till midnight, I should at least have something to occupy myself with."

He could kick himself for the lack of foresight. Then again, he hadn't known—and neither had Aloysia—that he would be trapped here for the day, half-terrorized into hiding by his own mother. Edouard sighed and rolled his eyes. Why should he even be surprised by that fact?

"See, brother? Had you taken the trouble to expand your mind beyond those horrible books, you'd have learned to shapeshift, like me, and you wouldn't have to depend so much on books to keep you occupied. Me? I can fly all over the place without worrying about anyone finding me out."

"Not if you look like something a disease-riddled horse would vomit," Edouard retorted.

"Why practice magic if you're going to limit yourself to the mundane? I can blend in if I wanted to, but for now, I prefer to practice looking strange and horrific."

Edouard stared at the tree where Aloysia had hidden herself among the branches earlier. Thank heaven, indeed, that his sister had decided to hide herself instead of fly all over, looking exactly as Edouard had described. One look at her and anyone in his right mind wouldn't think twice of ridding the land of her plague by shooting her down with an arrow.

"Practice? You? You don't need to practice looking strange and horrific!" he said.

"Edouard? Ah, there you are! Guess who's here?" a voice suddenly cut in.

Edouard snapped his mouth shut, as did Aloysia. He turned quickly to find Queen Franziska and two other people watching him. "Auntie?" he stammered, his blood freezing. How much of his conversation with Aloysia had they seen or heard? "How—how long have you been standing there?"

His aunt took a quick glance around the small private space and then shrugged, smiling at him. "Not too long. Well, long enough to hear you talking rather heatedly with your sister, it seems, but I don't see her anywhere."

"Ah. Yes. My sister. She—uh—she just left, Auntie."

"Oh? We didn't see her leave. This is the only entrance and exit to this little niche."

Edouard swallowed. "Well—she felt a little daring and somewhat boyish, and she forced her way through the trees." He pointed in the direction of the flowering trees at one end of the private area.

"She did?" Queen Franziska followed his finger with her eyes, and she blinked. "I hope she didn't tear herself up among all those thorny bushes. They grow densely over there."

Edouard swallowed again. "I didn't hear her scream."

"That's good, I suppose. Anyway, my dear, I'd like to introduce—or, rather, re-introduce—you to some guests," Queen Franziska said, beaming, as she swept into Edouard's last retreat, a noblewoman, who appeared to be several years her junior, following her.

Edouard pointedly ignored the flowering tree, whose branches now shook wildly under Aloysia's large, misshapen, feathered body. How the girl managed to keep her balance, let alone fly, was a mystery to Edouard, but he sought to keep everyone's attention on him in the event that Aloysia lost her footing and tumbled from her perch, exposing her unsightly form and arousing suspicion. He stepped forward and bowed as gracefully as he could.

"You might not remember, but this is Queen Elfriede," his aunt said, and Edouard and the other queen exchanged polite salutations.

Then Queen Franziska stepped aside and pulled someone from behind one of the taller shrubs, and out stumbled a boy with a yelp. He appeared to be a little younger than Edouard, with short blond hair, blue eyes, and a slight and rather awkward build. He wore a dark violet suit, which seemed to bring out his best features, though Edouard could also see doubt edged with terror in the other boy's gaze as he regarded him.

"Now this young man, I'm sure you remember," his aunt said with a bubbly laugh. "Prince Hamlin, this is your old nemesis, my nephew, Prince Edouard. I daresay neither of you would've forgotten that marvelous little spat of yours. Hamlin, I say, came out the better fighter, but he did have his size going for him."

She paused and gave Hamlin, who continued to regard Edouard with clear suspicion, frowning at him and then at the flowering tree, a playful nudge with her elbow. He refused to step forward, and his body language screamed "cornered young deer ready to flee."

"I can't remember how long it took for Edouard's bruises to go away, but it was rather a while."

Edouard returned Hamlin's dubious frown with a practiced look of calm superiority. That is, he arched a brow while looking expressionless. "Yes, of course I remember," he said, and deciding to be the courteous one, he bowed. "It's a pleasure to see you again, Your Highness. I hope that we've grown out of childish silliness."

Hamlin hesitated, his gaze continuing to move from Edouard to the tree and back. For a brief, awkward moment, he said nothing. Then his frown deepened. "I grew out of it," he said, his voice gentle and lilting. And hesitant. And most certainly nervous. "You, though, seemed to have gone mad."

Chapter 11

Hamlin had certainly grown out of several things, but one thing he apparently hadn't was his mother's scolding. What amazed him the most was the fact that, despite Queen Elfriede's exhaustion and melancholy, she still somehow managed to keep a very remarkable amount of nagging energy in store for him.

Following that awkward reunion with Edouard—which drew a great deal of mad twittering from that unseen bird in the tree as well as a burst of suppressed laughter from Queen Franziska, which she disguised with a bout of coughing—Hamlin found himself being dragged away from company by a red-faced and profusely apologizing Queen Elfriede.

Feeling his mother's fingers dig into his arm as she pulled him away and in the direction of another private garden within a garden, Hamlin complained and protested all the way. His arm was going to be sporting some bruises on the morrow, to be sure. At least his mother had long stopped dragging him around by his ear.

"Ouch! Mama!" he cried once he stumbled inside the little garden, but his mother refused to acknowledge him till she pulled him over to a stone bench and unceremoniously pushed him onto it. There he sat, glowering and grimacing as he massaged the pain out of his arm.

His mother stood before him with both hands on her hips. "I did *not* raise you to be rude or troublesome, Hamlin," she barked. "You're not your half-brothers, and I hope that lightning would strike me dead if you turned out like any of them."

"That's a bit extreme, don't you think?" Hamlin countered, now sulking.

His mother merely raised a brow at him.

"But he was talking to a bird! Didn't you hear him?"

"He was talking to his sister, who left before we got there."

"Then why didn't I hear a girl's voice? Why did I hear him talk and then hear a bird answer?" Hamlin paused as his mind furiously tried to wrap itself around a number of things, none of which promised anything good for Edouard. Eyes widening, he looked back at his startled mother, and he leaned forward and whispered, "Mama—is Edouard's family enchanted? Is his sister a bird?"

"What on earth are you going on about?"

Hamlin's mind continued its furious analysis of things.

"That makes sense, then!" he whispered again. "No wonder I didn't hear a girl's voice! But—but what's even more terrifying is the chance that maybe Edouard and his family are really ghouls or monsters of some kind, and they've all cast some sort of glamour on us, so we only see their human forms!"

His mother sighed and shook her head. "Hamlin..."

"It all makes sense now, Mama, given Edouard's graveyard-like personality. What if—what if all this business about celebrations and Roderika's birthday is nothing more than an elaborate hoax?"

Oh, that was a lovely one right there. Hamlin couldn't stop himself, but then again, he really didn't want to. His eyes widened even more as excitement and dread spiraled along with youthful imagination.

"What if guests are being marked for meals, Mama? For all we know, a dozen people are already missing and being roasted in the kitchen for tonight's banquet."

Queen Elfriede's look of tired motherhood immediately switched to horror. "Hamlin!"

"How does one kill ghouls, anyway? I must admit that I never even thought that I'd find myself in a situation like this!" An ugly reminder made him droop. "I'm terrible in sword-handling, too. I barely passed that class."

"Hamlin! Stop it!" his mother cried. She waved her arms in frustration, but then again, it might have something to do with the disgust she might be feeling toward the subject. "Where on earth do you get these horrible, outlandish ideas?"

"Um. Audwin?" Hamlin replied in a tiny voice.

He watched his mother stare at him in speechless amazement—as well as outrage. She pressed her mouth into a tight line, stepped back, and paced in front of him. It was a familiar sight to Hamlin, who had grown up being scolded about anything and everything, regardless of his fault in the matter. Experience had long since taught him that it was in his best interest to simply slump down, look as defeated and pathetic as he could, and hope for pity.

"Your father warned me about that, and I should've listened," she finally ground out without breaking her momentum. She looked like a gowned soldier-woman being taught how to look lively while marching off to war to wreak complete annihilation. "He told me that encouraging you to keep invisible friends is a bad thing, and he's right. Now you're using this Audwin creature as an excuse for inexcusable behavior."

"But he *does* exist!"

"Yes, yes, he's a talking raven. How utterly charming. Not only that, he's a talking raven who teaches you how to be saucy to others—even to those who're your superiors."

Hamlin blinked as he watched his mother in shock. "Superior!" he echoed. "Who? Edouard? Why would he be my superior? We're both princes! You and his mother are both queens! Why on earth would you even consider the idea that you and I are lesser?"

That made her freeze in her tracks. For one strained moment, Hamlin watched his mother struggle for words with her face turned away from him, her hands clenching and unclenching at her sides. Her body was stiff, so much so that Hamlin began to worry sincerely about her state of mind. She calmed eventually, and her posture softened and relaxed, her initial tenseness replaced by that quiet dignity that Hamlin had always admired in her. With a deep sigh, she turned to face him, her features now calm yet earnest.

"I won't shield you from the facts, Hamlin," she said. "I'm sure you know very well what I meant by that, and no matter how much you disagree with the way people think, there's really nothing much you can do to convince them otherwise."

Queen Elfriede paused and made a vague and lifeless gesture with one hand.

"I was a commoner before I married your father, and in some people's eyes, I'll always be a commoner, crown or no. Do I regret marrying your father? Absolutely not. I love him, and he loves me *and* you. He was never obligated to marry me. We were never betrothed, and we both made conscious choices. That's enough to elevate my status as his queen in the eyes of romantics, I suppose, but not in the eyes of the aristocracy, and I willingly put up with the gossip and the mockery wherever I go if it means being happily married to the man I love."

Hamlin dropped his gaze to his hands on his lap. "All that gossip, though—it wears you out. I can see it, Mama. I don't understand how you think that this is worth being laughed at and talked about like some dumb beast."

"My marriage to your father gave you to us, didn't it? That's something to be proud of."

"But you still think of us as lesser than everyone else!"

"Fact, Hamlin—by birth, we are. I've no drop of royal blood in me, but you do, if only by half. In everything else? We aren't. You have to understand that you, especially, straddle that ridiculous fence that so many people are so keen on maintaining. You *must* be aware of your—your difference and your sameness with those other noble children your age. If you were to blind yourself to either fact about yourself, you'll never be the kind of nobleman that every kingdom desperately needs. Empathy, respect, and wisdom—those are rare qualities nowadays. An open mind born out of that empathy—how many 'real' aristocrats are blessed with it?"

"Queen Franziska likes you a lot."

"Who else?"

Hamlin sighed, pinching his mouth into a tight line. "You're just as keen on keeping that fence up, Mama."

Queen Elfriede paused, and Hamlin glanced up, startled, when she approached the stone bench and sat beside him, taking his hand in hers.

"I'm not very good at verbalizing my thoughts, darling," she said with a rueful little smile, and she pressed her lips against Hamlin's hand. "But I'm sure that you'll understand my meaning in time. Let's just say that I'm a great deal more aware of my place, and each day is a constant struggle to determine where I stand."

"But what's there to understand? You love Papa, and that's all you need. Didn't you just say that?"

His mother sighed heavily, bowing her head and falling silent for a moment, though she never let go of his hand. "It does wear on me, darling. I'm saddled with doubts that come out at the worst times, and my confidence isn't enough to weather things as well as I wish." She shook her head, still looking down. "I ought to be stronger for you and your father, not be shadowed by contradictions, but—I'm only a merchant's daughter."

"Yet you're far better than most of the noblewomen I've seen." Hamlin watched her, swallowing. "And you're stubborn, just like Papa. You're two of the most stubborn people I know, actually."

"And you're the product of this double stubbornness?" Queen Elfriede looked at him again, smiling fondly. "You might not think it, but you've enough courage for two people, Hamlin. In time, you'll be given a chance to prove it. I don't know why I'm saying it, but I feel it deeply. Maybe it's premonition if you believe in that sort of thing."

"So for now I should stay away from Edouard," Hamlin said, sighing, and his mother chuckled and then shrugged.

"You do what you want to do," she replied. "But no more quarrels, please. No more provocations. I don't care who's at fault. Neither of you is a child anymore."

Hamlin nodded, and this time, his mother smiled, gave his hand one final squeeze, and then stood up. "Well, I suppose I should rejoin my friend. I want you to be present during the banquet, all right?" She bent down and gave Hamlin a kiss on the top of his head before hurrying away. Within seconds, Hamlin could hear his mother's voice mingling with Queen Franziska's, and the two queens were once again deep in conversation and laughter, their voices slowly fading away as they made their way out of the garden.

Hamlin sighed and looked around him. The little private area looked no different from the one where that mad Edouard had ensconced himself, and even as an occasional person or couple walked past, deep in thought or conversation, Hamlin took a great deal of delight in the serene beauty of the area.

He stretched his arms above his head and yawned, and then he turned and stretched himself out on the stone bench, closing his eyes against the vivid sky and ignoring the hardness of the bench on his back, both legs bent and feet flat on the bench, hands clasped over his stomach. Hamlin luxuriated in the fresh air and the distant sounds of revelry that were only broken up by the gentler whispering of the breeze.

His mind wandered back to his reunion with Edouard, and he wondered what the other prince was doing now. He could still see the look of shock and then mortification that cast a comical shadow on that insufferable boy's face, and Hamlin wished that he had his wits about him at that time, for he'd surely have come up with even better things to say that would've driven Edouard into an apoplectic fit.

What a pity it was, he couldn't help but note rather wistfully, that his nemesis had grown up into a very handsome young man. What a greater pity it was that Hamlin kept fixing his mind on the mad boy, and with every gentle touch of the breeze against his skin, he conjured up images of Edouard's dark eyes and lean figure, even conceding to the rather delicious fact that the other boy's haughty mien only added to his irresistible charm.

The insanity, though...

Hamlin's eyes flew wide open when he felt something land on his knees with a wild fluttering of wings and a squawk. That the animal fought to keep its balance by digging its claws into his legs and was the ugliest, most ungainly bird ever to be created only made the shock worse.

It was a gigantic bird—like a massive brown chicken. But it could fly, and it didn't have a comb on its head, and its eyes looked big and frog-like, its beak curved into an odd hook. It struggled to keep itself from tumbling off Hamlin, which only made its grip worse.

"Ouch! Get off! Get off!" Hamlin cried, waving his hands wildly and causing the bird to squawk and screech and flap its wings ineffectually. "You're shredding my knees, you monster!"

He sat up, and it was with a great deal of willpower that he managed to straighten out his legs despite the horrific pain, and his eyes watered as he kept trying to shoo the strange bird. It finally lost its grip on Hamlin's legs and tumbled off him, landing on the grass in a wild mess of flapping wings, flying feathers, and beastly shrieks that only that kind of a bird would be capable of.

It rolled over a couple of times before righting itself, still squawking hysterically, before it flapped its wings and flew away. If it could truly be called "flying." Hamlin, massaging his knees, watched the creature bounce across the grass as though to gain some momentum, and then with a mighty heave of its oversized body, the bird finally flew off, leaving a trail of brown feathers in its wake. Hamlin had no idea where it was headed, but he wondered if other people would see it, become frightened, and then try to bring it down with a well-aimed arrow.

He turned and put his feet back on the ground, shaking his head in astonishment. "What a horrible, insane animal," he muttered. "I wouldn't be surprised if it turned out to be Edouard's blood relation. Ow, that hurts."

With another grimace, he continued to massage away the pain, cursing under his breath at the sight of his torn hose.

Chapter 12

Edouard managed to sneak back inside the castle, tiptoe past the revelers, and find his way into his aunt and uncle's massive library, where he hid himself. He did, of course, attempt to find hidden passages somewhere in the room, and after plucking a random book from one of the shelves, he spent—or, rather, wasted—a great deal of time feeling around the walls for a telltale outline of a door, sometimes knocking against the stone or pressing his ear against it to see if he could detect any hollowness behind the wall.

After completing a circuit around the room, he was forced to give up, especially after he realized that he could've explored the floor as well, but a mere glance at the area stretching out before him made his stomach turn. In the end, Edouard was forced to concede that there was only so much desperate searching he could do before pride and dignity reasserted themselves.

With a defeated sigh, Edouard cradled the book against his chest and escaped the library, this time moving in the direction of the rear stairs. Surely there was an empty room on an upper floor where he could hide himself until midnight or whenever the damned celebration ended.

He didn't catch sight of his mother anywhere, which was a great relief, but he did spot several of the young women to whom brainless gossips were already linking him, and the less cause for further sordid speculation he gave the bored and the witless, the better. It was all he could do to stay out of sight till he was safely in the shadows of the southern stairs.

Glad that the echoes of revelry were rapidly fading behind him, Edouard hurried up the stairs, ignoring the cold and slightly damp air of disuse. Countless stone steps led him up in what felt like an endless spiral. That surprised Edouard, because he realized that he'd somehow found his way to one of the towers. The stairs led nowhere, in that they never led him to a door that might have opened onto one of the upper floors. Instead they kept going up, with nothing but weathered stone flanking Edouard, the darkness of his way eased by an occasional narrow window on his right.

"I think I might've made a mistake," he muttered several minutes later as he sagged against the wall, perspiring and panting.

He'd sought privacy, and he certainly got it. He'd absolutely no idea how far up he'd gone, but it certainly felt like he'd just walked the distance between the sun and the moon with nothing to show for it but damp clothes and a book he'd now lost interest in. He sighed, drawing a sleeve across his sweaty brow, and he allowed himself to rest for a moment.

"Another few minutes of this, and if I don't find anything, I'll just turn around and go back down."

Eventually he found himself standing before the door of an isolated room at the top of the stairs. The door was ajar. Edouard stared at it, frowning.

"Shouldn't this be shut?" he muttered. Quietly stepping inside, he pushed the door till it was completely open, and he stopped short.

A little girl was the only occupant of the tower room. She sat on the floor, dirty with disuse, a quiver of arrows lying before her. She didn't seem to be aware of Edouard's presence as she played with the arrows, pulling them out and examining them one by one before setting them down on the floor beside her.

"Roderika!" Edouard barked. "What on earth are you doing here?"

Roderika's head snapped up, and the princess's eyes widened in surprise as she stared at her stunned cousin. Then she grinned, blue eyes shining, pink cheeks flushing, rosy lips pulling back to show little white teeth. "Hello, Cousin Edouard!" she cried. "See? I'm playing! Aren't these pretty?"

"No, they aren't, and what on earth made you come all the way up here?"

Roderika shrugged. "I don't know. I just wanted to play in a tower room."

"What do you mean, you wanted to play in a tower room? You never used to think about them." Well, not in Edouard's company, anyway.

The little girl shrugged again, this time making a comically puzzled face. "I don't know, cousin. I was minding my own business, and then I just wanted to leave everyone behind and find a tower room."

Edouard leaned against the doorway, sighing. His cousin was compelled again, this time to find and play in a tower room that any normal child would have avoided. Here was yet one more inexplicable urge of hers coming to the fore, and Edouard wondered what other strange needs awaited her with every year that passed. Why hadn't those damned "wise women" left her alone?

No, he quickly amended; this was all his aunt and uncle's doing, displaying his cousin and making a grand show of the wise women's presence. It all came down to pride, plain and simple, and he wanted to chastise them despite his fondness for them—such silly, blinded parents.

"It's not good for you to stay in here," Edouard said after a moment. "It's cold, it's damp, and it's filthy. You should be outside, playing with your friends."

"But I can't help it! I want to be here!"

"Uh—no, you don't. That's not you talking, Roderika. That's the so-called blessing that's doing it. Come along. I'll take you back outside."

Edouard stretched out an arm and raised a brow as the princess frowned at him, clearly disapproving. For one tense moment, Edouard was afraid that he was going to be forced to drag her away, screaming and wailing. Then he realized that the mental image of Roderika being hauled out of the tower room in hysterics quickly and easily matched that of Hamlin all those years ago, with the spoiled little prince making a tremendous amount of noise in front of everyone in court.

What shocked Edouard even more was what Roderika said just a few seconds later.

"Why are you smiling? You look stupid."

Edouard gave a little start. "I'm not smiling. What gives you that idea?"

"Your smile?" Roderika retorted, rolling her eyes. "That was a stupid question."

"Look, arguing with me won't do you any good. Either I take you back down now, or I'll have to call your cousin Aloysia." Invoking Aloysia's name was always a very effective resolution to the young princess's behavior problems. All the same, Edouard hoped he wasn't blushing or that, if he were, his cousin was too put out to notice. He beckoned to Roderika. "Come on! Let's go!"

Roderika simply glared at him, pinching her mouth into a tight line, and then stumbled to her feet. With another emphatic glare, she stomped her way to her cousin, her dress soiled, her hair escaping the headpiece so that golden curls tumbled down her back. Edouard could only shake his head at her as he claimed her hand.

"Idiot spells and curses," he muttered as he led her out of the tower room. "Sharp, pointed objects for toys, and now hidden tower rooms. What's next?"

"I'm learning how to embroider!" Roderika suddenly piped up, her initial sullenness now gone and replaced by a surge of sprightly energy. She actually skipped down the stairs beside Edouard. "Isn't that lovely, Cousin? I'll be making all kinds of patterns soon, but I want to embroider roses with the biggest, thickest thorns the most."

Edouard groaned. "Let me guess—you can't help but be drawn to them."

"The thorns, silly! I love the thorns!"

"Of course."

"When I'm queen, I'll have a special crown made. I want one that's all in pure gold, with fifty sharp and very tall points all the way around. I want those points to be so sharp that you cut yourself badly and bleed all over yourself when you touch them."

"Charming."

• • • •

ONE OF THE GREATER universal truths, Edouard was quick to learn, involved good deeds not going unpunished. He'd managed to bring Roderika back down, but since the general alarm had been raised at her disappearance, he was now not only hailed as her savior and hero, but he was also the darling of every woman present in court.

He stood in the massive courtyard, surrounded by dozens upon dozens of admiring young noblewomen, while his mother—of course—stood nearby, practically bursting with pride, as she crowed endlessly about his virtues, of which he apparently had about fifty heroes' worth.

He didn't realize, in fact, that he was not only courageous, but also immensely gifted in languages, being fluent in about twelve. Healers had determined that his brain was five times as large as an average boy's, which, of course, meant that he was painfully, *painfully* smart. He was also a very fast runner who could challenge the leanest and quickest wild beast, and he was blessed with a perfect set of the most charming freckles, which he really didn't have.

But who wished to argue with a queen who adored—simply worshipped—her own flesh and blood?

Edouard felt like a prize bull up for auction, surrounded by wide-eyed and blushing beauties of noble blood, his brain and ears filled with their endless chatter about his incredible bravery in fighting his way past monstrous spiders and dark, dangerous stairwells in order to rescue a trapped little girl and restore her to her family, while his mother's loud, grating voice rose as she continued to praise him to the skies. He wondered how much of an effort it was for Queen Clarimond to raise her voice in order to be heard; his mother was the firm, quiet type who asserted her authority in a tone of voice that always chilled him.

Edouard tried to see over the tall headdresses, vainly searching for a reason to leave, but he only saw people and children going about their business. Offering his admirers a vague and rather uncomfortable smile, which some girls delighted in calling "shy and adorable," Edouard bore the awful tedium of the moment while his mother chattered on and on about his somewhat pricey eligibility, even going as far as to indicate that "We simply would never give him up for just *any* noblewoman, mind you!"

As he glanced back up in another attempt at distraction, he spotted a little group of youths just off to his left, all of whom not only made a great deal of noise because they were obviously drunk, but also seemed to be tugging and pulling at someone who put up quite a resistance. Edouard frowned as he watched them now, craning his neck to avoid having his vision blocked by an excessively elaborate mountain of a headdress on a young lady's head.

He saw that there were five young men about his age, possibly a year or so older. They were all well-formed and muscular, at that stage where the lankiness of boyhood was being shed for the fuller, thicker figure of an adult man, but the hapless creature they were dragging about and laughing at was decidedly their inferior both in age and build.

Even from a distance and with those ridiculous headdresses mostly blocking his view, Edouard was sure of the details about the hulking brutes' victim, for he recognized that the poor bugger who was now being bodily carried away was none other than Hamlin.

"What on earth?" Edouard murmured, blinking in amazement, as he watched the group hoot and holler and melt away into the crowd. No one seemed to care about what was going on, for everyone was not only too caught up in the celebratory mood, but more than half of the adults appeared to be just as drunk as those fools.

Well, *there* was an excuse right there.

"If you'll all forgive me, I see an old friend I need to talk to. It's been years since we last spent time together," he said, which was a half-truth, at least, unlike his mother's claims.

Amid a chorus of disappointed sighs, Edouard pushed his way past the girlish throng, ignoring his mother's little exclamations of surprise. He hurried through the crowd, straining to keep Hamlin and his tormenters within sight.

"Oh—Edouard! There you are! You'll never believe what I just found out!"

"Aloysia, go away!"

His sister stumbled into view, slightly disheveled, soiled, and flushed. She grabbed hold of his arm and forced him to stop. She was even panting for breath.

"Gossip, brother! Gossip!" she said, practically squealing, her fingers digging into his arm. Then she froze, her eyes widening even further, as she stared just above Edouard's head. "Oh, lord!"

"I said go away, woman! Leave me alone!"

"You've got—oh, my goodness! What, you and—no! I don't believe it!" she spluttered, looking shocked and delighted all at once and pointing at something just above him.

With a mighty tug of his arm, Edouard managed to wrench his way free, and before Aloysia could recover from her surprise, he'd already jogged away. Thank the heavens for the noise around him, for it overwhelmed his sister's calls and made it easier for him to ignore them. She might have said something about "handsome" and "special" in reference to someone, but Edouard couldn't bother himself to care a jot.

Chapter 13

Hamlin never realized just how much "hunger" meant "leading to instant death." Not once had the association crossed his mind and, had he known, he'd have satisfied himself with tearing leaves from trees and bushes and gnawing away like a cow till his stomach was full.

He wouldn't have abandoned his quiet little escape in search of food in the castle's bowels. He wouldn't have risked crossing paths with his drunk half-brothers and their new drunk friends in one of the larger rooms he'd accidentally stumbled into. Ironically, it turned out to be the armor room, where his half-brothers and their friends were busy showing off their inane knowledge of armor and weaponry to a group of princesses who seemed to actually believe in their expertise.

And he wouldn't have given them reason to mock him for looking like a girl—clearly to impress the princesses further—and then threaten him with a slow, excruciating death after he defended his honor by giving Otto a hard, clean, precise kick in the balls, much to the delight of their hoped-for conquests, who tittered and clapped their hands for Hamlin.

Much help those girls turned out to be, he huffed, after his brothers collared him and dragged him out of the armor room. Hamlin struggled and fought all the way, his energy waning as time went, and his world spun around him. It wasn't because of the rough handling he endured, but mostly because his demonic tormentors kept belching around him, filling the air he breathed with the stench of ale or beer—or whatever home-brewed vermin poison they'd imbibed—as well as roasted meat and fruit.

Hamlin was convinced, in fact, that had his captors decided to tie him to a tree and taken turns breathing in his face, that would have been an effective enough method of killing him.

He didn't know where his mother was. For that, at least, he was grateful. Nothing pained him more than subjecting Queen Elfriede to the miserable sight of her only son being publicly humiliated before a castle full of nobles who all looked down on her.

Hamlin found himself outside before long, though the world continued to spin, and he refused to be led away to his execution quietly. He tried, whenever he could—or at least whenever he was sure he was still upright and alive—to subtly call out for help. It was bad enough, after all, to be seen being carried off by a group of loud, intoxicated, and physically daunting boys who shared only half a brain between them. The least he could do was to reach out and show himself to be above the animal-like crowd in which he'd now found himself by showing politeness and restraint.

Then again, if he were to stop and really think about his reasons for doing so, it was because he was frightened out of his wits and was this close to suffering a full hysterical breakdown. Forcing politeness and restraint on himself was nothing more than a final, desperate attempt at keeping himself from exploding, and giving his tormentors the satisfaction of having caused it.

"Pardon me," he cried as he caught the eye of a knight who wandered the grounds in full armor. He'd been told that the castle grounds were littered with dozens of these intimidating men—for security purposes, of course. "If you please, I need help!"

The knight simply stopped in his tracks, watching them scuttle past. He did nothing else beyond reaching up and scratching the side of his armored head, baffled.

"I'm about to be slaughtered!" Hamlin yelled more loudly. "Would you be so kind as to stop them? Isn't that what you're paid to do?"

The idiot fellow simply stood there, watching them vanish in the crowd. Hamlin wished that Audwin were there. What he'd give to have his half-brothers' eyes pecked out. What he'd also give to have the rest of the insensible guests to look at the small, raucous group and question their purpose.

"Just stop your whining and let us get on with it!" someone hissed, giggling obnoxiously. It sounded like Mallory. "If you didn't fight so much, we'd be done by now!"

"I don't particularly care to be butchered in quick time, you idiot!" Hamlin snapped.

"Oh, in that case, we'll have to drag things out," one of their dull-witted friends said before belching for the hundredth time. Hamlin nearly gagged. "Didn't realize that you were one for naughty little games like this."

The rest of the group broke out in scattered giggles and laughter. At this point, they were outside the castle grounds, having pushed their way through the throng of revelers and servants. Hamlin saw nothing but an endless, rolling countryside before him, one that was dotted with woodlands and lakes. It was toward the nearest woods that the gaggle of gargoyles dragged him, laughing at their cleverness as they all exchanged suggestions on what to do with "the squirmy little shit."

They'd yet to reach a consensus by the time they crossed the first line of trees and plunged into the cold dark of the forest, though the thought of stripping Hamlin, leaving him in the middle of the wood, and using him for wild boar bait appeared to be the front runner.

Panicked or not, enough was enough. Hamlin redoubled his efforts despite the fact that he was completely overpowered, with each arm held firmly by a big, brawny bully.

"What do you oafs get out of picking on me, anyway?" he snarled. "It's a pretty sad picture you make, being five of you altogether, taking your inadequacies out on someone who's younger and smaller than any of you!"

Someone said something, but Hamlin didn't catch it, for they'd stopped all of a sudden, and he felt a hard slap on the back of his head. A million stars exploded behind his eyeballs, and another hard slap followed, this time to the side of his head. Mercifully, the two boys holding his arms let him go, allowing him to stumble and fall away from them.

"You just can't shut up, can you?" Otto snapped.

Hamlin lay on his side, waiting for the dizziness to go away, yelping when he felt someone kick his legs. He curled himself up into a tighter ball. His ear rang from the slap, and for one strange moment, he thought he could hear nothing but a string of jumbled phrases: bastard shit, whore queen, pretty bum, flaming sword of manhood (or was it "throbbing sword of utter masculinity"?), knight bait, wolf bait, freshly risen corpse bait, what-the-devil-is-that-thing, help-it's-a-demon-hound.

What followed was a sharp shift from drunken threats to a chorus of screams and curses and wildly moving air around Hamlin, the voices rapidly fading in the background, to be replaced by what sounded like a monstrous growl.

He cracked his eyes open, his body still curled up on the ground, and he looked around in terror. He saw nothing but endless trees and occasional streams of sunlight that broke through leaves and branches. The woods seemed innocent, with grass, brush, and rocks. His breath coming out in ragged gasps, Hamlin ignored the dull pain in his head as he struggled to sit up.

"Here. Let me help you," a voice said, nearly making Hamlin jump out of his skin.

He looked up to find, of all people, Edouard standing above him, looking grim as he bent down and offered his hand. "What are you doing here?" he stammered.

"I followed you here," Edouard replied, "after I saw those slobbering drunks carry you off."

Hamlin took his hand and gingerly stood up, blinking away the dizziness and leaning slightly against Edouard as he fought to clear his head. Edouard, bless him, said nothing about the imposition and allowed Hamlin to use him for a prop. Hamlin eventually straightened up and let go of Edouard's hand. "Thank you," he said, barely able to meet the other boy's eyes, his face hot from the shame of being seen in such a degrading situation. "I should go back."

"I'll walk with you."

Hamlin could only nod, dropping his gaze to the ground, his spirits deflated. It was painful beyond words, being humiliated like that, especially before strangers. Hamlin had grown used to being picked on, to be sure, but those moments had always been private, outside his parents' castle and beyond earshot.

He desperately wanted to break down and rage, but he knew better than to follow that embarrassment with a show of extreme sensitivity that one would associate with children, not fourteen-year-old princes. All the same, Hamlin found it very difficult fighting back angry tears, and he spent the time blinking the mist away and dreading Edouard's conversation.

They walked in silence for a moment till they broke through the trees and were back in sunlight. Hamlin sniffled, drawing a sleeve across his nose. "Thank you, by the way," he said after another awkward moment, still staring at the ground. "I'm surprised that you were able to scare everyone off, even with you unarmed like that."

"Oh—you're welcome, but you'll have to credit my sister for chasing those idiots away, not me."

Hamlin frowned, his distress vanishing all of a sudden. What did he just say? He looked up and turned to Edouard, who met his glance without a hint of emotion and without breaking his stride. "Your sister?" Hamlin echoed. "I didn't hear a girl's voice."

"Well, you did, in a way. In the form she took, she was still female. Whatever sound you heard, then, was quite girlish."

"Eh?"

"She'll have to explain things to you when you see her," Edouard replied with a vague shrug. He paused, turning to face Hamlin and regarding him with a thoughtful little frown. "You're a mess," he said, clucking and shaking his head.

"It's difficult staying neat and clean with someone kicking me on the ground and forcing me to stay there."

A shadow darkened Edouard's features for a moment. With another shake of his head, he reached up and plucked bits of grass and woodland debris off Hamlin's hair.

"I'm sorry you were treated like that." He paused, still frowning, and lightly brushed dirt off Hamlin's shoulders. "I recognized two of the dribbling oafs but not the others. The ones I know are nothing more than sons of barons. I'll make sure to talk to my aunt about what they did. With any luck, she'd have their families banned from future visits. The others, I don't know."

"I think it's best for you not to say anything," Hamlin stammered, blanching. "The others were my half-brothers, and if someone tells, they'll come after me again and make me pay."

"That's ridiculous. You're not the one who'll be telling on them. I will. And I dare them to lay a finger on me."

Hamlin shook his head. "You don't understand. It doesn't matter who tells. They'll leave you alone, but they'll take it out on me. They'll use any excuse they can find to make my life a misery, can't you see that?" He swallowed, pressing a hand on Edouard's arm. "Swear to me that you won't say a thing! Swear it!"

Edouard regarded him incredulously for a moment, his sense of honor most likely stung, but he dropped his gaze to look at Hamlin's hand before meeting Hamlin's eyes again. "Very well," he said, his voice tight. "I promise I won't tell."

"Thank you." Hamlin withdrew his hand and turned around, more depressed than ever.

The sound of hurrying footsteps ahead slowed them down, and from around a small grove of trees a young girl appeared, flushed and excited, disheveled and soiled. She grinned when she caught sight of the two boys, waving at them and running faster, her skirts gathered up around her shins. Edouard stopped, and Hamlin followed suit.

"Ah, there you are!" she cried, panting and breathless, as she skidded to a halt before them. Her headpiece was askew, her hair tumbling out around her shoulders, but she didn't seem to care. She glanced at Edouard first and then looked at Hamlin, her grin broadening. "How do you do? I'm Aloysia, Edouard's younger sister."

"A pleasure to meet you," Hamlin said, bowing.

"Lord, but those idiots can run when they think their manhood's on the line," Aloysia said, her eyes twinkling. "And it was awfully fun making them run for their lives like that! What a great joke it'd be, watching the looks on their faces, when they find out that they were running from a girl!"

Hamlin stared at her, grimacing in confusion. "What? What? Huh?" He turned to Edouard with a helpless little sound escaping his throat. "Huh?"

Edouard shrugged. "Aloysia was the one who chased your bullies away. She made a remarkable demon-dog, actually, with oversized fangs, matted fur that reeked of shit, and long forelegs with grasping claws. She even ran on two hind legs, which I think was a fabulous touch."

Hamlin just looked at him, despairing. "Huh?"

Chapter 14

Edouard would have laughed himself sick if he weren't so tired. But he kept reminding himself that he was the oldest noble in the group as well as the one most inclined to intellectual pursuits, so the burden of propriety and dignity lay squarely on his shoulders. It was all he could do, therefore, to sit straight in his chair, his hands clasped on the table as he watched the sorry exchange that was taking place between Aloysia and Hamlin.

The two sat next to each other, across the table from Edouard, and Aloysia had turned her chair to face Hamlin, who clearly wished that she hadn't. In fact, Hamlin looked as though he heartily wished that he were somewhere else, far away from an insane princess.

The trio had sequestered themselves in a small chamber on the second floor of the castle. For the past several minutes, Edouard had had the questionable pleasure of watching Aloysia explain her powers to Hamlin, who shrank from her, his eyes growing larger and larger, while his complexion hinted at an alarming loss of blood.

Aloysia, for her part, didn't seem to notice her companion's increasing terror. From what Edouard could see, it appeared as though his sister took Hamlin's reactions as speechless awe of her powers. The more horror poor Hamlin showed, the more Aloysia emphasized her abilities to transform into the nastiest beasts ever to be conjured up from nothing.

"So, yes, I was the mutant chicken that startled you out of your reverie," she said, beaming with immense pride. She hadn't even bothered to tidy her headpiece and hair. If only their mother could see her now. "I was trying to observe you from the air, but even mutant chickens aren't able to stay airborne for too long. Too heavy, you know."

"I see," Hamlin replied, inching his chair away from her. "I—I hope your experiment yielded something good for you."

"It did, thank you." Aloysia paused for a brief moment as though to consider what she would say next. Her gaze turned thoughtful as she regarded Hamlin, then she turned to look at Edouard, who narrowed his eyes at her in warning.

"What?" he demanded.

Aloysia pursed her lips as she looked at one prince, then the other. "I see tangled thread between the two of you. Like, uh..." Her words faltered, and she raised a hand and, with her index finger pointed, drew strange patterns in the air, starting from Hamlin and ending with Edouard. "Like that."

"Like cobwebs spun between two objects, you mean." Edouard shook his head. "Silly magic stuff again, sister. Illogical and, really, quite beneath you, even with your penchant for turning into ugly creatures."

"I noticed it first when I saw Hamlin," she said, pointedly ignoring her brother. "But I couldn't see where the thread ended then because Edouard wasn't there. I did see how it stretched out beyond that area of our aunt's garden, though. Then when I saw my brother, I noticed the thread above his head as well. I tried to tell you that, brother, but you wouldn't listen."

When the two boys said nothing, she sighed. "Part of my education in magic requires me to read eastern lore, and this is precisely what I read about. How amusing—and here I thought it was nothing but legend about destiny. Huh. What do I know, eh?" Aloysia giggled.

Hamlin stared at her and then at Edouard. His expression hadn't changed, looking like a cornered beast about to be slaughtered most horribly. "I don't believe in such things," he said after swallowing. "Destiny and all that—it's nonsense. I believe in being the master of my own fate."

"Well said." Edouard nodded. "But I suppose we need to be lenient toward my sister, though. She's still in the process of mastering her craft—whatever on earth it is. She could very well be prone to seeing things that her mind perhaps wishes to see."

Aloysia made a face at Edouard. "Oh, go ahead and joke. We'll see who'll be laughing last."

"But I don't understand what that even means. A thread?" Hamlin glanced at Edouard. At least his expression had shifted to one of complete confusion, which seemed to be less painful than the one before it. "A thread connecting us both? What are we supposed to do? Become allies or enemies? I mean, does this mean we're bound to come back to each other again and again in friendship, or are we bound to hack away at each other till we're both dead?"

Edouard couldn't help but feel impressed with Hamlin's dry sense of humor, largely because it skewered a subject that he'd always disliked. When he saw Aloysia open her mouth to speak, he quickly unclasped his hands and knocked firmly on the table.

"I think Hamlin's fully recovered from his ordeal, sister," he said, earning himself a withering look from Aloysia. "It's bad form keeping him trapped in here, slowly starving to death." He turned to Hamlin. "I'll join you. I haven't eaten anything in a while, and the stresses of today are taking their toll. Shall we?" He pushed his chair back and stood up, watching Hamlin nod, relief flooding his face, and following suit.

Aloysia just shrugged and clucked. "Well, I'm not going to force my beliefs down your throats," she said, standing up and fumbling with her headpiece, at long last. "But I'm not changing my tune. I know what I see, and that's that. Whatever happens next is—well—we'll just have to see, won't we?"

Then she paused, smiling deviously.

"Then again, with the results determined by the gods or whatever higher power you believe in, it's just a matter of going through the challenges that'll lead you to those results, yes? On one hand, one can argue that the predictability of something like this makes life a bit dull. On the other hand, it's the journey to the predetermined end that makes it all worthwhile. I can go on and on and philosophize about this, now that I see it's all true. Isn't this exciting?"

"Oh, what I'd give to have Clovis show up right now," Edouard muttered. "Aren't you joining us?"

His sister shook her head as she now turned her attention to her appearance. "I have to find a lady-in-waiting to help me with this damned headpiece." She waved them away. "Now go on and enjoy yourselves."

Edouard wasn't sure, but he thought he caught a sly gleam in his sister's eyes as she spoke. But Aloysia had turned her back to him quickly enough to make him doubt it. He just shrugged and moved away, slowing to let Hamlin catch up with him. He led the other prince from the room, and they walked in silence down the corridor for a few moments.

Edouard waited till after they rounded a corner to speak up. "You'll have to excuse my sister," he said, taking care to keep his voice low because heaven only knew how their voices carried, and one could never be sure with a princess-magician not too far behind them. "She's obsessed with magic and everything connected with it. And that includes superstitions and other nonsense. I'm afraid you can't really expect much else from her."

"I really don't mind," Hamlin replied, matching Edouard's volume. "We're all odd in our own ways, aren't we?"

"Frankly, I don't care to be lumped together in the same group as Aloysia. I've nothing odd about me."

Hamlin coughed, and when Edouard glanced at him, the other boy simply bowed his head and looked at his feet. Edouard shook his head at his companion, clucking softly as his gaze swept over the prince's soiled and disheveled state.

"I still think it's a big mistake for me not to say anything about the abuse you were subjected to earlier," he said. "We're only encouraging them to continue their bullying of you."

"Maybe, but if we don't tell, their bullying will stay the same, not worsen. Knowing that I betrayed them to your aunt and whoever else will only justify worse violence. I'd rather take the lesser of two evils."

Edouard frowned. "How long did it take you to convince yourself to believe this rubbish?"

"Since the day I was born. I mean—everyone's done everything they could to remind me of Mama's place. I'm not much better than a bastard in their eyes."

A moment's silence followed, with Edouard not seeing any reason to add anything more to that because he happened to be one of those who'd always believed Queen Elfriede to be an upstart, and he knew that it was pointless giving his opinion so freely regarding that matter. Nothing would be accomplished by it, seeing as how Hamlin was doing quite well on his own in accepting that fact and knowing his place.

Edouard toyed with labels, and the best he could think of in reference to Hamlin's royal standing was "half-prince." Yes, that sounded reasonable enough. Quite a pity, too, that Hamlin would be doomed to be less than a real prince, considering his good luck in inheriting the best physical characteristics from his mother.

All the same, he remained very much against the idea of anyone's honor remaining undefended, half-blooded royalty notwithstanding. He'd just have to broach the subject with Aloysia when he had a chance—that is, only if he remained stumped as to the logic behind Hamlin's request.

The two princes had reached the ground floor, and cacophonous noise and endless activity once again swallowed them.

"Edouard! There you are! Where on earth have you been?" a voice managed to make itself heard above the din.

"Oh, lord—Mama," Edouard muttered. He paused in his tracks and turned in time to see Queen Clarimond plow her way through the crowd, her face red and frozen in a grimace of anger. "I spent time with Hamlin," he said, raising his voice. "He's…" Edouard stumbled over his words when he felt Hamlin jab him from behind. "He had a bit of an accident, and I was there to help him."

Queen Clarimond reached them, screeching to a halt and panting a bit perhaps from her efforts at moving quickly through the dense throng of revelers, though Edouard suspected that it was nothing short of rage that made her gasp for air.

"Help who?" she retorted. Then her gaze moved past Edouard and fixed itself on Hamlin, who stood behind him. Her eyes narrowed. "Oh, I see. Then again I suppose it's quite natural for a commoner's child to require the services of a prince. Though I must admit to finding such a demand quite selfish, considering Edouard's obligations."

"Oh, for heaven's sake, Mama," Edouard said, sighing deeply. "Hamlin's more than a commoner's son. His father's still a king, which logically makes him a half-prince or even commoner-prince if you think about it." He turned to face Hamlin. "At least it's a step up from being called a bastard, don't you agree?"

Hamlin stood before him, staring at Edouard in wide-eyed shock, his pale complexion getting whiter and whiter by the second. Then his eyes narrowed into angry slits, his mouth pinched itself into a tight line, and his bloodless complexion was suffused with red, making Edouard wonder if something had just broken inside Hamlin, flooding the boy's body with a rush of blood.

Before he could decide, Hamlin raised a fist, swung it, and struck Edouard squarely on the cheek. An explosion of multicolored stars filled Edouard's vision as his head snapped to the side, and the noise around him seemed to diminish under his mother's furious shouts and demands to have Hamlin arrested and summarily executed without trial.

Edouard wasn't sure if he fell backwards, but the ground certainly shifted under his feet, and he cursed the damned thing for moving about too much without waiting for him to regain his balance. By the time the world righted itself and his vision cleared, Hamlin had gone. His mother stood behind him, holding him almost painfully by his arms, who continued to let loose a string of abuse on Hamlin's head despite the other prince's absence.

"Nothing good ever comes out of having that woman and her demonling around," Queen Clarimond raged, now dragging Edouard away. "Where's Franziska? I'll have a word with her—make sure she never invites that gold-digging strumpet and her savage brood again. How dare he! No one ever touches you that way! No one! Why, if I get my hands on that little barbarian, I'll..."

And the threats of physical destruction went on and on and on. Edouard grimaced and rubbed his face gingerly while allowing himself to be dragged away by his arm like a wayward child. He'd grown quite good at shutting his mother out, but in the midst of his embarrassment and outrage a quiet little voice nagged at him, leaving him even more confused than ever.

"What on earth did I say?" he murmured, both frowning at the thought and wincing from the pain that made the left side of his face throb. "Damned obnoxious of that little prick to attack me for speaking the truth—and after I helped him? What cheek!"

He had no idea where his mother was taking him, but he did spot his sister at one point, standing off to the side, ignoring Clovis's lovestruck attentions, and staring daggers at him. She even had the audacity to stand there with her hands on her hips. Poor Clovis, red-faced and probably sweating, seemed to be doing everything in his power to get her attention, even holding out a bundle of flowers that Edouard suspected was the size of a haystack.

Did Aloysia see what had happened? Edouard wouldn't doubt it; his sister could use her powers for anything, and she wasn't above spying. If she did, though, shouldn't she be redirecting her ire toward Hamlin instead?

"Everyone's gone mad!" Edouard ground out. Since his mother didn't care to stop and explain things to Aloysia, it was all he could do to pointedly look at his sister and roll his eyes at her.

Chapter 15

Hamlin sighed heavily as he turned the pages of the book without giving the text much attention. Even the beautifully embellished illustrations did nothing to curb his boredom, and at length, he pushed the book away and sagged in his chair, scowling at the pile of books on the table.

Crossing his arms on his chest, he thought about the events leading up to that moment, and no matter how many times he turned them over in his head, he couldn't find a single argument against his violent response to Edouard's insult.

"Well, well, well—what do we have here? Do I see a prince neck-deep in trouble with his parents?"

Hamlin turned to find Audwin perching on the window ledge of the tower room. "I'm being punished for hitting that stupid, arrogant bastard earlier."

"I see. And how long are you expected to stay in the tower room like this?"

"I don't know." Hamlin shrugged. "Until I understand what I did and apologize for it, I suppose."

Audwin cocked his head and regarded Hamlin with wise, button eyes. "And have you, Your Highness?"

Hamlin snorted as he stood and ambled over to the single bed across the little tower room. He threw up his hands. "He insulted me! What else do they expect? That I ignore him and pretend deafness? Wouldn't silence be something like agreeing to what he said about me?" Hamlin threw himself onto the bed, rolled over to his back, and stared angrily at the ceiling. "I swear, I've never met anyone so arrogant as that—that—arrogant—prince of all arrogance!"

"You seem to be overflowing with insults today."

"I can't think of anything worse to call him. My brain hurts too much."

The sound of flapping wings filled the air, and Audwin flew across the room and perched himself on the chair that Hamlin had just vacated. "Your Highness, I've heard about the insult through the grapevine—in a manner of speaking. I'd say that a little bird told me, but it was more like several birds passing on the news to several more till it reached me."

Hamlin closed his eyes and crossed his arms on his chest again. "Gossips, the whole lot of you."

"My question is, why react that way to Edouard, when you've heard that same insult from others before, and you'd managed to keep your temper?"

Hamlin frowned, keeping his eyes closed. That was a good question, and it took some doing for him to grapple with it and to find the answer. He squirmed on the bed and opened his eyes to look at Audwin.

"I don't know," he said, his voice tiny.

"Oh, yes, you do. Out with it."

Hamlin hesitated, chewing his lower lip. Then he sighed. "Because it stung, hearing it from him."

"And why's that? Because he's a prince? I'm sure you've heard other princes mock you that way, so what's the difference?"

"I wish I knew. It just—I don't know. It just got under my skin, hearing him say those same things other people have said about me." Hamlin shrugged, feeling his face burn. "I don't understand it, myself. I don't even like him, considering our pasts. He's a snob and a bully, and I really shouldn't expect anything better coming from him."

"And yet..."

"And yet it stung. And—and it was horrible."

Audwin shook himself, his feathers puffing up. When he looked at Hamlin again, he seemed to be about twice his normal size. "That's something you'll have to think about, Your Highness," he said. "I don't understand it, myself, but I'm a bird, and I'm guessing that I'm not meant to philosophize about human behavior despite the endless annoyances it gives me. And, by the gods, human nature's irritating beyond words."

"I don't care," Hamlin grumbled, turning his attention back to the ceiling and regarding it with growing resentment. "Mama and Papa might order me to spend a week in this tower room and then expect me to see the error of my ways and send a formal apology to Edouard and Queen Clarimond, but none of those change the fact that no one cares for how I feel about being called a half-prince or a bastard. Mama puts up with all the stupid things that other nobles say about her, but I won't. She'll preach forbearance, but I'll never take disrespect from anyone without defending myself."

"I see. And yet, Your Highness, you don't fight back where your half-brothers are concerned. If you demand respect, I daresay you need to be more consistent in your expectations."

"I'm outnumbered and outsized, you absurd bird."

"And they find safety in numbers, which is the coward's way. Besides, I'm not talking about physical violence. I'm thinking about your wit. Guile. Brain-work. Something that's too vague a concept to your half-brothers."

"I suppose I can always lure them toward a cliff and then sidestep them at the very last minute."

"Well, keep that thought in reserve—for emergency purposes only, mind you. Something more civilized and becoming of you would work better, I think."

Hamlin fell silent. Being one-upped by a talking bird had always been a thorn on his side, and while he didn't mind as a little boy, such a thing at fourteen didn't sit well. Queen Elfriede would call it pride, as though it were something dirty, but to Hamlin, pride was what kept his head held high despite ongoing misery he endured in his half-brothers' company. Had it not been for that, he'd have long been reduced to a mere shadow of himself.

"I don't want to cause more trouble for Mama," he blurted out at length. "Given the lack of respect my brothers show her, the least I can do is put up with their idiocy and show them that they can't destroy my spirit and give Mama some measure of comfort that way."

It was Audwin's turn to fall silent for a moment. Then he said, "As I said, I'm only a bird. I doubt if I'll ever understand the workings of human nature. I must go and scavenge around for carcasses."

Hamlin clucked and turned to frown at Audwin. "I thought you told me before that you were getting too fat."

"As I said, Your Highness, human nature irritates me to distraction. Now I need to tear away at a dead animal to let the aggravation out. Good day." Without another word, Audwin flapped his wings and flew out of the tower room. He even left a couple of feathers fluttering down behind him, which only emphasized Hamlin's belief that the crotchety raven was also prone to dramatic flourishes.

• • • •

A DAY AND A HALF HAD passed since Hamlin was "domestically banished"—or grounded, in a word—to the dreaded tower room of his father's castle. He wondered why it had never been used until he was unceremoniously tossed into the world screaming, toothless, and dismayed. It was nothing more than "extra space" throughout his half-brothers' childhood, and not one of those princely wretches was ever "domestically banished" until he'd learned the error of his ways.

What was so different about Hamlin that his own mother would agree to subjecting him to isolation and "hours best spent in earnest contemplation" of his sins? He couldn't figure it out, and at length he resigned himself to the fact that he was regarded as the black sheep of the family, while his half-brothers remained free to run about, terrorize every person unlucky enough to cross their paths (namely him), and still go unpunished.

Queen Elfriede arrived, followed by a servant who came to whisk away Hamlin's soiled clothes. She swept in and stood next to the open door, waiting for the servant to go about her business. Hamlin remained seated on his bed, an illuminated manuscript spread out in front of him, and pointedly ignored his mother.

The air in the tower room crackled, as they say, with the poor servant hurrying, practically cowering under the weight of unspoken anger and resentment between mother and son. She took the pail that Hamlin had used to clean himself, all the while keeping her head bowed and her shoulders stiff and drawn up as though to protect her ears from a possible boxing. When she left, she barely managed a clumsy curtsey before scurrying away as though a pack of demonic hounds were nipping at her heels.

It was Queen Elfriede who closed the door behind her.

"I'm still not apologizing for something that I'm justified in doing, Mama," Hamlin said without looking up. He turned a page and glared at the vividly colored designs of the massive book.

"I'm not sparing you, Hamlin, even though you're my son, and it hurts to punish you. I just don't understand why you had to behave the way you did."

"I already told you, and I'm tired of repeating myself."

"Then you'll have to follow through on your week-long sentence." When Hamlin refused to respond, Queen Elfriede sighed. "What are you reading?"

Hamlin shrugged and turned a page. "One of the manuscripts you and Papa commissioned for me for my birthday. It's an adventure story."

It was, of course, a bit of a lie. The manuscript was a pornographic one, which he'd stolen from Otto's bedroom. Gloriously colorful illustrations of naked women filled the pages, none of which stirred Hamlin. It led him to wonder what on earth was the big deal about naked women that Otto would have amassed a magnificent collection of illuminated smut manuscripts. That said, Hamlin took care to turn the pages until he reached a point with no saucy images that his mother could spot.

"Do you enjoy your books?"

"Of course I do. The characters in them live far more interesting lives than I do, anyway. That's one thing about being 'domestically banished' to this room. I've been rediscovering my favorite stories, and I'm enjoying living vicariously through them."

"We're no longer welcome in Franziska's castle, Hamlin. I don't know if you're aware of that." When Hamlin glanced up to stare in surprise at his mother, she continued. "She didn't want to, you know, but Clarimond was insistent, and I'm afraid that I'll have to agree with her. If putting you and Edouard together in a room means the end of civilization as we know it, I think it's best to keep you two permanently separated."

"But that's not fair to you!" Hamlin stammered, blushing. "It's not your fault that Edouard's a snot-nosed bore! Why do you have to be dragged into this? If they don't want me, that's perfectly fine, but Queen Franziska's your friend—your *only* friend—and it isn't fair to keep you two away from each other!"

His mother just watched him with a sad look, and she gave a little shrug. "It's not my place to say anything, Hamlin. It's Franziska's castle, and we abide by her rules. We're the outsiders—remember that."

Hamlin shook his head, fury now spiraling. "No, I won't accept that. I'll write her and tell her what I think. She shouldn't do this to you, Mama. And you know what I think? I think Queen Clarimond's a right bi—"

"Hamlin!"

Pain now marred Queen Elfriede's features, and Hamlin wilted. "I'm sorry, Mama," he said after a moment's strained silence. "But I still think it isn't fair to you. I don't care what happens to me, but this shouldn't fall on you."

Queen Elfriede merely shook her head and sighed as she walked over to the bed. She took Hamlin's face with both hands and gently raised it to meet her gaze. "Do the right thing, Hamlin. Be good. That's all I ask." She searched his face in silence for a few seconds before bending close to kiss his forehead. She smiled when she stood up. "I'm sorry you have to stay here for a week, darling, but it's for your own good. I hope you understand."

Hamlin nodded, and Queen Elfriede left the tower room. Hamlin stared at the door, his mind whirling at the look his mother gave him just before she left him. It was an odd look—the kind of look that told him she knew something or she'd just glimpsed the future. His future, anyway, and was saddened by what she saw.

Hamlin was nothing if not practical, however, and he quickly shook off that strange thought, set the illuminated smut manuscript aside, and hurried over to the window. Leaning out, he whistled, and after several attempts was able to summon a dove. Dropping his voice to a gentle whisper so as not to startle it, he conveyed his message and then watched it fly away in the direction of Queen Franziska's castle. Hamlin hoped that the message wouldn't be garbled and twisted, but he trusted birds despite their propensity for gossip and silly rumors.

Chapter 16

Edouard's eyes watered terribly, and his nose felt like it had swollen to twenty times its size. The sneezing fits refused to die down, however, and after a momentary respite, the itch started all over again, and soon it was another strung out series of "Ah-choo!" And Edouard would, if he could, blow his nose for relief—if not flee the room and its hellish contents. Unfortunately for him, he was quite stuck.

Groaning after the last sneeze, he sniffled, tilting his head back to keep his nose from dripping. It was utter misery.

"I'm not above telling Mama and Papa about this," he said at length, his voice sounding nasal and weak. Blinking away the tears, he gazed around him for the umpteenth time and took in the sight of thick cobwebs that filled his chamber. He tried to move his limbs again, but the giant, thick, sticky web that held him fast wouldn't allow it. "Aloysia, I need to blow my nose."

"You will when I let you go."

"And when will this be?"

"When I'm satisfied with my punishment."

Edouard sighed and raised his head, a touch relieved by the feeling that he wasn't about to have another sneezing fit. From where he was trapped in a giant cobweb, which suspended him above the floor, he glared at his sister, who'd been busy moving about the room, inspecting the mess of cobwebs her monster form had spun earlier in a fit of rage.

"My, but this is very impressive!" she said, breaking out in a broad, proud grin. She reached out to a particularly thick cobweb that encased Edouard's table and chair and started plucking at it. The odious stuff actually let out a dull twang, reminding Edouard of traveling minstrels and their lutes.

"And what exactly do you expect to gain from trapping me in stuff that your monster form just shat out?"

"Oh, I don't know—common sense, I suppose." Aloysia paused to look at him, her eyes wide and questioning and sparkling with hellish intent. She even clasped her hands behind her and tilted her head in a show of faux innocence. "You're such an atrocious troll, and I daresay you've earned this."

"Troll? I don't guard bridges and demand payment in blood. I've no idea what you're talking about."

"Oh, well—too bad for you, then. I'll have to go and do a bit more reading about transformation spells. I've been tempted to practice on you."

Edouard's blood ran cold. "Don't you even dare consider it!" he spluttered, struggling against his cobweb bonds and failing to give his sister a pretty impressive show of defiance and strength.

Aloysia actually shrugged. "It'll depend, of course," she said, her manner still light and provoking. "I'll have to wait and see if you improve your personality. I'd provide you with a challenge and expect you to see the error of your ways within a certain length of time, but I have a feeling that such an approach will be, sadly, useless."

Edouard rolled his eyes, which felt raw and sticky from his sneezing fits. "There's absolutely no incentive for me to see the error of my ways if you're talking about that ghastly little commoner prince. I was well within my rights to say what I said, and seeing as how *he* was the one who first referred to himself as a bastard, I was merely echoing him. Not only that—I was echoing him in a very civil, thought-provoking manner despite the too-real fact that he has absolutely no grasp of logic." Edouard paused to sneer at his sister. "I must say that people's memories hereabouts are miserably deficient. But I suppose I shouldn't expect better from those who prefer to fritter away their time in silly pursuits like—oh—magic. And in Hamlin's case, being completely devoid of sound reason."

Aloysia merely listened in silence, even nodding her head now and then. When Edouard fell silent, she asked, "Are you finished?"

"Well, yes, I am. Now get rid of these stupid cobwebs and leave me alone!"

His sister didn't say anything for a few maddening seconds. It was very clear that she was spinning more hellish schemes in her mind. At length she shrugged, pursing her lips. "Let the cobwebs go, then," she said. She waved a hand, creating strange patterns in the air and muttering something under her breath.

Edouard was about to say something, but he suddenly felt himself sag, and before he knew what was happening, the cobwebs in his room faded away. He hung suspended in the air for a fraction of a second before falling to the floor and landing hard on his rump in an explosion of dust.

He waited till the pain and the rainbow-colored stars vanished before opening his mouth to verbally abuse his sister. And perhaps he said something ("Oh, lord, my backside!"), but his brain remained frozen despite his mouth's movement. He did vaguely hear his own voice without its usual firmness; in fact, it seemed as though he'd undergone an age change and was once again at that dreadful, awkward period where his voice catapulted itself up and down the scale.

The whole time, he could also vaguely see Aloysia through the mist that had formed after the sparkling stars, and she appeared to ignore him completely as she surveyed the room, moving from one point to the other—no doubt to revel in her unearthly powers and congratulate herself for ascending one more rung up the ladder of princess-magicianhood.

His vision eventually cleared, and he found his sister walking to the door and opening it. "Mama!" she said. "Edouard's here, if you're looking for him."

"I am, yes."

As Edouard stumbled clumsily to his feet, Queen Clarimond swept inside his room, with Aloysia standing by the door and feigning innocence.

"Edouard," their mother said, her voice as tight as her face, "I've just received word from Franziska that she's relented in her decision to ban that cheap commoner and her spawn from visiting her castle."

"That's her choice, Mama," Edouard said, biting back a groan and the reflexive need to massage his buttocks as he straightened himself up. He sniffled and rubbed his nose. Thank the heavens for clear air once again.

"No, it wasn't. I'm sure that Elfriede had something to do with this—ingratiated herself to Franziska the way she ingratiated herself to Reinhard, no doubt." The queen paced back and forth, dragging her thick robes behind her majestically. Edouard wasn't sure, but he thought the floor where she paced appeared cleaner and cleaner with each sweep. "And now we're to be subjected to their barbarism every time we're invited to Franziska's castle."

Edouard sighed again. "It's Aunt Franziska's choice, Mama. We should at least respect that. You're more than justified in banning Queen Elfriede and Hamlin from *our* castle, of course."

"Oh, and we're supposed to put up with Elfriede's demonling every time we're visiting to enjoy ourselves? Rubbish! I don't know what possessed Franziska to change her mind, but this isn't over yet. I'll make sure of it." Queen Clarimond paused in front of Edouard and narrowed her eyes at him, raising a threatening finger. Edouard fought hard not to yawn. "For your sake, Edouard, you need to stay away from that little savage. If he ever lays another finger on you, I swear I won't be responsible for my actions."

"Mama, there's no reason for you to threaten Hamlin. I was completely at fault."

Silence fell on the room, and for a moment, Edouard froze, stunned. Where on earth did that come from? He was supposed to say something else—something along the lines of agreeing with his mother regarding Hamlin's animal-like intellect!

"I beg your pardon?" Queen Clarimond said, her voice low and ominous. "What did you just say?"

Edouard shook his head. "I said that what happened at Aunt Franziska's was my fault entirely. I provoked Hamlin with a very stupid—very ignorant—remark, and I shouldn't have." Edouard gaped, feeling his blood drain away from him. What was happening?

"You do *not* apologize for something that wasn't your fault, Edouard," his mother hissed, her narrowed eyes narrowing further till they were nothing more than slits. Her threatening finger remained raised. In fact, it looked as though it, like Edouard, had drained of blood. "You had every right to say what you said because it was the plain truth. What that little beast had no right to was put a fist in your face."

"Hamlin was hurt by what I said. It was only natural for him to defend his honor." Dear heavens, stop it! Edouard felt cold sweat break out on his forehead. Stop it! He clamped his mouth shut, but it refused to stay still. "In fact, I aim to write him, Mama, and apologize for my actions. I only hope that he finds it in himself to forgive me."

Realization suddenly dawned, and Edouard turned to stare, wide-eyed and drop-jawed, at Aloysia, who stood by the door, examining her nails. Oh, the little turd!

"I must call for the physician immediately," Queen Clarimond said, turning to hurry toward the door. "You're not well, Edouard. You should have told me sooner; subjecting me and your sister to all this nonsense is cruel, and the heavens know what's really happening to your brain right now."

"I'm sure his brain's quite fine, Mama," Aloysia piped up, smiling at Edouard and even having the gall to wrinkle her nose at her horrified brother. "Though I'll agree to the physician bit. I daresay Edouard doesn't look at all well. Isn't he paler than usual?"

"He is, yes. He looks about ready to faint. Don't delay me, Aloysia. Your brother's in desperate need of healing." With that, Queen Clarimond sailed out of the room, leaving Edouard standing in shocked silence as he stared at Aloysia, his tongue fused to the top of his mouth.

Aloysia waited till their mother's hurried footsteps faded in the distance. She continued to hold the door ajar as she regarded Edouard. "What?"

"You did that! You tricked me!"

"How did I trick you? All I did was open you to Mama—or more like open you to the truth." Aloysia wrinkled her nose at him again. "It's a new power I'm practicing, brother. I quite like it. It enables me to dig through the rubbish that's piled up in there," she paused to point at Edouard's chest, "and to pull out what's nice and clean and shining under all the debris."

Edouard felt a crippling headache coming on. Pressing both hands against his temples, he marched toward the door. "Get out of my room, Aloysia, before I throw you out the window." Grabbing his sister's shoulder, he roughly steered her toward the corridor outside.

"What—don't you want to hear what I learned about what you really think of Hamlin under all that pretentious mass you call your heart?" she cried as he pushed her. "I swear you'll be just as tickled as I am!"

"Go away!" With another mighty shove, Edouard got rid of his sister, slamming the door in her face as she turned around, her mouth wide open and ready to drive him insane with more ridiculous claims of "seeing" into his heart.

Chapter 17

Thank the heavens for war. Hamlin had had enough of peacetime; he'd been praying desperately for war, and now he finally had it. Well—at least war in their country, seeing as how England and France didn't seem to be keen on easing the mutual slaughter anytime soon. Indeed, several brave souls had begun placing bets on how long the war between those two would last, with some going all out and declaring "a hundred years war, give or take five hundred at the rate those two were going," while wondering how that could be confirmed down the line, since they'd all be dead by then.

Hamlin and his half-brothers were summoned to the castle study—their father's sanctuary, that is—and there were apprised of some ominous rumblings in a somewhat distant kingdom. It wasn't a full-on threat yet, but matters were getting dire enough to spur King Reinhard to take precautionary measures.

That is, he was bent on sending his three older sons, a gaggle of ministers, and a pack of knights for maximum intimidation effect, to the offending kingdom. He wasn't alone, either.

"Baldemar, Ingelbert, and Jurgen are doing the same," he said, his voice dripping with confidence. "The sooner we impress that none of Orbert's neighbors are to be trifled with, the easier it'll be for everyone involved to defuse the situation."

"And other kingdoms are well aware of King Orbert's sauciness, Papa?" Otto asked.

Hamlin wondered if his half-brother had just gained a few pounds simply by showing their father a touch of the warlord in him. Indeed, Otto's chest seemed to swell to three times its size, though his waist—already thick as it was—maintained its girth. For a moment, Hamlin mulled over what his half-brother would look like once he ascended the throne—most likely abnormally top-heavy unless Otto's pride and arrogance were to crowd his heart and squish it to pieces. In that case, Baldrick would have to replace him, and the very idea of one wrong thing replacing another made Hamlin shudder.

King Reinhard nodded, sitting back in his chair and smiling with smug pleasure. "All have been warned, and all are behind us. I doubt if Orbert will be foolish enough to challenge us alone. He knows he has no allies in this." He tapped his thick, bejeweled fingers loudly against the table.

"Why even threaten us if he's alone?" Mallory asked. Only he of the three older princes didn't look at all thrilled with being sent off on a diplomatic mission. Then again, Mallory didn't really have much to show for by way of ambition. He'd always been quite happy in the shadows, free to do whatever he was entitled to as a prince and not bothered by the little irritations that came with ruling a kingdom.

"Too much peace, I'm afraid," their father replied. "Orbert comes from a line of extremists, and a few decades of nothing but goodwill can be a sore test of one's nerves. He could very well be on the verge of a breakdown. We hope to prevent it—maybe convince him to go on holiday for a month—enjoy the world a little and get his bearings."

"Well, I can't wait to show myself and rub his oily porcine nose in our kingdom's might," Otto blurted, his chest expanding some more. Hamlin couldn't help but stare nervously.

"I can't, either," Baldrick chimed in, nodding firmly and looking grim and determined. "Besides, it'll also be a show of strong youth versus decrepit old age." He paused and looked around at his brothers. "Otto's twenty, I'm eighteen, and Mallory's seventeen. That's a pretty impressive showing, considering King Oink's eighty-something years."

"Orbert's sixty," King Reinhard corrected, rolling his eyes. At that moment, the door opened, and a minister appeared, apologizing profusely while begging for the king's presence.

"It's regarding the diplomatic mission, Your Majesty," he said, inclining his head in the princes' direction.

"Very well." King Reinhard pushed his chair back and stood up, nodding at his sons. "Remember your place, Baldrick. You're not to provoke Orbert by any means. I'll summon you three again before you leave." Then he left, the minister shadowing him.

"It doesn't matter! We'll make you proud, Papa!" Baldrick spluttered, even hammering the table with a fist, and he went on about their kingdom's superiority in all things martial, making Hamlin sigh inwardly and fight hard to avoid yawning in everyone's presence. Luckily for their father, the king had just escaped the study and wasn't able to suffer through Baldrick's blustering.

"Good thing we're not taking Hamlin with us," Otto said once Baldrick had exhausted himself and had slumped back in his chair, panting and sweating. He turned to Hamlin and sneered. "Though I'll have to admit that our little princess here can be useful. He'll make a good diversion for the restless savages—their own little bum boy, eh?"

The three older princes broke out in titters and snorts, elbowing each other (they sat together across the table from Hamlin) and making loud kissing sounds at him. Hamlin shrugged and pushed his chair back to stand up.

"Not really sure why Papa even bothered to send for me if I'm not needed," he said.

"He meant to put you in your place, I'm sure," Mallory piped up, still looking unhappy with the mission. "Only his *real* heirs are good enough for something as important as this, and you'd better remember that."

"Yes, well—I'm sure you'll all do what you do best—make total fools of yourselves." With that, Hamlin retreated—or more like fled the study—because his half-brothers didn't particularly care for what he said and were on their way to falling all over each other in a race to get their thick, sticky hands on him.

The good thing was that Hamlin, being fourteen and around two-and-a-half-persons smaller, had also mastered the art of running in abject fear, and it didn't take much for him to outpace his bigger, more muscular, and slower—mentally and physically—tormentors.

Thank the heavens for war, indeed—or the threat of war, at least. It meant that his half-brothers would be far, far away and unable to make Hamlin's daily hours a living hell.

Before long he was safely in another part of the castle, in a favorite little hideout of sorts. His father's castle boasted several tower rooms, most of which were unused, and it proved to be a very easy task to find a nicely situated one, clean it out, and claim it for his own.

It was similar to the tower room that he'd been "domestically banished" to not too long ago, and he'd furnished it with a smattering of old pieces that had been accumulating dust in some of the duskier corners of the castle. The tower room now contained a table, a chair, and a cot that he used whenever the need for a nap came, and he didn't feel like going outdoors to enjoy one. Then again, he'd also grown tired of being shat on by birds that flew above him, and after a while, not even the beauties of the outdoors could convince him to continue his occasional naps snuggled against Nature's bosom.

Complaints to Audwin, of course, fell on deaf ears, for the irritable raven claimed that he wasn't the bird world's keeper. "Build a canopy above you, then!" he'd cried, feathers falling from his quivering body. No, he obviously didn't get Hamlin's need to be exposed to the sky and the breeze, and it was utterly pointless arguing about it.

Then again, Hamlin also realized that the need for solitude, which included thick, impenetrable walls and a location far removed from civilization, was a significant phase in his maturation. In addition to ensuring that he wouldn't be crossing paths with his half-brothers as much as possible, of course.

So this was his happy little escape, with a window that overlooked a gorgeous corner of the countryside. Beyond the gray stones of the battlements and the brilliant pennants flapping in the wind stretched rolling hills, colorful meadows, a distant forest to his right, and, on a clear, sunny day, the stately silhouette of a castle sitting grandly atop a hill.

here was something distinctly romantic in the sight, and Hamlin couldn't help but lean on his elbows, feeling the hard and uneven surface of his window ledge, and stare at the castle for several moments together, his mind awhirl with all kinds of pictures, stories, and other things, all inspired by the simple contentment that could be had in enjoying a lovely scene.

Discreet inquiries led him to the discovery that that distant castle was Queen Clarimond and King Rikard's, and by extension, Edouard's. That such a proud and snobby family would live so close—Hamlin made a face and sighed.

"It's a pretty scene, all the same," he muttered, pulling away from the window and walking over to his desk, where a pile of illuminated manuscripts awaited his pleasure.

He sat down and sorted through his books, eventually pulling one out and preparing himself for a long, pleasant afternoon lost in stories on chivalry. He loved knightly adventures, though he'd never been impressed with knights in person. Everyone was entitled to a few fantasies, he decided.

Hamlin didn't know how long he was immersed in his reading, but at length an insistent twittering tore his attention away from a particularly bloody battle between a knight and an army of demon-possessed gnomes.

He sat up and looked at the window, where a sparrow sat, blinking and twittering.

"Oh, hello," he said, turning in his chair. "Are you here with a message?"

Hamlin had all but forgotten the note he'd sent via avian carrier to Queen Franziska. He'd done so for his mother's sake, guilt overwhelming him over his role in severing ties between Queen Elfriede and Queen Franziska, the only person of noble birth who'd accepted the "commoner-queen" without hesitation. Hamlin had apologized for his behavior and begged not to have his mother pay for his unprincely outburst; he'd even voluntarily banished himself from Queen Franziska's castle as long as his mother remained welcome to the good lady.

Apparently, Queen Franziska had taken heed of the message and had sent a note of her own by private (human) messenger. While she'd playfully scolded Hamlin for his behavior, she'd also gladly taken him and his mother back, excusing her own rash decision under quite a bit of pressure from Queen Clarimond. It was with a great deal of pleasure that Hamlin watched his mother read the letter, her complexion and her eyes reddening. And it was with that final glimpse of his mother's happiness that Hamlin withdrew and amused himself quietly with his books.

So with the sparrow making a sudden appearance at his window, Hamlin wondered if this was another message from Queen Franziska, though it was puzzling, sending it by feathered carrier.

"Do you have something from Mama's friend?" he prodded when the sparrow paused in its singing and gazed around the tower room critically.

The bird shook itself, spreading its wings, and then proceeded to twitter, filling the calm air with light sounds. Hamlin listened intently, curious at first. As the message went on, his look of concentration slowly shifted to one of indignation and then outrage. He waited till the bird was done before speaking.

"Oh, so that's what he thinks, is it?" he spluttered, and the sparrow cocked its head to the side, blinking and listening and letting out an occasional chirp in answer. "You can go back to that consumptive snot and tell him that his head's so deep up his bony bum that his brain's been affected by what he's been breathing! And that's my way of saying that he'll never get an apology from me! What gall!" The sparrow chirped a few times. "Yes, you can quote me directly, and that's all I have to say to him." Hamlin paused and mulled things over. "Oh, and give my regards to Princess Aloysia, if you please."

The sparrow bowed its head, chirped again, hopped around, and flew away with Hamlin's message.

Chapter 18

"**O**h, lord, another party," Edouard muttered, fighting hard not to slump in his chair and slide halfway off it. The very idea of having to mingle—no, display himself for the matchmaking pleasure of desperate mothers—made his blood curdle and his strength vanish.

He kept his hazy gaze on the open book before him, all the while automatically saying, "Yes, Mama" and "Mm-hmm" to his mother, who'd been chattering his ears off since she'd unceremoniously swept into the library. Not that he was missing much by ignoring her, anyway. Ever since she'd had her first taste of aristocratic matchmaking, she couldn't seem to enough of it. What a travesty it was for Edouard's two older brothers to be already married!

When Queen Clarimond finally fell silent, and Edouard swore he could hear her gasping for air, he sighed and looked at her.

"And what occasion would this be, Mama?" he asked, all patience and forbearance. "Didn't we just survive a celebration in honor of Roderika's tenth birthday?"

"Why, it's a celebration of another year without incident!"

"Another year without incident. You mean to say another year of barely escaping that cranky, toothless crone's curse? That would've been Roderika's recent birthday, wouldn't it? This is all so redundant."

Queen Clarimond regarded her son as though he'd just sprouted a furry hump on his back. "Edouard, don't be difficult. You know very well that your poor cousin's days are numbered, and there's nothing Franziska and Friedrich could do but to live each day to its fullest. I mean, really—just the thought that you're on a path to a terrible fate that you can't control should be reason enough to live as though every day's your last."

Edouard listened to her, grimacing. "What a rotten way to live. I don't understand why everyone believes all that superstitious nonsense. Even Roderika behaves as though she were born into great beauty, singing talent, and brains, but I'm convinced that this is nothing more than a demonic possession of this..." He paused to tap his skull emphatically. "All because people around her believe superstitious rubbish, and they've absorbed it and somehow infected her with false ideas about who she really is."

"You philosophize too much, dear. It's also odd hearing you argue against the curse, when you actually believed in it not too long ago."

That much was true, Edouard was forced to concede. "It's called reading a great deal more and being enlightened as a result, Mama," he replied. "Aunt Franziska and Uncle Friedrich have taken on a very fatalistic turn, and their mania for celebrating every little milestone in Roderika's life seems to grow more and more desperate each year. Why they decided against placating that witch and convincing her to reverse the curse is beyond me."

Queen Clarimond merely sighed heavily, and it was her turn to cock an eyebrow at her son.

"Edouard, this conversation is tedious. Your cousin was cursed, and that's all there is to it. It's a terrible thing to live under one, to be sure, but you can't rationalize curses away." Shaking her head, she turned around and glided majestically to the library doors. "Make sure you're thoroughly scrubbed and dressed in your best clothes for this party," she called out, not once slowing her pace or glancing back.

She swung the doors open and sailed past them, and Edouard finally found himself alone and enveloped in precious silence after the doors shut.

He still didn't feel comfortable, however. He tried to pick up his reading where he'd left off, but his mind was spinning so many ideas that he was forced to give up entirely. Sighing heavily, he stood up and slowly walked around the long, narrow table, listening to his footfalls.

Yes, his opinion about things had changed considerably (from no to yes and back to no), only because he'd bothered to think things over and even consulted not just his books, but also his own understanding of the world. It was simply too easy to fall victim to superstition, he saw and, because of that, it also made personal responsibility a dangerously impotent concept. It was too easy to blame something else for one's behavior and choices, when one clung too much to the belief that life was shaped by Fortune and only Fortune. No free will, nothing.

"No, I can't accept that," Edouard muttered, frowning at the floor as he paced, clasping his hands behind him. "Too risky."

But he was only seventeen—coddled by his family and, in peacetime, just one more eligible bachelor to toss onto the auction block. Well, he thought with a wry smile, as far as that was concerned, the workings of Fortune were the culprit, and there was only so much free will could do to delay the inevitable. The heavens knew, Edouard had been doing his utmost to buy more time, and it wouldn't be long before both his parents would grow fed up enough to compel him to marry a princess.

He stopped at length, his shoulders and spirits drooping at the prospects. "Oh, this is going to be hell," he said.

• • • •

THE COACH SLOWED TO a halt, and both Edouard and Aloysia gazed dully out the windows. "Haven't we been here not too long ago?" Aloysia asked, her voice dripping with depressed resignation.

"Don't remind me," Edouard replied. He supposed that the only good thing in this was the fact that their parents rode in a separate coach—largely because of the desire for ostentation. Not many nobles in the country owned more than one coach, after all, and Edouard had a sinking feeling that it was also another way for his mother to herald their wealth, ensuring a more positive response to Edouard's marriage prospects.

"I'm going to vomit," he whispered, dragging a clammy hand across his brow. "I've got to get out of here."

He managed to stumble out and not trip, and he was barely even aware of turning around and helping his sister alight.

"Edouard!" Queen Clarimond's voice sliced through the fog in his brain. He turned to find her scowling at him while attendants scrambled about to make sure her robes had cleared the coach before allowing the driver to move on. "You and your sister are supposed to wait till you're attended to!"

Edouard sighed, throwing his head back and staring dourly at the blue, blue skies. "We're not invalids, Mama!" he said, irritated. "Besides, you and Papa are keeping them busy enough. Aloysia and I don't have the luxury of time."

"I told you that you spoil him too much," King Rikard said, his eyes flashing as he glared at Edouard. "You'll not talk to your mother like that!"

Edouard could only shake his head and purse his lips as he watched his father guide his mother away, their chins up, looking down their noses at everyone and everything, regardless of rank. His parents joined several other new arrivals as they entered the castle's front doors and were lost in the golden glow from within.

"Psst—Edouard, I think we can jump back in our coach and ride back home," Aloysia hissed as her brother led her to the doors on his arm. "It's not too late, you know."

"Yes, it is, and you know it. We're stuck here, and there's nothing we can do but grin and bear it."

"Is there a way for you to eat something really awful and be sick enough to be sent home?"

Edouard was only peripherally aware of their slowing pace as they neared the doors. It felt as though their feet were turning into tree trunks, sprouting roots that began to cling to the stones beneath them. Oh, if only!

"Seeing as how you're the one with the magic powers, Aloysia, I should be depending on you to get us out of here!" he hissed back. "And why should I be the one to get sick?"

"Because it's typical for girls to swoon, and I'm not a typical girl."

"You're telling me."

"Anyway, I haven't mastered transportation spells yet. Maybe I can make Roderika disappear and distract everyone that way while we run. What do you think?"

"I think you're insane as ever, and we're plain stuck here."

They finally entered the castle, and Edouard's melting brain suffered further injuries at the sight of the same faces and the same scenes, all of which he'd seen more than a millions times in just this past year. Unfortunately for him, quite a few of those familiar faces appeared to notice him, and several pairs of interested eyes targeted him, no matter where he turned.

For several moments, he silently cursed his good health (he wished he were stuck at home, desperately ill), his handsome new clothes (he wished he'd somehow tripped and fallen into cow manure before climbing into the coach), and his reputation (he wished he'd been turned into a toadstool that was lost in the undergrowth of the largest forest in the world).

"Quick," he said, "this way!"

He was about to drag Aloysia down one of the smaller corridors when they were both accosted by someone—a servant especially dispatched for the sole purpose of finding him and his sister for a full day of torment.

"Your Highnesses, Her Majesty, Queen Clarimond, requests the honor of your presences in the banquet hall," the fellow said with a graceful bow, sweeping his hand out to indicate the general direction.

"How soon?"

"Now, Your Highness."

"Bugger it," Edouard muttered as he led Aloysia to the place.

He decided to surrender to the inevitable. Aloysia seemed to have done so much sooner, and she walked beside him, hollow-eyed and lifeless. Then again, he could never tell with his sister; for all he knew, she'd just cast a spell on herself to look like the walking dead in a bid to draw sympathy from their hosts.

Walking through the dense crowd of colorful revelers and liveried servants, Edouard tried to amuse himself with some people-watching, his eyes sweeping the place.

As they neared the final corner leading to the banquet hall, he spotted Hamlin standing off to the side of the massive corridor. The bright-haired prince instantly got Edouard's dander up, though Hamlin appeared to be completely isolated from everyone, with his mother nowhere in sight. He merely stood against a wall, looking awkward, uncomfortable, and miserable as he watched the guests move around, ignoring him. Hamlin was well-dressed and looked quite beautiful, and Edouard was sure that, had Hamlin been born to a better set of parents or blessed with a personality, he would surely be smothered in adoring attention from all quarters.

But he lingered for a moment before making his mind up about something, and he walked through the crowds and eventually disappeared, not once noticing his archenemy.

Edouard shrugged the thought of him off, though, and eventually found himself in the banquet hall, which was thick with noblemen and women. He heard his name called and found his father beckoning to him from the opposite end of one of the long tables.

There were about seven long, massive tables standing parallel to each other, each weighed down with food and wine and fully occupied. At the middle table sat his aunt and uncle, both of whom were lost in lively conversation to notice their surroundings. To his parents' table he led Aloysia, and he sat next to his mother, who nodded her approval.

He gave the table a quick look and saw Queen Elfriede seated farther down near the opposite end, looking pale and alone and worried, but she was well-bred enough to converse with an old lord who sat beside her despite her clear distraction. Every once in a while, she'd look around and crane her neck, searching the crowds.

"I didn't have the power to keep her away from the table," Queen Clarimond said quietly in his ear. "For Franziska's sake, I allowed it. But I took care to make sure that her little savage stayed away, with you here. Your aunt doesn't know, and it's not necessary to tell her, is it? Besides, she's too busy entertaining to notice." She paused and smiled, again fixing her eyes in Queen Elfriede's direction. "You see, darling? I'm quite capable of compromise. Now let's eat and enjoy ourselves."

Edouard merely looked at her before helping himself to the nearest platter while a servant poured wine into his goblet. He felt ill at ease, though he didn't understand why. After all, his mother did what she could to ensure his protection. All mothers were expected to do that, weren't they? It sure sounded logical enough, but Edouard still couldn't help but feel guilty as he ate his food, not even tasting it.

Chapter 19

"Trouble finds you everywhere you go, doesn't it?"

Hamlin snorted, frowning at Audwin. "I never asked to come with Mama, but she insisted. I told her it was a bad idea, and look what happened—forever forbidden to wander within twenty leagues of Edouard."

Audwin clucked, hopping on the grass and inching closer to Hamlin, who sat on the ground, his back against a tree, his legs stretched out and crossed at the ankles. With a great heave and two quick flaps of his wings, the raven perched himself on the tip of Hamlin's shoe.

"Isn't that what you wanted, anyway? I sure do. I'm not one for bloody quarrels, and the heavens only know what would happen next if you and Prince Edouard were to set eyes on each other."

"I was hungry after the trip," Hamlin said. He dropped his gaze to the little collection of mushrooms beside him, and he gently touched the soft caps. "I'd have loved to have something to eat, even if it meant sitting down with the servants. I'm sure they're enjoying themselves right now."

Audwin was silent for a moment. At length he sighed. "I'm very sorry you have to put up with this, Your Highness. Shall I go peck away at Queen Clarimond's eyes for you? Righteous vengeance is very fashionable in this day and age, you know."

Hamlin blinked and looked up. "No, thanks. It's bad enough that she hates me and Mama enough to do this. I don't want her blood on my hands."

"Her blood would be on my beak, not your hands."

"No. No, thanks. I should rise above this." Hamlin paused, scowling. "Isn't that what you've been teaching me since my childhood? Whatever happened to those lessons of virtue? Now you're advocating violence?"

"It's a product of age, Your Highness. One gets irredeemably grumpy and resentful of anything and everything."

"Pfft! I'm glad I'm not a bird."

"No, you're too soft and would be dead well before your time, gobbled up and shat out by predators in two seconds." Audwin looked around, his little eyes blinking as he scanned the vicinity. "I'll go search for possible places for you to find food, Your Highness. I'll be back soon."

Without waiting for Hamlin's answer, he flew off, squawking. Hamlin sighed and made a face as he glanced back down to marvel at the mushrooms beside him. What were the superstitions involving mushrooms again? He tried to divert himself with those as waited out the time, his stomach growling and his brain growing fuzzy from starvation.

He'd abandoned the castle to wander into the woods where his half-brothers and their drunk friends dragged him not so long ago. His initial intentions were to sulk and feel sorry for himself, and for one glorious moment, wallowing in self-pity made the self-directed poison taste all the sweeter. The woeful "Why was I ever born?" sounded like the screeches of a mistuned lyre—perfect for what Hamlin wanted.

As was his habit, though, Audwin appeared, having managed to track him down, and ruined Hamlin's plans for an afternoon of self-indulgent woe. How did Audwin find out about his predicament? Why, a little bird told him, of course.

Hamlin wondered why he was so closely linked with birds. Only princesses communed with woodland creatures! What did that say about him? He sighed, scratched his head, momentarily dislodging the velvet and feathered cap that perched jauntily on it. He'd told Audwin the truth; he'd never wanted to attend this party, having been to a recent one, and he thought that Queen Franziska, however well-intentioned, was getting carried away.

But the good queen wanted to see her friend again, and Queen Elfriede was both humbled and delighted to be so warmly welcomed despite all the social forces working against her. Hamlin couldn't bear to disappoint his mother, who'd also insisted that, with his half-brothers off on a diplomatic mission, she was afraid of Hamlin feeling lonely if she left him back at the castle.

"Considering what just happened, it would have been much better if I hadn't come," he grumbled. He looked around and his mind cleared all of a sudden. Self-pity was well and good, but it was quite dull after a length of time. Now he felt nothing but boredom, sitting in the shadows of a pretty woods, with no one else for company but a collection of delicious-looking but most likely dangerous mushrooms.

At length, Hamlin scrambled to his feet, brushing off dirt and grass and looking himself over. No stains on his good clothes. He decided to go back and stay invisible in the crowd for as long as he could while looking for something to eat. Perhaps he could flatter a stray page into bringing him something.

Would Queen Clarimond be watching the staff of both the castle and its guests in hopes of keeping Hamlin from a day's nourishment? Hamlin wouldn't doubt it. He still remembered his meeting with the queen on his arrival; she'd taken advantage of a moment when Queen Franziska had whisked away his mother for a friendly chat, leaving him trailing behind and susceptible to the surging powers of the demon world.

"You're not to set foot in that banquet hall," she'd snarled, raising a white finger in warning. "You've done enough damage to last ten lifetimes, you insufferable brat, and while that social-climbing commoner you call your mother has managed to subvert my request to ban you both, I'm still within my rights to keep you away from my children at all costs."

She'd said other things, but since she'd pulled Hamlin aside with a painfully tight grip of his arm, Hamlin's attention had been fixed more on the agony of her claws digging into his skin. It was all he could do to retort, "I didn't want to come to this stupid party, anyway, and I'd sooner be drawn and quartered than spend a moment in your son's company!"

"I'm pleased to see that you're a good deal smarter than I thought."

"I'll keep my distance if you swear to me that you'll leave Mama alone and let her enjoy her time with her friend."

Queen Clarimond regarded him in mild surprise at first, an eyebrow raised, and inclined her head in a graceful nod. "I promise. Now go. Get out of my sight."

He'd managed to yank his arm out of her grip without tearing his sleeve—or his flesh, for that matter—and stormed off. When all the nobles were summoned to the banquet hall, Hamlin took care to lose himself elsewhere, making sure that everyone had gone in, including his mother. He could pretend that he was distracted by something and had missed the call.

That sounded easy enough, but soon, even stung pride didn't mask the hurt, and Hamlin had to go to the woods for a moment of solitude, reflection, and, yes, self-pity. Then Audwin appeared and ruined things for him.

He grimaced as his stomach growled more loudly. He pressed a hand against it as he once again found himself on the wide dirt road that led to Queen Franziska's castle.

He wondered if there was a way for him to change his situation—his fate. True, no one ever chose his or her parents, and for better or for worse, he was born to a young woman scorned by her husband's peers for being a commoner, and that scorn had become his birthright.

Had he done anything to earn it? Edouard would most likely say that his propensity for melodramatic outbursts was clear enough, but what of that? Hamlin, like other people, had too much self-respect to allow others to verbally abuse him over something he'd no control over. His half-brothers already gave him enough grief—in words and actions—day after day. He didn't need any more that from strangers outside his father's castle walls.

Then he thought of his mother, and his heart ached for her. Self-respect notwithstanding, Hamlin realized that he'd rather offer himself up for constant humiliation if it meant that his mother would be left alone. It was only too bad that the cursed court of King Friedrich and Queen Franziska operated rather fatalistically, and it was very likely that each moment that Roderika spent not subject to her curse—not pricking her fingers on a spindle—would be celebrated with a desperate joy.

And it meant that there'd be several future occasions like today, where Hamlin would have to grit his teeth and endure the embarrassment of being the unwanted dog that everyone kicked.

Hamlin sighed irritably as he entered the courtyard, which swarmed with people. Perhaps there was a way to change his fate somehow. Even he was forced to admit that, at the tender age of fourteen, he was getting more and more tired of being an outcast. Still, he had to remind himself that he needed to do this for his mother's sake.

So many things confused and depressed him, but not hunger. That, at least, was one thing that was real, and it was a problem that he could easily solve.

. . . .

FINDING A MOMENTARILY idle page was easy. Convincing the baffled boy to sneak away some food from the kitchen was a bit more challenging, so thank the heavens for money. A couple of gold coins later, Hamlin was once again fleeing the castle grounds for the haven of the woods, carrying a small sack packed with food—bread, fruit, roast meat, and even a small flagon half-filled with wine. The wine was the reason that Hamlin carried his food sack gingerly. He desperately needed the wine.

He retraced his steps to his earlier spot, stopping abruptly and gaping when he saw someone pacing back and forth on the path that led to his tree.

"Oh, for the love of—" Hamlin's heart dropped, his spirits sinking, at the sight of none other than Edouard, looking as though he were lost in thought, his head bowed, his arms crossed over his chest.

The other prince didn't seem to have heard him. Absorbed in his own concerns, as usual, Hamlin thought, shaking his head. And since Edouard stood in the way of Hamlin's escape, Hamlin had no choice but to clear his throat loudly and break the other boy's concentration.

"What the—oh." Edouard blinked, and he blushed for a moment.

"What on earth are you doing here?" Hamlin asked, frowning. "Are you going to tell me that I'm not allowed to sit under the trees as well?"

"No," Edouard replied, momentarily looking abashed and uncertain. He looked around him as though he were just waking up from a dream. Then he regarded Hamlin solemnly. "No, I'm here for you."

Hamlin sighed. "To tell me to bugger off, I suppose."

"To bring you something to eat."

Silence.

"Huh?"

Edouard beckoned to him and turned around, plunging deeper into the woods. Hamlin wondered if a band of hired cutthroats waited for him. He wouldn't put it past Queen Clarimond's spawn to have his enemy ambushed and disposed of once and for all.

All the same, he couldn't help but follow Edouard deeper into the shadows, the fresh air and the soft breeze allaying some of his doubts. His grip on his food sack tightened, and he wondered if bread, fruit, and roast meat could be used as defensive weapons.

At length they reached a small open area—a little circle of grass flooded with sunlight. And sitting in the center was another sack similar to what Hamlin carried. Edouard walked up to it and knelt down to untie it. He glanced up when Hamlin paused, hesitating and staring at him dubiously.

"I know what my mother did," the other prince said matter-of-factly. "And I disagree with her. It's petty, childish, and utterly illogical, regardless of our mutual enmity."

Hamlin blinked, now completely confused. "She's going to find out about this, you know," he said, his resistance wavering. "You'll be in big trouble, and I'm sure she'll blame me for manipulating you."

Edouard shrugged, looking nonplussed. "No one's perfect."

"That's supposed to be comforting?"

"Hamlin, sit down and eat."

Hamlin cocked an eyebrow. "I beg your pardon?"

Edouard looked comically baffled at first, and then realization dawned, his frown disappearing, and he sighed, indicating the open sack. "Please sit down, Hamlin, and eat something. I'm not going to fight with you. It's neither the time nor the place, and I'm really not in the mood for a row."

"That's a relief, to be sure," Hamlin muttered, rolling his eyes when Edouard turned away to busy himself with pulling out food. Hamlin walked over to him and carefully sat down. "I brought my own food. It cost me quite a bit, but I'm just grateful to have had the foresight to bring coin with me today."

Edouard looked dismayed as he listened. "You shouldn't have to pay for what's meant for you," he said. "That's wrong."

"I didn't have choice, did I? Your mother made sure of it." Hamlin couldn't help but spit that bit out, and it felt good watching Edouard wince. But the other prince rallied himself quickly enough.

"Point taken," Edouard replied, sitting down opposite Hamlin. "Let's call it a truce, all right? I'm trying to right what's obviously so wrong, and I'm not interested in fights like I said."

Hamlin nodded, falling silent, and he soon busied himself with inspecting his food, which he offered to Edouard. With Edouard's stolen food, the two appeared to have a feast on their hands. Hamlin soon indulged himself, while his companion nibbled here and there, claiming to be full already.

No conversation passed between them the whole time, and while Hamlin was relieved, he still felt a tad uncomfortable having Edouard there with him. He kept his eyes down and glued to his meal, but good breeding reprimanded him for being so rude. Unfortunately for good breeding, discomfort turned the screws more tightly, and Hamlin refused to look at his companion as he silently ate. Besides, Hamlin was also dangerously close to tears, the humiliation of the moment just too much to bear.

Chapter 20

Discomfort and boredom proved to be a bad combination for Edouard. One result was stomach pain brought on by continuous, mindless eating in order to fill the excruciating time spent in awkward silence. The other result was the emergence of a new conundrum involving Hamlin's hair color—what shade was it, exactly? That last bit occupied Edouard's mind the whole time, which could partially account for his continuous, mindless nibbling.

Since Hamlin refused to look up and engage him in conversation, Edouard shrugged and contented himself with simply observing his companion, seeing if he had the ability to look beyond his prejudices.

He took note of Hamlin's clothes, which were very nicely made and quite flattering to the younger boy. The feathered cap was a nice touch, but Edouard wasn't sure if it was chosen to purposefully draw attention to Hamlin's hair, which he now was able to observe more closely. It was blond, yes, but it seemed to be a curious shade of blond.

As he absentmindedly sampled fruit, Edouard stared long and hard, his mind working on all variations of yellow and gold that he knew, and somehow he still couldn't come up with the right one. For one mad moment, he willed Hamlin to look up and meet his gaze so that he could decide the matter, but a sudden twinge in his gut shattered his concentration, and he was forced to toss a half-eaten apple behind him.

"Oh, I'm done," he said, grimacing a little as he pressed a hand to his stomach. "I overdid it, I'm afraid."

Hamlin looked up, finally, blue eyes startled and unblinking. "What?"

"I have to go back. I'm sure my family's searching for me." Edouard paused to indicate the food he'd brought. "Do you want to keep this? I can bring it back if you're not interested."

"Oh—I'm getting full on what I have," Hamlin stammered, blushing. He actually looked around him, the confusion on his face almost comical. How far lost in thought was he, anyway? "I'll be going back to the castle once I'm done."

"You're staying, then?" Edouard thought it was a bit silly and self-indulgently depressing, purposefully isolating oneself like that. He started to gather the food he'd brought and carefully put it back in the sack.

"I am, yes. I think I should enjoy the peace and quiet for another moment."

"Very well, then." Edouard stood up in one quick and graceful movement, stooping down to pick up his sack of food. "Don't worry, I won't tell Mama about this, and I hope you won't, either."

Hamlin's pale features darkened. "Your mama and I have nothing more to say to each other. I daresay that won't be a problem at all."

Edouard bowed. "Of course. That's understandable. Good day."

He walked around Hamlin and started back on the path that led them there.

"Edouard."

He paused and glanced back to find Hamlin half-turning and regarding him earnestly.

"Thank you. I really appreciate it." Hamlin didn't smile or overtly display pleasure or friendliness. In fact, his manner was very matter-of-fact yet sincere, though Edouard could also detect a faint edge of reluctance there. Pride, perhaps? He wouldn't doubt it. Hamlin was an intractable, proud little bugger.

"You're welcome," he said, inclining his head again before walking off. Once he cleared the trees and was once again awash in sunshine, he felt a great deal better. That was well played on his part, and he congratulated himself for a job well done. Now his conscience would stop bothering him, and he could carry on with the rest of his day in peace.

· · · ·

"EDOUARD! WHERE ON EARTH have you been?"

"Oh, lord, Mama," he muttered, rolling his eyes. He paused and turned around to find his mother pushing her way through the crowd with—egad!—a young lady in tow.

"Enjoying the party, of course," he replied in a louder voice. He hoped he sounded cheerful and careless, seeing as how all hopes of freedom were about to be dashed, stomped on, and set on fire. "You know how easy it is to be swallowed up by the crowd in any of Aunt Franziska's parties."

Queen Clarimond reached him, looking a bit put out and flushed from her efforts. She merely made a face at her son before tugging the young lady to the front. "I want to introduce you to Princess Melisande, who hails from the country southwest of ours."

When Edouard said nothing and stared hard at her, she added, "It's France, of course! My dear, she's a year younger than you, and she's visiting our country with her parents and brothers and sisters—quite a large family, too!"

She paused to lean forward, her eyes widening. "Seven children in all, mind that!" she whispered and then straightened up. "You *will* look after her, won't you, darling? I'm busy entertaining her parents—good diplomatic relations are essential in this day and age, you know—and Aloysia's off with Prince Clovis." Queen Clarimond added through gritted teeth, "Hopefully not ignoring or putting off the poor boy."

Then she turned to Princess Melisande and smiled brightly. "This is my youngest son, my dear—Edouard. He's terribly brilliant and indescribably handsome, and I'm quite sure that you and he will get along quite swimmingly. Here you go."

Without ceremony, she gave poor Melisande's arm one more yank, and the girl stumbled forward, almost falling against Edouard.

"My, you two look like a charming pair!" Queen Clarimond said, beaming. "Now go along and enjoy the party. Go! Shoo!" She flapped her hands at them in a very unqueenly way. She was also red-faced, extremely happy, and a touch giggly. Edouard sighed. Apparently his mother had been in his uncle's favorite cask of exotic wine again. That explained a few things. He also knew that she'd be waking up to a black cloud of shame the next day, not to mention a crippling headache. The things monarchs did for good diplomatic relations.

His dander up, Edouard offered an arm to Melisande, who first stared at it as though it were some demonic tentacle about to melt her skin before taking it. Edouard gave his triumphant and glassy-eyed mother a baleful look and led his partner through the crowds.

"I must apologize for my mother's behavior," he said once they'd reached a quieter section of the courtyard. "She fancies herself a skilled matchmaker, I'm afraid. Her perceptions get progressively worse with every goblet of wine she downs."

"It's no problem at all," Melisande replied, her voice cheerfully singsong and edged with an accent. "You should meet my mother. That's why they get along very well together. I think they're on their way to breaking open the second cask."

Edouard nodded, falling silent. He hated small talk, and he hated being forced into awkward situations. Finding himself in two awkward situations in a row, in fact, rankled, and he desperately wanted his sister to appear, do what she did best—transform into something unspeakably ugly—and terrify the rest of the world into avoiding him for the rest of his natural life.

For better or for worse, Melisande didn't appear to be inclined to talk. In fact, she kept sighing and looking around her, clearly bored and simply waiting out the time. And since Edouard didn't have a clue as to how long he was supposed to keep her occupied, he wracked his brain for a list of things to talk about—small-talk subjects that would help eat up whatever time they were meant to spend together.

"And how is the weather where you live?" he asked, turning to smile at the princess, who blinked in confusion before answering.

"Very mild and pleasant right now, thank you," she said, returning his smile before looking ahead again. Edouard took note of the fact that she was blonde, but her hair color was easy to describe: recently harvested hay.

Another moment of silence fell on the two. Edouard had recovered from the previous conversation and moved on to the next item.

"How does your country's cuisine compare to mine?"

And so on and so forth. Edouard didn't try to keep track of time, but by the time he'd exhausted all ten items on his conversational list, the two of them had completed two-thirds of an idle circuit around the courtyard. When he realized that he'd fallen short of one complete circuit, Edouard tried to come up with a few more spontaneous subjects, but he couldn't. As another heavy silence fell on them, Edouard frowned, pursed his lips, scratched his head, coughed, sighed, looked up at the sky, and did everything he could to rattle his brain into a better state.

Shaking his head at himself, he scanned the crowds to see if he could see something worth discussing. It was humiliating, of course, to be reduced to nothing more than useless gossip for conversation, but as with his previous efforts at brainstorming, he found nothing worth talking about.

A flash of gold just off to his left drew his attention away from his desperate efforts, and he spotted Hamlin walking through the crowds in the direction of his aunt's private garden. He watched the younger boy till Hamlin eventually vanished from view, and he once again found himself marveling at Hamlin's hair and, to his surprise, drawn to the other prince's profile.

Embarrassingly enough, Edouard not only remained at a loss for words in his zealous attempts at finding the right word to describe the shade of Hamlin's hair, but he was just as handicapped in his attempts at describing Hamlin's profile beyond "very fine."

This was a bad thing. Edouard immediately stopped, annoyed. "Melisande," he said, turning to his partner, "it was a great pleasure to meet you, but I'm afraid I must leave for a moment."

"What's wrong? Did I say something wrong? I was quiet, wasn't I?" the princess stammered, blushing. She looked so alarmed that Edouard's tongue nearly stuck to the roof of his mouth. Good heavens, did she like him? Did Edouard overplay his hand and somehow engage her too much in intimate conversation with those ten items? Hopefully not!

"No, it isn't you," he replied, trying to squelch his panic. "I just—I need to go find something for my stomach. It's been hurting for a while now."

"Oh—I'm so sorry for that. Should I order my servant to look for a healer?" Melisande beckoned to someone in the crowd and, like magic, a young girl appeared and curtsied.

"No, thank you, but I'll be fine. I appreciate your time and company."

"Will I talk to you again?"

Good heavens.

"You will, I'm sure. It's a pleasure." Edouard bowed and then moved away, ignoring the irate mental voice that was now practically screaming at him for his lack of manners. He didn't care. He'd done what he could to entertain the princess, and it appeared as though his efforts worked, though perhaps too much. If he were to find himself once again forced into a similar situation, he'd have to cut back on his subjects for small talk—halve it, in fact, to five items. That ought to keep single, interested young ladies at bay.

He hurried inside the castle and headed straight for Queen Franziska's library. There he hid himself, pulling out manuscripts. He needed one whose subject was language. Surely there was a way for him to find those elusive words that were now bothering him. Carrying a stack, he brought them over to the table and immediately lost himself in their contents.

He gave up within the hour, and it was all he could do to rest his chin on his folded arms and lose himself in thoughts of Hamlin, pulling out the image of the prince's profile in the sun and placing it in his mind's eye. After another minute of fruitless brainstorming, he sighed and cursed under his breath. It was pointless. He was forced to resign himself to "very fine."

Chapter 21

Had three years passed already? Hamlin shook his head in disbelief as he put his head out of the coach. It seemed as though one day he was overwhelmed by Queen Franziska's many festivities, and the next day he was studying under the steady guidance of austere scholars in the battle-crazy northwestern kingdom beyond the channel called England.

Now seventeen, Hamlin was on his way home after a summer spent touring the continent with a tutor. The two had parted ways ten miles ago, Hamlin was now on his own save for his servant, and the trip back to his father's castle had been nothing short of amazing.

The countryside had changed considerably, but not for the worse. Peace continued, and it looked as if Nature were celebrating accordingly by painting the landscape with a breathtaking, vivid palette. The sky was also cloudless and a brilliant shade of blue, and the breeze was gentle and warm. Stretching his neck a bit farther, Hamlin could glimpse his father's castle just beyond the next hill.

Smiling and misty-eyed, he sighed and sat back inside the coach, waiting on the stiff seat. He was exhausted beyond words and sore from all the jostling, but all he could think about was just how excited he was to be finally home after so much time abroad. He'd visited his family for as many holidays as possible, of course, but those were rare because traveling was simply too difficult.

It was a good thing, then, that King Reinhard was able to negotiate with a local abbot to take in Hamlin during those weeks when he couldn't return home, compensating the monastery handsomely for looking after a prince. Those times had proven to be wonderful, though Hamlin didn't take to the brothers' faith, let alone their daily rituals. He'd been given his own private room and was allowed to wander about the grounds and gardens, and to amuse himself with the secular books he'd bought for himself.

The tranquility and simplicity of his life during his schooling was unsurpassed, though he missed his parents terribly, and he was still able to adjust to his new life without much difficulty. The best part, of course, was the great distance between him and his half-brothers. For three glorious years, Hamlin remained untouched by their crudeness; his too-brief visits home found him alone with his parents, for Otto, Baldrick, and Mallory were always on one diplomatic errand or another.

The flapping of a bird's wings interrupted Hamlin's thoughts, and he opened his eyes to find a familiar black creature sitting on the seat across from him, barely able to keep itself upright on the rough ride.

"Well, what do we have here?" Audwin squawked, flapping his wings every time he pitched sideways. "A young prince traveling alone with no royal guards for an escort? What's the damned world coming to, I ask? Oh, blast this coach!"

Hamlin grinned and patted his lap. "Come here, you oaf," he said, laughing, and Audwin happily accepted his invitation. The raven flew across to perch himself on Hamlin's arm, which Hamlin had raised for him. "And as for my invisible escort, Papa said it wasn't necessary."

"What the blazes does he mean? You're not in danger of being stopped and carried off for ransom, with a thorough ravishing thrown in?"

"That's not going to happen, Audwin. Good grief, your imagination's gotten pretty wild. Is this what age does to a bird?" Hamlin didn't know how long ravens lived, but he was pretty certain that Audwin's life span was miraculous, to say the least. Then again, he didn't know of any other raven that talked, so he just resigned himself to being good friends with a feathered creature that was bewitched.

Audwin snorted, eyeing Hamlin and shaking himself a bit. "All kinds of awful things happen with age, Your Highness, but one thing seems to be very obvious here. Am I the only living creature who worries about you?"

Hamlin's grin softened, and he ignored the soft pang in his chest. "I think it's wonderfully sweet of you to fret like that," he said, gently stroking the bird's head, which felt like silk.

He kept his free hand up to let Audwin lightly peck at it—a sign of affection, he'd long learned, which was the closest he'd get to being kissed by a bird.

"But I'm perfectly safe, and there's no need to worry so much. I miss your crotchety company, you know. The birds up north aren't very friendly to foreigners." Hamlin paused, mulling things over a bit. "Come to think of it, the people up north aren't very friendly to foreigners, though they treated me well enough. At least they were very polite."

"It's your station in life, of course."

Hamlin shrugged. "And Papa's money."

"You could've been spirited away in the dead of night for your papa's money while studying over there."

"For heaven's sake, no one did, and now you're coming up with all kinds of sordid scenes that won't happen, now that I'm done with schooling. I'm surprised you're still alive and not a victim of your own wild imaginings and temper."

Audwin snorted again. Hamlin realized how funny that sound was, and he fought off the urge to burst out laughing in his long-suffering friend's face. "Wild imaginings? Pfft. There's nothing wild about ensuring the safety of one who's fated to do grand things."

"Princes are always fated to do grand things," Hamlin replied, rolling his eyes. "Save princesses from curses, pass a dozen dangerous tests to prove their worth, sacrifice themselves in the name of love, et cetera, et cetera. Stupid, predetermined fluff, I say."

"Yes, well, try to convince the wind that."

"Is she still bothering you?"

"Birds and the wind have never seen eye to eye, Your Highness. And she's a horrible gossip to boot. Birds can't help but be subjected to her pointless chatter."

Hamlin chuckled. "Birds are just as bad as the wind, I think."

"It's a parasitically dependent relationship we have with her, I'm afraid. Now," Audwin paused and cleared his throat, "I suppose you wouldn't be interested to know more about your old friend and how he fared while you were away, laying to waste foreign lands with your charm."

Hamlin blinked. "Friend?"

"Edouard, I mean. What, how many friends do you have?"

Hamlin fell silent, blushing.

"You can have my head lopped off by royal decree if you'd like for embarrassing you, Your Highness, but let me finish giving you the news first."

"I won't have you executed, you ridiculous bird. Now out with it!" Hamlin still felt the heat suffusing his cheeks, and it refused to abate.

"Tsk, tsk, temper, temper. Anyway, I thought you'd be interested to know that your royal friend was sent away for his schooling as well."

Hamlin sighed irritably. "That's no news. All princes must be learned."

"Lord, child, you'll kill me at this rate! Let me finish!" Audwin retorted, puffing up his feathers till they appeared to stand on end, making him look obese. "His mother tossed him in a finishing school—of sorts."

Silence fell, and Hamlin took some time to process that piece of news.

"Finishing school of sorts?" he echoed at length, frowning. "For a *boy*? What kind of curriculum do they have? How to shoot arrows at a target and say 'excuse me' before slaying it? Or how to apologize to the corpse afterward? Is there a genteel way of running an enemy through with a sword? Maybe the proper way of placing a crown on one's head?"

Audwin stared at him. "Forgive me, Your Highness, but you're hopeless. I'm afraid you'll have to find out from him yourself."

"No, I won't. I haven't seen him in three years, and I doubt if we'll be crossing paths again, let alone be on friendlier terms than before."

At this, Audwin shook his head, sighed deeply, and flew off Hamlin's arm. "Positively hopeless," he said. "You'll be meeting him soon enough, when that brute half-brother of yours marries!"

The raven escaped the coach, flying through one of the windows, and vanished. Hamlin watched him go, bemused. Whistling low, he settled himself back in his seat. Audwin had left him with quite a bit to consider, and he was only too glad to lose himself in that curious news regarding Edouard.

Finishing school "of sorts"? Hamlin burst out laughing at the idea. Oh, yes, he could see that now. It was one thing that he and Queen Clarimond would see eye-to-eye on, no doubt, and Hamlin soon reveled in one mental image after another as Edouard and his mother, the latter announcing her plans to fix his lack of manners and personality. Taking that idea further, Hamlin tried to picture his nemesis in such a school, forced to learn social niceties and the fine art of being agreeable.

For the next few minutes, Hamlin amused himself with one mean-spirited scene after another until he imagined the unlucky Edouard reduced to behaving as meekly as an old, tired horse. It took some doing, but he pulled his thoughts away to another item: Otto's upcoming nuptials.

"Poor Princess Hedda," he muttered, gazing out the window again.

Hamlin meant it, too. He'd met his future sister-in-law on his first visit home from his schooling. He'd found her to be just like his mother in beauty and temperament, and he wondered what on earth had made her agree to marry a coarse brute of a prince like Otto. The two had nothing in common, and the match wasn't even fixed. They'd met during one of Otto's diplomatic travels east, and apparently they'd fallen in love. Hamlin remembered being so flabbergasted by their engagement that he'd begged her to repeat her story five times.

"I can give myself a headache just trying to understand this," Hamlin said, shaking his head.

Two years later, he still could hardly believe it, and nothing made sense, no matter how many times he turned possibilities and rational arguments about the match in his head. Love really *must* be blind—at least in Hedda's case.

He could only wish her the very best, and he looked forward to having her for his sister, as she'd shown him a great deal of kindness, effectively silencing Otto's usual criticisms and insults. The older prince wouldn't dare cross her, it seemed, and for that, Hamlin would be forever grateful for Princess Hedda's existence.

Otto's royal wedding was in a fortnight. Hamlin braced himself for the chaos of his father's court, with everyone in an excited frenzy. It was going to be a grand celebration befitting the heir to the throne, and both nobility and the gentry from neighboring kingdoms were expected to come. And that included Queen Clarimond's family. Hamlin couldn't suppress a devious grin. He couldn't wait to see Edouard again, just to bear witness to the effects of a "finishing school of sorts" on the prince's behavior. Revenge was sweet, and Hamlin didn't even have to throw a punch. Fortune was on his side this time.

Chapter 22

The doors to the great library swung open—rather dramatically, at that—and in swept Queen Clarimond, gesticulating and talking a mile a minute, showing off her immense pride in her home and her family. Immediately behind her followed a group of women, one of whom was a queen, and the rest, her daughters. All five of them.

"And this is the room where my Edouard spends much of his time," Queen Clarimond declared, pausing to allow her guests to walk around and inspect the library. She smiled at them and encouraged them to explore. "He's a great reader—in fact, he's the intellectual of my children, far surpassing everyone else in matters of the mind."

"What are his favorite subjects?" one of the young women asked as she gazed around her, wide-eyed and breathless.

"Anything and everything, my dear. The boy's just gifted in that regard, and it's our duty to make sure that he's encouraged in what he does."

"Oh, look at this—Prince Edouard likes to read about plants? I hope he likes flowers. I do so love flowers—especially roses," another young woman said, eagerly pointing at a shelf where illuminated botanical manuscripts were neatly categorized. If she'd been more attentive to the texts, she'd have noticed that half of the books dealt with poisonous plants and flowers and the countless ways they were used by witches and sorcerers for dark magic. But those were Aloysia's books.

"Yes, he loves flowers of all kinds," Queen Clarimond agreed, nodding her encouragement. "His favorite sanctuary happens to be his aunt's private garden, and he does get very sentimental whenever the subject of roses pops up in conversation. Vastly fortunate would be the young lady whom he'd lead into that garden for intimate conversation."

That was certainly a bald-faced lie, but Edouard was in no position to argue against it. In the disguise that Aloysia had fashioned for him when they'd heard the women approach, he wasn't in a position to do anything but wait, fixed and silent. The women moved around the library in a continuous whirl of girlish chatter and rich gowns.

"And what can an intellectual do for a kingdom?" the visiting queen asked, meeting Queen Clarimond's proud gaze with her own. Both queens regarded each other with hauteur.

"Oh, come now, don't be silly," Queen Clarimond replied stiffly. "Intellect brings a great deal more to the management of a kingdom than brute strength, my dear. A man needs to be cleverer than his enemies, wiser than his counselors, and sharper than his heirs. Much bloodshed can be avoided with sound judgment grounded firmly in reason, with every possibility weighed."

Her defense of Edouard's intellect carried on for a while, and Edouard just wished that they would stop. Only the visiting queen was interested in what Queen Clarimond had to say, and her five daughters continued to explore the library and talk among themselves about Edouard's thousand and one virtues. And judging from the animated conversation between the sisters, it was clear that a rivalry was growing. If Aloysia's disguise had left Edouard with a head, he would have shaken it in amazement at their conversation.

He made do with waiting, amusing himself with thoughts about entering some sort of monastery, vanishing from the world. Not only would he be left in peace, but he'd also be in the company of ascetics who wouldn't care a jot about anything but their spiritual lives, and Edouard's attraction toward the male sex could be stifled and ignored.

His propensities had become clear to him just before his mother booted him into that confounded school. He didn't know how it happened, but he'd somehow found himself hopelessly in love with a duke's son, and he'd panicked and had thrown himself into his education with fiercer energy. Of course, no amount of reading had gotten rid of his pining, and Edouard had lived in miserable silence since then.

Unfortunately, his mother had also redoubled her efforts at finding him a wife. Edouard was now twenty years old, and she was feeling desperate. This, he'd long realized, was the downside to peacetime: bored and idle nobility He sighed as he waited. And waited. And waited. At length, the women swept out of the library, still chattering, the visiting queen still skeptical as to Edouard's virtues and each princess convinced that she was fated to be The Lucky One. Yes, even the youngest, who was twelve years old.

Edouard waited until the doors had closed behind them and their voices and footsteps had faded away. He sighed in relief and stared at one of the windows high above.

"They're gone, Aloysia," he called out.

A figured appeared in the window, its shape distorted by the sunlight that streamed through. "Ah, just in time!" Aloysia said, sounding pleased with herself. Then she leaped off the window and sailed down.

No, she wasn't in bird form, and neither was she in human form. She was—in a form of some kind, one that Edouard had long given up identifying. In fact, he reminded himself, he really should just stop trying to figure out his sister's chosen appearance because it might drive him insane.

Aloysia had become a hybrid of goat and fish, and she could fly without wings. That was the best Edouard could do. Once she neared the floor, she shifted back to human form, and he watched her land lightly, leaving a trail of small, sparkling stars in her wake. As the glamour faded, she primly adjusted her headpiece and brushed off her gown before walking up to Edouard and regarding him critically, her hands on her hips.

"You know that I can't keep doing this forever," she said.

"Really? I thought you enjoyed using me for practice spells."

"I've long gone beyond that, brother. I'm a master now, or haven't you heard the news? All this is just child's play for me." She indicated Edouard's situation with a careless wave of her hand.

"It isn't child's play to me, for heaven's sake. My life and my sanity are at stake!"

Aloysia rolled her eyes. "You should've fled to a monastery a long time ago, Edouard." Then she muttered a string of incoherent words, made strange gestures with her hands, and Edouard found himself engulfed in white nothingness and slowly receding warmth. In another moment, he was standing before his sister.

"Thank you," he said. "I appreciate the disguise."

"You made for a very interesting stain on Papa's old chair."

That rankled a bit. He was sure that his sister had turned him into a stain that discolored King Rikard's heirloom chair as way of amusing herself. "You could've turned me into a book or a footstool."

That earned him a cheeky wrinkling of a nose from Aloysia. "Nonsense. Those would've been too predictable, even for you. I think turning you into a stain was the best disguise. Even Mama didn't notice, and you know how fastidious she is when it comes to heirlooms and sentimental objects."

"And if she noticed, she'd have me scrubbed off or even burned," Edouard retorted as he walked over to the chair he'd abandoned just before his sanctuary was invaded.

Aloysia just sighed. "That's gratitude for you."

She walked over to the table where she perched herself, idly scanning her books. They'd lain ignored for a while now. "I hope you're not going to ask me to cast more spells on you at Otto's wedding. That's another opportunity for Mama to sell you off, you know."

"Maybe you can cast a spell on Mama instead. Come to think of it, maybe you should cast a truth spell on her now and make her confess as to why she agreed to go Otto's wedding, considering who his mother is."

Aloysia just shrugged, picking up a book and flipping through without much interest. "More matchmaking opportunities, I suppose? Or very likely a smart diplomatic move? She doesn't have anything against King Reinhard, you know."

"Unless Papa had something to do with it."

"There you go." Aloysia sighed as she hopped off the table. "Well, I have to go and play hostess to our guests. I promised Mama that I'd spend time with the princesses—ten minutes, to be precise."

"You don't mind at all, eh?"

"What's there to mind? I can easily practice spells on them without their knowing anything." Aloysia grinned, looking terribly pleased with herself. "I've also mastered subterfuge, brother. It's quite good fun!" She patted his shoulder and then walked off, leaving a faint smell of lavender.

Edouard turned his attention back to his reading.

"Oh, by the way," she said, startling him out of his book. "I heard that Hamlin's back from his travels."

Edouard blinked and frowned, but he didn't turn around to look at Aloysia. "And why should I care about that?"

"You already do. You just don't know it or won't admit to it."

"It's been three years since we were at each other's throats. We've both moved on from childish things to that stage we call 'I can't get myself to care.'"

"Indeed. Three years can do all kinds of odd things to a person, apparently. Enjoy your books!"

Edouard swore that Aloysia actually cackled, witch-like, as she exited the room, and once silence fell, he realized that his hair was standing on end. Grimacing, he shifted uncomfortably and shook off the feeling. He had too many things to worry about, things that were much more important than the presence of an old enemy.

All the same, he soon lost himself in thoughts of Hamlin. How had his schooling changed him, he wondered? The word was that Hamlin had been sent to a foreign country for his studies and that he'd even spent time in a monastery. Would academic or even spiritual discipline have made a difference in the boy's unruly behavior?

Edouard tried to picture Hamlin in a monastery. Oh, that was precious. A wild, spoiled brat of a prince suddenly surrounded by nothing but prayer and strict austerity? One could only pity the abbot and the brothers. He also tried to picture a complete reversal in Hamlin as a result of his studies and travels. Edouard forced himself to picture it, at least, and for some reason, he couldn't quite come up with an image of the younger prince grown up and reasonable.

"Maybe he's a hopeless case," he said, shrugging. That possibility seemed easier to accept. It was very realistic, as far as he was concerned.

And Otto's wedding was rapidly nearing. Edouard would have his answers soon enough, and he swore to himself that he wasn't going to laugh in Hamlin's face when they met. His mother's injunction for him to keep his distance from Hamlin was still in his mind, even after three years.

Chapter 23

The crush of people was incredible, and Hamlin wanted nothing more than to run as far away as he could; unfortunately, being the youngest son of the bridegroom's proud parents, he didn't have much of a choice but to spend as much energy as he could on keeping his humor. His clothes did him no favors, either.

Though his parents wore their ceremonial robes and heavy crowns while he and his half-brothers simply wore their finest formal attire, the amount of decorative embroidery, tiny gems, and gold thread made his clothes feel as though they weighed a blasted ton. Even Hamlin's cap—with its requisite collection of feathers—seemed as though it was bent on crushing his skull, if not tearing his head off his neck. If it worked, it'd be a rather crude method of decapitation.

The exchange of vows was long and dull, for Otto and Hedda couldn't help but get overly sentimental, embellishing their vows with one cooed endearment after another till Hamlin felt the bile rise in his throat. Around him, practically every noblewoman sighed and let out happy little sounds, with some whispering, "Oh, how terribly romantic they are!" or "I know that they'll never, ever be apart, or they'll surely die!"

Hamlin could only raise his eyes and stare dazedly at the ceiling and the colorful pennants hanging down, muttering, "Oh, help."

What a pity Audwin wasn't there. Hamlin would give anything to have his cantankerous old friend with him, diverting him with sarcastic observations and threats of annihilation. Then again, seeing as how Otto's wedding meant a gargantuan collection of humanity, Audwin wouldn't likely come around until everyone had gone home. The poor bird could only take so much where human beings were concerned, after all.

At length the ceremony ended, and the festivities began with ripples of cheering throughout the castle and even beyond. For his part, Hamlin turned and frantically searched for a free chair. He found one, eventually, and, as luck would have it, it was in his room.

"Well, that's only because the other free chairs out there are situated in the most inconvenient places," he grumbled as he slumped against the backrest, pulling off his cap and fanning himself with it. Those "inconvenient places" happened to be in locations that swarmed with guests and servants.

Once he'd rested enough, Hamlin stood up, tossed his cap onto his bed, and walked over to look out the window. The courtyard was a sea of color and movement. He glanced at the battlements, and he wondered how many of the peasantry were gathered beyond the castle walls, celebrating the wedding. Perhaps he should take an idle stroll along the battlements. It would be nice to watch the festivities on both sides and not be harassed by guests wherever he turned.

Hamlin yawned and stretched his arms above him. "Then again," he said when a more brilliant idea struck him, "maybe I can get away with disappearing from the crowd by resting here. I'm sure Mama won't miss me, considering how many people she has to entertain."

A knock on the door broke into his thoughts, though, and a servant came in at his command and curtsied. Like the rest of the servants, she wore her best clothes for the occasion, and the girl looked a bit uncomfortable in her finery.

"Your Highness, I have a message from the queen. She said, 'I know you're hiding in your room. Come downstairs at once and mingle. And don't give me any excuses, or else,' Your Highness." Blushing deeply, she scratched the back of her neck with a little whimper.

Hamlin sighed and walked over to his bed. He snatched his cap and set it back on his head. The servant vanished, leaving the door open, and he walked out. For one mad moment, he'd give anything to be Audwin right now.

• • • •

AUDWIN WAS RIGHT, HAMLIN reflected. He didn't have friends. He walked through the crowds, smiling and nodding and exchanging pleasantries with whoever stopped him, and he realized with a sinking feeling that there was no one with whom he could talk and pass time. There were many people his age surrounding him, but he'd never felt so alone, and this was his father's castle, his home, to boot.

Weaving his way through the crowds, he entered and left corridors, large halls, the stables, the main courtyard, and his parents' private courtyard. He walked a circuitous route, counting how many times he passed the same tired and bored knight standing at attention. He entertained the cheeky idea of sticking a flower in a joint of the knight's armor each time he passed until the man stood like a decorative garden in gleaming metal, flowers sprouting from the most interesting places.

He paused before a traveling minstrel performing to the delight of a small, appreciative audience and watched, momentarily diverted. When he grew tired of it, he moved on to another performer at the opposite corner of the main courtyard. This time the colorful fellow was doing funny acrobatics for the children, who howled, yelled, clapped, and begged for more.

What time was it? Hamlin was half-afraid of finding out. Something told him that only ten minutes must've slipped by since he was ordered to mingle.

"And to think this will have to be repeated with Baldrick and Mallory's weddings," he muttered, frowning at the lively scenes around him. And his? Hamlin shuddered. He refused to entertain the idea, and with that, he turned and walked on, taking a random direction toward—somewhere.

"Hamlin, my dear?"

He stopped, blinking. He was being acknowledged by someone? No, surely this was a party trick played by some drunken sorcerer. All the same, he turned around, amazed, and found Queen Franziska walking toward him. She smiled and he relaxed, bowing as she approached.

"Young man, I'm so pleased to see you again," she said, taking both his hands and giving him a kiss on each cheek. "Look at you! You've grown some since I last saw you!" She laughed and adjusted his cap on his head. "There. Now you look every bit the dashing young bachelor that you are."

Hamlin, abashed, engaged her in light conversation, taking advantage of the moment to ask after the queen's family. At length, he learned that the weight of that old witch's curse had become worse with time.

"One can't be too careful, you know," Queen Franziska said, linking her arm with Hamlin's.

Very unqueenly, to be sure. And, considering his situation as the son of a very unpopular queen, the show of friendliness was also scandalous, to say the least. For his part, Hamlin couldn't help but look left and right and see if anyone had noticed anything and, sure enough, quite a few raised brows met his gaze.

"Poor Roderika's thirteen now, with only two years left before—well, you know."

She paused and sighed. "All we can do is to ensure that she goes nowhere near sharp objects, though she's still predisposed to finding the oddest needle-pointed things in the most unexpected places. It's almost as though no matter where she looks, she's reminded of her destiny. We used to panic and order all those things confiscated as soon as she saw them, but it's pointless, really. We realized—silly us!—that no matter what happened, her curse would come true on her fifteenth birthday, when she pricks her finger on a spindle. All those strange artifacts she sees won't bring her day of reckoning any closer. She'll prick her finger on a spear or a needle, to be sure, but nothing will come of it because it's not the appointed day, hour, and method. Still, we try to get those things away from her if only to keep her from cutting herself up horribly."

"And you still can't have the curse reversed?"

"Curses don't work that way, my dear. This witch has been particularly stubborn and truculent, and I suspect that pride's her biggest sin. I mean, think about it. If she capitulated, it means admitting defeat."

That didn't make much sense. Hamlin frowned at his feet as he walked an idle pace with Queen Franziska. It sounded too easy and too simple an excuse for not insisting a reversal. Surely, being monarchs, she and her husband could spare a chest of gold coins as a way of bargaining with the slighted old witch. Who could say no to gold?

"Begging your pardon, but don't you think compensating her with gold would help?" he asked, hoping he wasn't being rude.

"We've thought about that, yes, but we decided against it in the end."

"How come?"

Queen Franziska was silent for a moment, concentration showing on her face as she considered her response. Hamlin didn't push, though, and he simply allowed himself to lead and be led till they neared his parents' private courtyard.

"We decided that—this curse was meant to be," she finally said. "That it's not only Roderika's fate but also ours. There's something odd about the way the witch spelled out her curse, with all those things about pricking a finger at sundown on her fifteenth birthday, falling asleep for a hundred years, and the curse lifting after the final minutes of the century go silent."

She turned to smile at Hamlin, who blinked, still confused.

"We believe in destiny, you see. In the beginning, when the curse was placed on our daughter, we fought against it, tried everything in our power to prevent it from happening. But as time wore on and Roderika grew older, we started to realize that, by some heavenly decree, we were meant to endure this curse and—have our story turned into legend for the good of future generations, I suppose. A cautionary tale, maybe?"

That still didn't make any sense, but Hamlin felt the resignation in the queen's voice and the desperate hope edging her words. He suspected that none of them wished for this but, as with other unhappy accidents of Fortune, there was no sense in fighting something that couldn't be changed. But free will and autonomy—whatever happened to those?

"And how's Roderika?" he asked, shaking off dour thoughts.

"She's growing up to be a very popular young lady, all things considered. Then again, one can argue that she's popular because of the curse. Mind you, she doesn't seem to care. She's lively, chatty, and loves to sing and dance, though she's never had formal instruction in either."

Hamlin nodded. More effects of that blasted day involving those wise women, he thought. Having seen Roderika a couple of times since her presentation, he was convinced that most of her actions were was nothing more than compulsion, no thanks to those "gifts" bestowed on her.

Unless time was kind to the princess, he expected Roderika's singing and dancing to be quite dreadful at best, despite her overriding need to exhibit herself in such a way. Had she grown up to be a great beauty as well? It was one of the gifts the wise women had given her: unsurpassed beauty. Truth be told, she'd been a pretty little girl, but unexpected things tended to happen to one's body beyond ten years of age, and he knew he was bound to see her for himself soon enough.

"You'll find out how far she's gone, my dear. I was on my way to her when I saw you in the crowd." Queen Franziska gave Hamlin's arm a friendly squeeze, and she smiled at him again, making him feel terrible for thinking so uncharitably about Roderika.

They passed through the little gate that opened into a smaller courtyard, which echoed Queen Franziska's own garden, though this retreat was mostly stone and potted flowering trees.

There was a little alcove, which used to be his favorite hideaway from his nurse as a child, and it was a tiny haven of lush grass, flowers, and shrubbery, all sequestered from the rest of the private courtyard. That spot remained strictly off-limits to visitors even today, and Queen Elfriede had taken care to have some potted plants moved to block the garden's opening for that day. Hamlin adored the courtyard, and he'd spent countless idle hours reading or playing there when he was younger.

Now it was a hive of activity, though not as much as the rest of the castle. Only a few guests seemed to have discovered it.

They walked past benches on which couples sat, lost to the world but alive to each other. More lovestruck pairs strolled, their gazes locked, their voices hushed. Hamlin tried to ignore both them and the slight discomfort that had begun in his chest, forcing his attention back to his companion. The feeling of being alone came back, and this time, it stung.

Eventually they stopped, and Hamlin recognized the farthest corner of the private courtyard—the corner with the old stone fountain where the endlessly gushing water seemed to sparkle with fairy magic in the sunlight, though Audwin had always mocked it, calling it "an invisible giant's perpetual pissing."

There, before the fountain, stood Roderika, commanding an audience, so to speak, with her performance. Dressed in a gorgeous gown, her hair gathered under an elaborate headpiece, she sang and danced in very much the same way Hamlin had seen her sing and dance when she was years younger. The only difference was that her voice was lower, and her steps were more elaborate. Hamlin fought back the urge to grimace.

Roderika was out of tune, and she had absolutely no rhythm and no grace. She also had grown up to be a pleasant-looking young lady, though still nowhere near a great beauty. If Hamlin were to be brutally honest, he'd say that Roderika was agreeably plain.

Yet the princess was compelled to do exactly what those wise women "told" her to do through their gifts. She danced, she sang, she dressed splendidly—and yet she had nothing to show for it, having been born with very average abilities at best. Simply put, she couldn't help herself, and she didn't know any better.

"Poor Roderika." Hamlin sighed. "It looks like this is a far worse curse than a hundred years' sleep." He hoped that Queen Franziska, who stood beside him with an indulgent and proud smile, didn't hear him.

Sighing again, Hamlin let his gaze sweep the area, past the dozen young noblemen and women who'd gathered to watch and listen. Perhaps they, too, were merely staring in morbid fascination. He froze when he spotted a familiar figure standing away from the group, watching the proceedings from the safety of a potted rose tree.

Edouard had turned his attention to Hamlin at that same moment, and their gazes met. They both stared at each other in surprise, then embarrassment. Hamlin would have liked to have looked longer, but Edouard's unwavering stare flustered him, and he was the first to blink. Mortified, he turned his attention back to Roderika, who was now busy thanking the lifeless, scattered applause following her performance.

"I shall now sing a nocturne," she said, grinning, unaware of the few people who were tiptoeing away and the looks of horror on the faces of those who were too polite to flee.

Chapter 24

Was that Hamlin? It took some time for Edouard to get over his surprise—no, amazement. What on earth did that English school do to him? Or was it the monastery? He didn't even know where to start, and it was all he could do to pick up his scattered thoughts.

The last time he'd clapped eyes on Hamlin, three years ago, the other prince had been a skinny, gangly, and terribly awkward fourteen-year-old. All thin limbs, blond hair, and blue eyes, with a personality that curdled milk.

The Hamlin of the present was still thin (perhaps the monastery had been a bit too austere), but the childish awkwardness was nowhere to be seen. The younger prince moved with visible grace and even a hint of confidence, though Edouard could still see a bit of shy self-consciousness in the way Hamlin carried himself.

Hamlin's face had lost its childish softness, and had developed subtle angles that made him beautiful. No, handsome. All right, "beautifully handsome" would probably be a more accurate way of describing him, and Edouard continued to stare at the other prince in spiraling amazement even as Hamlin, mortified, turned away.

What on earth was the shade of Hamlin's hair again? He couldn't remember, but it didn't matter anymore. What stroke of Fortune was this? Edouard had been forced to chaperone Roderika, and he'd been so bored that he'd found himself agreeing to it. Not once had he expected to cross paths with Hamlin and, to his embarrassment, he hadn't expected it to happen while he was monitoring his cousin, who seemed to be bent on winning admirers with her misplaced gifts.

"Besotted, aren't you?"

Edouard nearly wet himself and bit off his tongue as he jumped, but it took him all of two seconds to gather his wits for a passionate retort.

"Don't you ever sneak up on me again!" he hissed, turning his head to scowl at Aloysia. She'd appeared behind him and was now observing the proceedings on tiptoe, as she struggled to peer over her brother's shoulder for a good view.

"Sorry." Aloysia's tone didn't convince Edouard of her earnestness. She craned her neck, her eyes wide and twinkling with mischief, as she stared at Hamlin, who continued to ignore them as he watched Roderika entertain her shrinking audience. "Well, I must say that your Hamlin's coming along very well, don't you agree?"

"I don't know what you're talking about."

"You don't know what I'm talking about? Oh, I'm going to enjoy making your life a daily misery, brother."

"You already do."

Aloysia merely laughed, obnoxious little snorting sounds coming out of her as she fought hard to stifle her amusement, while peering over Edouard's shoulder.

Edouard sighed and glanced back at her again. "You know, there's plenty of space in front of me. I'd prefer it if you'd attempt two or three measly steps to get there."

"I'm comfortable here, thank you. Oh—did you see that? Did you?"

Edouard turned to look around him, utterly baffled. "What? No. What on earth are you talking about?"

"Your Hamlin! He looked at you again! What a darling he is! Look, he's doing it again! Wave, Edouard!" Aloysia hissed. Edouard could feel her nose pressing against his shoulder. To his horror, she actually reached an arm around his shoulder and waved at Hamlin.

"Oh, for..."

Horrified beyond words, Edouard kept his eyes glued on Roderika, who was now serenading the fountain. She'd momentarily turned her back to her audience, and half of those who remained took advantage of the situation and scampered away. At this point only seven people were left. Edouard wasn't even registering her singing, which he was sure was utterly horrendous. He was too embarrassed and self-conscious now that Aloysia had made a mess of things, drawing Hamlin's attention to them.

"He's coming our way, Edouard! I think he is! Aunt Franziska's letting him go!"

Their aunt was definitely letting Hamlin go. She'd abandoned him in order to march up to Roderika and put an end to the princess's performances. Apparently even the girl's doting mother had her limits. Or maybe it was pride. Or pity for the remaining young people, who were probably too polite to run away. Whatever the reason, it was mercy on the queen's part.

"Make yourself look presentable. Straighten your back. Stop slouching like you're dying to shrink into yourself and vanish from the world. Chin up. I don't think Hamlin's going to appreciate a lazy-looking beau."

What the—*beau?*

Edouard sighed and turned to stare at the sky, wondering what he'd done that earned him both a meddling mother and an equally meddling sister. Maybe it was something in the female brain that made them do unspeakable things to unlucky male members of their families.

Hamlin was still a bit of a distance from them when Aloysia peeled herself off Edouard's back and sailed off to meet the other prince. She'd never been one for patience.

"Hamlin! It's a pleasure to see you again! How are you?" she cried, laughing, and reaching out to take hold of Hamlin's hands.

Hamlin looked suitably startled by the energetic—aggressive, he thought—welcome, and Edouard couldn't help but allow himself the luxury of watching Hamlin's eyes, which he now thought were as remarkable a shade as Hamlin's hair. He'd have to consult his books later to find an appropriate description for them.

"I'm well, thank you," Hamlin replied, coloring when Aloysia had the audacity to kiss him on both cheeks as though they'd been good friends since the dawn of time. "And you?"

"Oh, I'm fine, but you don't need to know that, I'm sure," Aloysia said, waving his question away with an impatient flick of a wrist. "Come along, come along, I know that you're simply dying to talk to my brother again despite your quarrels, which are legendary, by the way. I think Mama took care to log every moment in the family archives for posterity's sake. I daresay she's thinking of having her writing illuminated."

Edouard realized all of a sudden how nervous he was, and he squirmed uncomfortably, angry at himself for losing control of the situation. He'd have been very content simply watching Hamlin from afar and perhaps spending time afterwards pondering things—beyond Hamlin's hair and eye colors, that is.

Never had he expected to be thrust into a situation that not only befuddled him, but also terrified him. By all the demons below, he didn't even know what this uncertainty was about. But it was uncertainty piled atop uncertainty till Edouard couldn't tell up from down or why on earth his eyes kept locking onto Hamlin's mouth.

"Are you all right?"

Edouard blinked. Had he pissed himself yet? He tried to move his legs and felt no dampness between them. Yes, he was safe. "What?"

"You look a bit ill," Hamlin said, frowning a little and sounding tentative. "Should I call for a healer? Papa has a very good one in his employ, though he's a bit gruff and not very sympathetic." He paused, thinking. "Come to think of it, I think he's just as pleased to watch you waste away and die as he is in curing you with every stinky herb he has at his disposal."

"Oh, I'm sure that whatever ails my brother can't be cured by ordinary medicine. Don't you agree, Edouard?"

He stared at his sister. "The cure for what ails me, sister, lies in your marriage to Clovis, which you've been putting off year after year."

Aloysia sniggered, even wrinkling her nose at him, getting Edouard's dander up. Again. "You'll have to excuse my brother, Hamlin. He's just spent the last two years in a finishing school of sorts after Mama and Papa decided that he was a bit too surly and withdrawn where the ladies are concerned." Then she added in a whisper that Edouard just knew the rest of the world could hear, "If they only knew why."

Hamlin looked at Aloysia, stunned, before turning his attention back to Edouard, eyes wide. "So it's true then!" he cried, grinning. "What on earth could you learn from a finishing school 'of sorts'? I've never heard of any man being tossed into one. Was it terrible? Were your tutors tyrants when it came to your posture and table manners? Did they teach you how to stab your enemy in a way that's proper and genteel?"

Edouard's brows furrowed as he listened. He could feel his cheeks burn more fiercely with every ridiculous question coming out of Hamlin's mouth. Embarrassment gave way to shock, which gave way to seething anger. He fought against the urge to snap back, but his ability to keep himself in check proved to be a great deal weaker than he'd first expected.

Of course, it didn't help that Hamlin seemed to be amused with Edouard's ordeal. He wouldn't even stop his stupid chattering, for heaven's sake.

"So what made your parents decide to send you to one? Girls? I thought that you were one of the most accomplished princes from my generation. Your Mama kept telling everyone that, anyway. Did you spill drink on a princess's gown? Did you trip her by accident? Run away from her? Talk to her in a most unprincely way?"

Aloysia, confound her, just stood beside Hamlin, grinning broadly, her eyes darting back and forth between them like the insufferable enabler that she was. Luckily, Roderika, who was now being whisked away by her mother, called out to Aloysia and begged her cousin to go with them.

"I'll leave you both to it, then," she said, releasing Hamlin's arm. "Have a wonderful reunion, you two." She left them, humming to herself, and joined her cousin and aunt, and the three walked away, lost in cheerful girlish chatter. Edouard waited till he and Hamlin were finally alone.

"Let's just say that I benefited more from my education than you did from yours," he replied in a calm, icy voice. "If I were your parents, I'd demand my payment back, considering how you came ended worse off than you began. I also heard that you spent time in a monastery."

Hamlin's smile faded as he listened. "Mama decided that it was best for me to stay there and not travel."

"Oh, did she? A prudent move, then, though it isn't enough, judging from what I see. If you were my spawn, I'd forego school and just have you cloistered and your crudeness beaten out of you, which I understand is typical in a monastic environment. Apparently a short time spent in isolation and prayer did little to improve your manners. Then again, I suppose I should content myself with the obvious fact that you're not one to improve in time."

Edouard barely took note of the way Hamlin's face paled as he listened, and while he braced himself for a physical altercation, he was relieved when Hamlin didn't respond with a fist.

The younger prince just looked at him, shocked and bewildered at first, before reddening and stepping away. His eyes now fixed on the ground, Hamlin turned and walked off. Edouard's initial bitter exhilaration was intense but short-lived. He crowed silently as he watched Hamlin slink away, chastised, but once Hamlin had disappeared from view, Edouard's triumph immediately dwindled to a nagging, twisting ache in his gut. Taking a deep, shaky breath, he rubbed his face with both hands and cursed softly.

"I need a drink," he muttered, shaking his head at himself.

Just as he turned to leave the private courtyard, he heard a wet splat near his right ear. Glancing at his shoulder, he saw fresh, massive bird droppings on his best suit. He looked up and saw a raven flapping its wings wildly above him, and when they locked gazes, it squawked. Or more like screeched in his face over and over again, like a foul-mouthed, black-feathered harridan. Edouard scowled at it.

"Oh, bugger off," he retorted and walked away, leaving the ridiculous creature still flapping about and screeching obscenities at him in bird-talk.

Chapter 25

"**Y**ou didn't!"

"Yes, I did, and he damned well deserved it, too."

"What—how?"

Audwin snorted as he tried to groom himself while perched on Hamlin's shoulder, his body rocking forward and backward. He tried to raise a wing and peck away underneath, but keeping his balance proved to be a touch challenging when one was clinging to the shoulder of a boy who was pacing in an agitated circle.

"Your Highness, would you be so kind as to slow down or moderate your pace a little more?" Audwin retorted after a few irritable sighs.

Hamlin did, though slowing his pace into an easier rhythm did nothing to quell his anxiety and crushing guilt, which had twisted his gut into a painful, tight mass. He hugged himself, but it did nothing to soften his agitation.

"You didn't have to do that, you know," he said after another moment. "He'll hate me all the more."

"He already hates you. And you, apparently, hate him. So why fret over well-aimed shit?"

Hamlin untangled his arms from his waist and started wringing his hands. It was finally evening, and he'd just finished nibbling away at his meal and fled the banquet hall to barricade himself in his private tower room. He'd been spending the past several minutes agonizing over what had transpired earlier, and if it weren't for Audwin's appearance, he'd have knocked himself unconscious by banging his head against the stone walls.

Outside, the festivities continued, and the heavens only knew where Edouard was at that moment. Hamlin wouldn't be surprised if the prince had already gone home, considering his shabby treatment.

"I don't want you to protect me or play the knight and be chivalrous. It was my fault entirely that he snapped back at me."

"Oh, by the demons, here we go again with the vagaries of human nature." Audwin flew off Hamlin's shoulder and settled himself on the table. "What on earth are you talking about now, Your Highness? You and that young man have been at each others' throats since the first moment you crossed paths. I saw you taunt him, and he mocked you in turn. Isn't that how things go when humans detest each other? My shitting on him was meant to be your final word since he was in your territory, after all, and you weren't able to have it yourself as the son of his host."

Hamlin wanted to chew a hole through his cheek, and he found that he couldn't look Audwin in the eye as he continued to pace and agonize. "I didn't mean to taunt him," he stammered, his face burning. "It just came out. I mean, I didn't know what else to do to pretend that I—"

"Lord, don't go there!"

Hamlin stopped and glanced up, still gnawing at his cheek. "What?"

Audwin was silent for a few seconds and then finally sighed, his body sagging. "What am I doing?" he muttered loudly enough for Hamlin to catch his words. "It's inevitable."

"What's inevitable?"

"Oh, don't play innocent with me, young man. You know very well what I'm talking about. You were about to say it and make it official and drive me to drink or to peck away at another carcass."

If Hamlin's face wasn't red then, it was now. His whole body felt like it was on fire, and it was dreadful. He gulped some air and commenced pacing again.

"He looks very fine, don't you think?" he asked, his voice shrinking into a meek little bleat. "I didn't expect him to turn out that way. I thought that in the intervening three years that he'd mature into a thin, sallow, ill-tempered, corpse-like bore, and I admit that I was shocked when I saw him today. I suppose I panicked when I realized that I needed to be the gracious host and welcome Aloysia and Edouard, and—um—I resorted to defensive measures instead." He paused and took another breath. "I thought it was easier for me to mock him than to show—I don't know—appreciation. He's—he's quite beautiful."

Audwin sighed after each sentence, but he was generous enough to remain silent and allow Hamlin to unburden himself in an awkward stream of words that seemed to grow more and more muddled.

"I should apologize. I really should. I just don't know how to do it without making a bigger mess of things."

"I can always shit on you, and you can show him that you're even."

"You're no help."

"Well, I'm sorry, Your Highness, but matters of the heart aren't my strengths. You should know that by now. Making scathing and sarcastic remarks about humanity, however…"

Hamlin finally stopped before his table and gazed down sadly at Audwin. "You're kind enough to listen to me," he said as he lightly stroked the bird's head. "It matters much more than you think, even if you're judging me right now."

Audwin's feathers immediately plumped. "What, judging you? What makes you think I'm judging you? All I'm doing is considering your behavior and, seeing that I'm a bird and you're not, it's not my place to pass judgment. No, I'm just trying to understand the way things are turning out because, as you know, that's the first step toward acceptance." He paused, shaking himself back to his normal size. "Though I must admit I question your tastes in beaux."

"You're biased against him."

"Considering your histories, you shouldn't really blame me. If anything, I should blame you for turning this into a brain-curdling melodrama, Your Highness," Audwin spluttered, shaking his head and plumping his feathers again. "I swear, there's absolutely no consistency in human behavior. It's no small wonder your philosophers never find the answers they need and turn to poison or the dagger for relief."

Hamlin stared at him, mystified. "You don't understand, and yet you say things are inevitable between me and Edouard."

"Well, it's that ridiculous red string thing that binds you together. I say it's nonsense, but apparently it's true."

Hamlin frowned now and walked to the window to peer out, his thoughts meandering. "Aloysia said that before," he said after a moment. "Apparently she sees it, but no one else does. I guess it's because she practices magic and all that, and she did say that she's been studying eastern lore. But what about you?" He looked back at Audwin. "How did you know about it?"

"Gossip, of course. The wind isn't known for her discretion. Besides, from what I know, it's quite common. I mean, you and Edouard aren't the only ones linked by that mystical red string. I daresay your mother and father are practically lashed together by theirs." Audwin shrugged. "It's always been part of legend in the East, but it isn't something we know much about in this part of the world."

"The wind told you that?"

"That and an infinity of other things, Your Highness, which I don't care to recall at the moment."

Hamlin pondered again. "Can you see it, Audwin?" he asked at length, his voice quiet and uncertain. "The thread, or string, I mean."

The raven shook his head. "I'm afraid not. I only know about it because I was told in the strictest of confidence by a gossiping force of Nature, so I assume that only those who practice magic are able to see it if what you said about the princess is anything to go by."

Hamlin sighed as he walked over to the cot. He sat down and stared at the floor. "If Edouard and I are destined for each other, it's got nothing to do with love, does it? I mean, how does free will figure into it? I don't particularly care for a bond that's nothing more than what Fortune decided in advance, and the people involved are no better than puppets with no say in the matter."

One idea melted into another, and confusion started to swell in Hamlin's mind. Frowning more deeply, he pulled off his shoes and stretched himself on the cot, staring at the ceiling. Outside the tower room the sounds of the festivities continued, providing him with something akin to background "music" as he turned things over in his head.

"If I find myself attracted to him, does that have anything to do with free will at all, or is it nothing more than additional manipulation from Fortune?" he asked. "Then what kind of a bond is this going to be when neither of us is in it of our own choosing? Would we turn out like Roderika, who's burdened by so-called gifts that are dreadfully incongruent with reality, and who's growing up being tugged around by invisible puppet strings? Ugh. What a horrible existence it is, poor girl. And I'm sure it'll be doubly worse for her husband, whoever that might be, and no one hereabouts will find out till after a hundred years have gone by. If that's how it is with me and Edouard, what a miserable pair we'd make. Imagine being forced to be with someone only because Fate decided that so-and-so should be your partner, no matter what."

What about their quarrels? Were they also predestined? Or did they quarrel as a means of exercising their will against a force that they'd no control over? Was it the only way for them to remain autonomous creatures?

Hamlin's brain hurt just sorting through these questions. The possibilities seemed awful, and he couldn't think of any way that he could sidestep his destiny.

"Oh, Lord, that's another consideration, Audwin," he stammered, feeling the blood drain away from him as he continued to stare at the ceiling. "If I were to fight Fate, what would happen? I've heard of some pretty dreadful things happening to those who try to outsmart their destiny, and they end up worse off than if they'd gone along with it. I mean, most of them, anyway, end up dead rather than living out an existence that they've no choice in. Then again, which is the lesser evil? Would I rather be dead, or alive but forced to follow a predetermined path? What a choice—death or prison?"

That was a hard question, and Hamlin didn't care for the alternatives. He sighed again. Why on earth did this sort of thing happen, anyway? Which god or immortal being or spiritual force decided to play destiny with his life—or anyone else's, for that matter?

"Audwin? What do you think?"

When his friend didn't respond, Hamlin turned to find Audwin fast asleep on his desk, his beak tucked under his wing, his body swaying a little with his gentle breathing. Hamlin rolled his eyes.

"You're no help," he grumbled, turning to scowl at the ceiling again. "And my blasted head hurts."

He'd have to read more about this strange legend. Surely this was nothing more than that, yes, a legend from eastern countries. Just as the west had its own myths that everyone knew weren't true, this silly red string of destiny thing shouldn't be any different. If Aloysia saw it, it perhaps meant that she was hallucinating as one of an unfortunate effect of practicing magic.

A tiny, insistent voice in the back of Hamlin's head accused him of overthinking things, but Hamlin ignored its nagging and turned his attention back to his intended apology. His guilt was painful, and he simply needed to do it and hope for the best.

Chapter 26

Edouard never thought that he'd take to chaperone duty very well, but then again, he simply felt that he'd no other choice. It was either be at his mother's beck and call—both of which had grown progressively more insistent, no thanks to his utter disinterest in every young lady who'd been thrown his way—or be absent for indefinite lengths of time in order to keep a close eye on a cursed princess. Though at first Queen Clarimond chafed at the thought that her youngest son appeared to be avoiding his duties (she wasn't wrong there, to be sure), she also felt a good deal of pride in the fact that Edouard's chaperoning of Roderika was essential, given the rapidly approaching day of reckoning.

"I suppose I shouldn't begrudge you your new responsibility, Edouard," she'd said, trapping her son's face between her hands and squashing it as a means of expressing maternal approval—that being a recent innovation. "Poor Roderika's time's running out, and your sacrificing your personal obligations for her sake is a very noble thing. Then again, I don't expect anything less from my wonderful boy."

Edouard could only nod—or attempt to nod, anyway, since his cheeks, nose, and mouth were all pressed into one puffy mass. By the heavens, his mother's hold was painful, and his eyes watered from the pressure.

"You're such a handsome bundle of chivalry. I daresay no one else in this world can outdo you in looks and virtue, and Roderika's a very, very lucky young lady to have you for a cousin. I'm more than happy to wait to see you married, Edouard. Take care of Roderika first, and when the time for her to fulfill her destiny comes around, we'll pick up where we left off with your marriage plans, all right?" She actually spared him a hint of a smile. Very unqueenly of her to do so, but at the moment, that was the least of Edouard's worries. "In the meantime, I'll improve on our matrimonial arsenal."

He nodded again, feeling a tear trickle down his left cheek. With a smirk, Queen Clarimond tugged Edouard's face closer so she could plant a quick and almost reluctant kiss on his forehead, and then she released him. She'd also begun to weave his new chaperone duty into her ever-lengthening list of eligible-bachelor virtues, convinced that no princess could resist the allure of a husband who was fiercely protective of the young and hopelessly cursed.

· · · ·

IT WOULD TAKE A DAY for the soreness and redness to go away, but after twenty-four hours, Edouard felt his face restored. He did, however, find some measure of relief in his mother's promise to delay any matchmaking efforts.

"Thank you, Roderika," he muttered, his thoughts finding their way back to the present. "I owe you quite a bit."

He was deep in the woods outside Queen Franziska's castle. It was the same woods where he'd spent some time with Hamlin three years ago, though their brief moment together had been strained and awkward.

Today, though, found him trailing his cousin, who was skipping down a path, singing passionately and dancing randomly along the way. She'd decided to spend the morning communing with Nature, which meant regaling all woodland creatures with her voice.

Unhappily for her, none of the squirrels, deer, birds, butterflies, or other animals seemed to be interested in what she had to offer, and she was forced to chase after them in order to subject them to her singing. Perhaps she'd expected her voice to lure them all out of their hiding-places, enthralled and mesmerized, and they'd follow her wherever she went like mindless, furry slaves.

After he watched the sixth doe stiffen and then turn tail and run at Roderika's approach, Edouard pursed his lips and rubbed the back of his neck.

"Uh—cousin, perhaps you shouldn't come too close to the animals," he said during a pause in the princess's singing. "They're not used to having people singing to them the way you are." He tried to be honest without being offensive, and it proved to be quite a feat.

Roderika just sighed and frowned at him. "Nonsense! They're all running away because my voice is too loud. I'll have to adjust my volume a bit and sing to them as though they're my babies, see? I know they'll appreciate it more."

"I sincerely doubt if volume's the issue here," Edouard muttered, but he didn't keep Roderika from experimenting with volume or even rhythm. Then again, he didn't have a clue as to what kind of music she was singing since she was not only off-key all the time, but also making up words along the way. He continued to follow her, keeping a respectful distance from the girl. Eventually boredom overcame him, and he thought of Hamlin yet again.

He barely took note of Roderika as she scrambled up an old oak, still singing, because a pair of birds fluttered up and tried to avoid her by perching on one of the branches. The princess seemed to be undaunted by their attempted escape and was now bent on coming after them. Not once did her chase interrupt her bizarre song.

Edouard, in the meantime, waited below, wondering what Hamlin was doing. It had been a couple of months now since he'd received a letter of apology from the other prince, and he'd responded with a dry and distant acceptance. His tone had been cool, an attempt at hiding behind his pride, and he'd regretted it once the letter was dispatched.

Hamlin never wrote back, and though Edouard was disappointed, he also felt a great deal of relief. The sooner their last meeting was put behind him, the better, after all, but he still found himself sulking over the way things got so ugly so quickly.

The birds, realizing their danger, had flown to a higher branch, and Roderika contented herself with sitting down on the lowest one and serenading them for the next few minutes. Seconds into her song, the birds broke out in a frenzy of wild chirping as though screaming at her to stop.

"We're incompatible, and that's that," Edouard noted, glancing down at a pebble near his right foot, which he idly kicked. "It doesn't matter what we do. We're just meant to snap at each other whenever we cross paths." He paused at the sudden recollection of a conversation he'd had with Hamlin and Aloysia a few years ago. It had something to do with a red thread or string that his sister claimed linked him to Hamlin.

Startled, Edouard blinked away the gloom as his mind caught hold of that brief scene and replayed it. At length, his shoulders sagged, and he shook his head again. "What a stupid idea. Obviously nothing more than superstitious nonsense that Aloysia actually believes in—unless she's making it all up." He certainly wouldn't put it past his sister. She took too much delight in provoking him, and unfortunately Hamlin provided her with ample ammunition.

Roderika eventually ended her singing—or at least that particular song—and climbed down the tree. She leapt to the ground, her dress now soiled and sporting some tears along with bits of leaves, twigs, and even cobwebs. Her headdress remained surprisingly intact, keeping her hair under control, but it had somehow captured an unsuspecting spider that was not only large, but also busy spinning itself a web on its new home.

"Come, Edouard, let's go that way," the princess said breathlessly as she pointed down one path that would take them deeper into the woods. "I thought I saw a family of deer playing. I'd like to join them."

"You know very well they'll only run."

"No, they won't. I just need to sing and dance for them."

Edouard pitied the poor animals, but it wasn't his place to complain or contradict his cousin. Roderika had been given a lot of freedom and was quite spoiled because of it, but he knew that it was likely a way for his aunt and uncle to compensate for the fact that the girl was under a curse.

He once again thought about that silly superstition regarding the red string. It was no different from Roderika's situation, he realized, because it had everything to do with destiny and nothing about free will. As a scholar, he bristled at the idea of not having much control over the course his life would take, let alone his relationships with others. Was he meant to be partnered with Hamlin in a romantic sense, or was he fated to be forever at odds with the younger prince?

"No matter how I look at this red string thing, I always come to the same conclusion, and that's fate." He sighed, scratching his head as he trailed behind Roderika. "Like my cousin, whose life's course isn't of her own choosing."

Which also affected the world around her because of the glaring incongruence between her compulsions and her true nature (and lack of talent). Edouard winced.

He couldn't help but—for the millionth time since he realized it—lay the blame squarely at his aunt and uncle's feet. Their pride and, obviously, ambition, had led them to turn to those wise women for their only child's gifts. What difference would it have made, he wondered, if they'd let things be and allowed Roderika to grow up as she was meant to without the interference of magic-wielders? No doubt his young cousin would've turned out to be a smart and sensible princess who'd know how to work within her abilities as well as strive for greater goals.

"Oh, Edouard, look what I found!"

He paused as Roderika bent down to pick something up. She turned, grinning at him, and showed him a dried up branch, which was curiously shaped like a crooked spear.

"Isn't it pretty? I so love how it tapers to a sharp point at this end!" Roderika said, indicating the spear-like tip. "It makes me want to touch it!"

Edouard sighed and raised a hand. "Give it to me, cousin," he said dully. "You know the rules. No pointed objects within fifty feet of you."

"But—"

"Now, please."

Roderika made a face at him and grudgingly walked up to Edouard to surrender the branch. "How can you be so boring?" she asked, scowling.

"Rules are rules, and you know that. If you want to complain, you'll have to go to your parents. I didn't make those rules. I only follow them."

"You always follow rules," Roderika grumbled, turning around and stalking off. "You're never, ever spontaneous and fun. I wish Aloysia were here instead. She'd let me play with it."

True, Aloysia was more likely to encourage the girl to play with sharp objects, but it was nothing more than caprice on her part, being sick and tired of having to follow Roderika around. When the princess's day of destiny came, Edouard wouldn't be surprised if his sister were to throw a wild celebration.

"Your cousin's with Prince Clovis," Edouard replied, but Roderika didn't seem to hear him—or care about what he said. She continued her trek deeper into the woods, distracting herself with more made-up songs and off-key singing, sometimes breaking out in spontaneous and rhythm-deficient dancing. The deer family never materialized; then again, they were sure to have heard her coming a mile away.

Edouard fell silent as he mulled over his cousin's sulky retort. Yes, he played by the rules. He was ruled by rules, in fact, and he'd never once sought to challenge them. So why on earth was he so glum about destiny and the loss of control over the course of one's life? His playing by the rules wasn't imposed on him. He'd willingly taken that route as a child, and now he'd become trapped in a life of rigid control. Edouard grimaced. So much for the value of willpower over fate, although...

He caught himself in time. "There's safety in rules, anyway," he murmured, and he believed it.

Chapter 27

"Welcome home, Your Highness."

Hamlin opened his eyes and smiled as Audwin swooped down to settle himself on the grass. It was a beautiful day, all sunshine, fresh air, and soothing breezes, and Hamlin had been spending the time since his arrival lying on the soft grass, his eyes closed and his mind drifting from one pleasant thought to the next. He'd been glad to come back here, to his favorite hideaway as a child, and he still remembered the day after he and his mother had returned from Roderika's presentation, with Hamlin smarting from his first fight with Edouard.

"Thank you, Audwin" he said. "What's the gossip hereabouts now? It's been a year since you last filled me in."

"Oh, this and that and those," Audwin replied, shrugging. "Nothing much has changed besides your next half-brother being betrothed."

It was now Baldrick's turn to be sacrificed at the marriage altar, and while the actual festivities were still a long way off, Hamlin's heart sank at the thought. Since Otto's wedding, Hamlin's social circle hadn't expanded, and while he didn't care much for its implications at this point, he still dreaded being reminded of his shortcomings when the day arrived. Perhaps he could plan another adventure overseas or elsewhere on the continent. He was, after all, eighteen years old now, and his parents left him alone by and large.

He'd just returned from a year-long tour, this time chaperoned by two young lords who were sons of one of his father's good friends. They'd proven to be a welcome distraction, given their gifts of conversation and wit, but they'd also been just as easily swayed by distractions of the female bent. Hamlin didn't have much choice but to pretend interest in relics and ruins while his companions rutted like overeager stallions, leaving a trail of former virgins in their wake. In the end, Hamlin found his adventure wanting, and he'd returned home both relieved and restless.

"Anything else worth noting while I was away?" he prodded.

"Princess Aloysia continues to drag her feet over her pending marriage, but her poor husband-to-be seems content with her decision. I suppose he's just happy that she'd agreed to marry him. The lad's not much to look at, I heard, but he's got a good heart and a bright future ahead of him. You really can't say the same about most of the younger generation of nobles, with their good looks and breeding."

"You're terrible, Audwin."

"And yet you love me."

Silence fell on the two, with Hamlin turning his attention back to the sky and closing his eyes against the brilliance above. He hesitated, listening to Audwin hop and flutter and do whatever else talking ravens did to pass the time. Hamlin swallowed, forcing himself to hold his tongue as the question clawed its way to the forefront of his mind. He wanted to ask, desperately needed to know the answer, but he fought against it till he felt sweat beading on his forehead.

"Your Highness," Audwin said, sighing, "come out with it, please. You're making me itch in discomfort, waiting."

"I've nothing else to say."

"Again—come out with it, please, before I peck it out of you. I might be old, but my beak's just as sharp as it was in my prime."

Hamlin held his breath in a last, sorry bid at staying silent on the matter but was immediately forced to inhale when his chest started to tighten. "How's Edouard?" he asked in as quiet and humble a voice as he could manage. By the heavens, this was all so awkward.

"Still alive and breathing, and he thanks you for your concern. Now, was that so hard?"

Hamlin rolled his eyes behind his eyelids. "You know very well it was."

"Makes no sense, but I'll take your answer all the same." Audwin followed that with a muttered sting of incomprehensible words, which Hamlin could only guess were obscenities in raven-talk.

"Is he betrothed to someone?"

"No. He's currently spared that, I heard, as he's looking after Roderika. To be sure, I don't know which is worse—a forced marriage or to be chaperone to a cursed princess who—lord, you already know how things fare with her."

"He's not seeing someone, is he?"

"I don't think so. Your Highness, do you have any questions that don't drip with lovestruck sentimentality?"

"No. You'll have to put up with it, you grumpy old bird. Human nature's what it is, and you can't get away from it."

Audwin snorted. "Oh, I can, but I'm bound to you as your protector and advisor and so am obliged to deal with it every hour of my life."

"And yet you love me," Hamlin said, grinning. He always enjoyed tossing Audwin's words back at him.

"Don't be cheeky, Your Highness."

It was one of those strange mysteries of their relationship, and Hamlin had only once questioned why, receiving nothing of any substance in return. Whether or not Audwin knew the reason behind their bond no longer puzzled him, and he'd learned to simply let things go and carry on as always.

There were so many unknown forces at work day after day, after all, and having a talking raven that outlived his species for his only friend was just one of them. He'd heard of fairy godmothers, which made him wonder if Audwin was a variation of them, and it was the closest possible explanation he could come up with. But were ravens, as a species, this hopelessly misanthropic?

"Any more questions about that stiff dandy you fancy?"

"He isn't stiff, and he isn't a dandy. Will you stop provoking me? I wish you'd fall in love with a wild boar and suffer with that the way I do."

"That insult falls far wide of its mark, I'm afraid."

What an insufferable little monster. Hamlin sighed and rolled onto his stomach, resting his chin on his arms as he stared at the grass.

"Your Highness, do fix your gaze on something a bit farther out. You're cross-eyed right now, and it's highly unnerving." Audwin plumped his feathers.

A very insufferable little monster, indeed. "Leave me alone, for heaven's sake. I'm brooding, which, by the way, is quite typical for young men in my situation."

Audwin sighed and hopped around, his feathers still sticking out. "Come along, come along, it's not healthy to keep it all in. I'll stay awake and listen if you need me to despite every pore on my body screaming against it."

"You don't have pores."

"That's neither here nor there, young man. Now out with it. Remember the beak."

Hamlin clucked and narrowed his eyes at his friend but proceeded to talk, anyway. He'd probably have to pull a handful of feathers off Audwin's cranky little body with a violent yank later.

"I went on another tour of the continent to forget about him," he said after a moment's hesitation. He felt his face burn and dared not look at Audwin again. Cross-eyed or not, he dropped his gaze to the rich, lush blades of grass and ignored Audwin's rough throat-clearing. "It didn't work, obviously."

He fell silent and frowned at the grass. Eventually he was forced to concede to the discomfort brought about by being cross-eyed for too long, and he redirected his gaze elsewhere. Nothing but the breeze and the soft rustling of leaves filled the silence for the next moment or so.

"And?"

"And nothing. That's it. It didn't work. It was a bit difficult not thinking about him when my companions kept jumping from one bed to another, and I was left to fend for myself without much success."

"I wouldn't be surprised if your two traveling companions were to come down with the most disgusting venereal diseases within a fortnight."

Hamlin sighed and raised himself onto his elbows, turning to glare at Audwin. "Have you any advice, or should I shove a stick down your throat and roast you on a spit?"

"Tut, tut, tut! Temper, temper, Your Highness. I was simply philosophizing about your traveling companions, and that's all. What I was trying to point out was the fact that you weren't as stupid as the pair of them, and you've got your nature to thank for it."

"I could've jumped into bed with one man after another all the same," Hamlin retorted, offended. He didn't know why he was offended, but he somehow felt that Audwin was being sarcastic about his proclivities.

The raven hopped closer and stuck his face close to Hamlin's, so his beak touched Hamlin's nose.

"But you didn't," he said slowly and with exaggerated emphasis. "That's my point. I don't care if you fancy pox-riddled goats. You were a great deal more prudent when it came to your physical needs."

Hamlin nodded, a bit unnerved by the closeness. He'd never been scolded this way by the bird before, but he supposed there was a first time for everything. Audwin stared deep into his eyes for another few seconds before giving an indignant huff and then hopping away.

"As for my advice," the irritated bird said once he seemed satisfied with their distance, "it's quite simple. Go see him and have a nice, earnest conversation about the two of you. You're eighteen now, Your Highness, which makes Edouard twenty-one. You'll both be aging one more year in a couple of months, five weeks apart from each other, just before Roderika's day of doom. I daresay you've shed all silly childish tendencies by now and don't expect you two to come to blows within ten seconds of opening your mouths."

"And if he doesn't like me the same way?"

"There's this curious little thing called the red string that binds you two together. I doubt if your question's legitimate." Audwin actually sounded smug.

Hamlin shook his head and frowned, tugging idly at the grass. "I still don't like the idea of not having a choice in something like this," he said. "I'm not too fond of destiny."

"That's rather unfortunate because you—and the rest of the world—are mired neck-deep in it, whether you wish it or not."

"I wish I had a choice in this matter."

"Perhaps you already do, and you just can't see it."

"Accident of birth, and that's all."

"Or perhaps it's free will that dictates your destiny, and that red string is nothing more than a glimpse into the future. Which, by the way, is the end result of all the choices you make along the way."

"Bah."

Audwin squawked and flapped his wings. "Your Highness, just go see him and talk if it means settling your doubts or satisfying some perverse need you have that requires you to pine away for him while wondering why you're pining away for him."

Hamlin pushed himself up and sat up straight, grimacing as he massaged his sore arms. "When the moment comes, I'll do it," he said. "This is all so embarrassing, so you'll have to excuse me when I hem and haw and so on. I normally don't talk about my private life to anyone, you know."

"And what a relief it is, pouring your heart out to a confidante, isn't it?"

Hamlin had to agree, and he nodded his head, offering Audwin a sheepish little smile. "Don't call him a stiff dandy again," he said.

"But he is, and you know he is."

"Yes, but you shouldn't call him that!"

"So you agree!"

"I don't care! Just don't call him that!"

Audwin let out an exasperated sigh, shook his feathers again, and flew off to perch himself on a flowering rose tree. "I swear to the heavens, human nature's far worse than twenty plagues put together," he retorted, shaking the branches, showering the grass with red petals.

Chapter 28

The day for Baldrick's wedding finally arrived, and Edouard was dreading it. Once again, he listened to his mother's grumblings about having to set foot in "that wretched commoner's castle—with all due respect to Reinhard, of course."

At least, according to Queen Clarimond, "Reinhard's three *real* sons are a great asset to his kingdom, unlike that surly little pup. Why Reinhard chooses not to toss that brat into a monastery for good escapes me, but perhaps he has plans of sending the boy to the front lines when war breaks out—enemy bait, you see."

Edouard could never agree with his mother's assessment of King Reinhard's older sons, considering his past experiences involving those three bullying brutes. Otto, Baldrick, and Mallory all fancied themselves to be good friends with him—or good friends when in company with him, anyway—but Edouard had managed to keep them at a cold distance, their manners and mental capacity ruining every precious minute of his time. Time, he'd often add, that he could never get back again.

The tedium of another royal wedding was a heavy shadow that hovered above him. With other young noblemen and women coming of age, there'd been a rash of weddings, and that didn't even count Aloysia's pending nuptials with Clovis. His sister had said that she wanted to wed her long-suffering beau a month before Roderika's fifteenth birthday, which was now well-known as "The Day of Reckoning" and was only a mere six months away.

"Give everyone one last celebration before the spell takes over," Aloysia had reasoned, and all had agreed. Queen Clarimond, of course, praised her daughter's decision for its selflessness and out-and-out kindness toward a cursed family.

And once King Friedrich and Queen Franziska's castle succumbed to a hundred years' sleep? Edouard shuddered at the thought that it would be his turn on the block, and he'd have no more excuses. In fact, he wouldn't even have Aloysia available to turn him into a stain or an unidentified household item should the situation turn dire.

He went through his preparations sunk in dark musings, the dread of the upcoming ceremony and celebration adding weight to his thoughts. He wasn't even aware of his servant helping him, nor was he cognizant of being shepherded into a waiting carriage with his sister and Clovis.

Did they have a conversation during that long, jarring ride to King Reinhard's castle? He was sure they did, but his brain appeared to have turned just as glassy as his eyes, and before he realized it, he was walking through a surging, colorful crowd of revelers, his senses filled with laughter, conversation, music, and the smell of good food.

"Will you be looking after Roderika today, too?"

"Huh? Oh." Edouard blinked, and his vision cleared. He turned to Clovis, who regarded him curiously. Was there even a hint of sympathy in his future brother-in-law's eyes? Yes, there it was. "Yes, if my aunt requires it of me."

"She will," Aloysia piped up, her look of sympathy a lot less subtle than Clovis's. "I can always transform you, brother. Just say the word. I promise I won't complain this time."

Edouard smiled, oddly moved by that. "No, don't worry about me. I'll be fine. Enjoy your time together, you two."

Clovis beamed, his freckles lighting up. Even his fiery red hair seemed to burst into brilliance. The boy—no, young man, Edouard hastily corrected himself—had always been extremely eager to earn his approval. Aloysia had said that Clovis looked up to Edouard for reasons unknown (she'd claimed to be utterly mystified, herself) and, for some time, Clovis even shadowed Edouard like an eager pup. Clovis was very lucky, indeed, that both King Rikard and Queen Clarimond approved of the shy prince.

Edouard wondered if they hoped that Clovis's quiet level-headedness and kind-heartedness would help to rein in Aloysia's fierce independence, but it looked clear that the pair respected each other and would allow each other space. That Clovis didn't bat an eyelash at the knowledge that his future bride practiced magic was proof enough of that.

• • • •

THE CEREMONY WAS JUST as tedious as Edouard had expected, but, thankfully, Baldrick wasn't lost to sticky sentimentality the way Otto was, and neither he nor his bride—a right warrior princess, perfectly matching him in size and temperament—was inclined to pepper their vows with one sordid, syrupy declaration of undying love after another. To be sure, all the noblewomen in attendance regarded the affair with some dismay after Otto's wedding.

"Oh, what a shame," some whispered. "Not a very romantic pair at all."

"I hope their bond lasts a long time."

"I daresay it will. She'll tear his head off with her bare hands at the smallest sign of trouble, from the looks of things." All were in agreement there.

Edouard, in the meantime, spotted Hamlin in the crowd, looking just as—*fine*—as he had a year ago. How did Edouard describe him again? Beautifully handsome or something ridiculous and redundant like that? He winced. For a scholar, he certainly didn't have much to show as far as his vocabulary was concerned. Then again, Aloysia would be quick to say, perhaps it was because of a stronger, more subversive force than a mere lapse in one's education.

Edouard didn't care much. He was grateful that Hamlin stood far enough away for him not to notice Edouard's occasional stolen glances, which lingered more and more as the ceremony went on. The prickly issue involving destiny reared its ugly and unwanted head, but strangely enough, Edouard found it much, much easier to push the unwanted thought aside or ignore it than he had before. Then again, whenever he contemplated it in the past, Hamlin was nowhere within sight, so perhaps that was the difference.

Now that he could easily stare without shame and without being caught, he was quite delighted. Relieved, even. He didn't even realize that he was smiling wistfully until a resounding cheer rippled through the attending nobles, signaling the end of the ceremony and the beginning of the day-long festivities.

The massive hall was suddenly swarming with activity as people fought each other to congratulate the happy couple first, and Edouard lost sight of Hamlin. Excusing himself to Aloysia and Clovis, he turned and pushed out of the room, heading for the main courtyard, where the gentry and other wealthy but untitled attendees mingled. Edouard would eat later. In the meantime, he needed fresh air and space. The hall was tightly packed with nobility, and he was shocked that he'd somehow managed to breathe and stay upright all that time.

Feeling himself relax, he idly strolled past groups and pairs, not realizing where he was headed until he saw that he was standing before the same private courtyard where he'd taken Roderika a year ago. He'd yet to be summoned for chaperone duty, and he'd no idea where his cousin was, but it didn't bother him. He wanted to savor the private time and do so at his leisure. Food would have to wait, and he was sure that he wouldn't be missed.

Strolling past the knight who stood guard outside the courtyard entrance, Edouard entered the pretty little sanctuary, relief washing over him when he saw that he was alone, what with guests now scurrying for something to eat. His solitude would disappear in time, but he was determined to revel in it for as long as he could.

For the next several minutes, he admired the potted greenery and the quaint approach to the place. He'd long been used to private gardens and courtyards made into miniaturized and overly romanticized versions of the surrounding countryside, but Queen Elfriede's tastes were quite different. Unique, even. And she loved roses, apparently, for every potted flowering tree or shrub was a variety of that plant in every imaginable color. It meant romance, if Edouard guessed correctly, which, given Queen Elfriede's history, made a great deal of sense.

He stood for a moment, lost in thought, before the fountain where Roderika had entertained a gaggle of reluctant guests last year. When a sudden, shrill squawking and the frantic flapping of wings jarred him back to the present, he looked up to find a raven settling itself on the wall behind the fountain. It eyed him, all avian malice and feathered evil.

"What do you want now?" Edouard demanded, scowling. He even recognized the little bugger. At least this time he wasn't shat on. "I'm just minding my own business."

The bird squawked again, flapping its wings but not flying away.

"You'll have to excuse him. He's a born contrarian, I'm afraid."

Edouard felt the blood drain away from him as he turned, startled, and found Hamlin standing not too far away, regarding him with a mix of doubt and wariness. The younger prince looked like a young deer on the verge of bolting at the first sign of trouble—a familiar look, to be sure, and a notion that struck Edouard hard because it tore at his conscience and forced him to remember his own stupidity the last time the two had spoken face-to-face.

No, he thought, staying put and allowing Hamlin to take one tentative step forward. No, he'd keep his head this time around, behave himself properly, and not give Hamlin any reason to despise him even more.

"It's all right. He surprised me, is all." Edouard paused, waiting, as Hamlin took another cautious step forward.

The other prince looked so tense and nervous, but what truly prickled Edouard's skin was that odd light in Hamlin's eyes. It was nervousness, to be sure, but there was something else there. Hope? Was it hope? Edouard was never a good judge of anything as far as people's emotions were concerned, and it was, he realized now, a shortcoming.

Hamlin took one more step forward, and he started to knot his fingers together, though he didn't seem to be aware of it, and Edouard's discomfort dissolved.

"I apologize if I startled you just now. I saw you leave after the ceremony and decided to follow you—and talk."

Edouard thought that Hamlin was on the verge of retching. "You didn't startle me. That bird did, though." He jabbed a finger in the raven's direction, earning a too-brief smile from Hamlin.

"It's been a year," Hamlin said after a lengthy and awkward pause. "How are you? I hope you're doing well?"

Hope. Yes, there it was again, shining in vivid blue, edged with fear. Edouard nodded, though he didn't know why. His brain seemed to have emptied itself. No thought, no reason, no internal debates about destiny and free will—there was nothing that made up his present reality save the brilliant shade of Hamlin's blue eyes, that he found himself drowning in.

Was he smiling? It felt like it. He definitely was, because Hamlin broke out in a little smile, too, though hope and fear still lit up his eyes. Edouard wanted nothing more than to offer him some reassurance that everything was going to be all right.

It was his turn to take a step forward, which he did, relieved by the fact that they hadn't come to blows. He hoped that their enmity belonged to the distant past. He was still smiling, even as he leaned close to press his mouth against Hamlin's, pulling away for the briefest moment to see if the younger prince would respond with a fist. When no blow came, and Hamlin stared at him in wide-eyed shock, Edouard took that for permission, and he pressed close again, this time moving his mouth to encourage Hamlin to kiss back.

Hamlin did, doubtfully at first, and then with growing confidence, though their kiss was clumsy at best, and Edouard took quiet delight in the belief that both of them had never done this with anyone else before. What they lacked in finesse, he figured, they more than made up in feeling. Yes, he quite liked that reasoning.

For the next few moments, they held each other close, lost to everything else and not caring who'd be stumbling across the scene. When they finally took a breath, they still held each other, with Edouard pressing Hamlin's face against his shoulder—a protective gesture he couldn't help but make as he gently stroked his fingers through Hamlin's soft, short hair. He felt overcome, lost, and quite terrified, and he sought relief in Hamlin's arms. Gathering his thoughts and barely keeping them together, he finally answered.

"I'm doing well, thank you," he murmured against Hamlin's temple. "I am now, anyway."

Chapter 29

Hamlin couldn't breathe, he had the overwhelming urge to throw up, and he wasn't sure, but he might've wet himself. Yes, he was most certainly in love. The fact that he didn't mind being embraced quite tightly by Edouard, his face pressed against the other prince's shoulder, which all but prevented him from breathing—no, he didn't mind at all.

Edouard smelled nice. He also tasted very, very nice. Never had Hamlin even considered just how acrobatic the human tongue could be, but what had just transpired between them provided incontestable proof of that little body part's remarkable abilities.

Hamlin wanted to cry in relief, but he heard Edouard's voice tremble and realized that the young man was perhaps feeling even more vulnerable than he, and he allowed Edouard the freedom to decide when to pull away. It took some time, but Edouard did. He was red-faced and stunned, blinking rapidly as though to dispel tears, and he bent his head to avoid looking at Hamlin for a moment as he gathered himself.

Hamlin waited with utmost patience, glancing past Edouard to look at Audwin, who remained quiet and watched the proceedings without plumping his feathers or showing a hint of displeasure in any way. Bless the little monster, Hamlin thought, braving a little smile. Audwin nodded and waited.

"I'm sorry," Edouard said, straightening up and drawing a sleeve across his face. He looked at Hamlin with a sheepish grin. "I'm rarely overwhelmed like this, and I have a difficult time pulling myself together. Losing control of any situation is—it's frightening." He paused, concern shadowing his features. "I didn't hurt you, did I?"

Hamlin shook his head. "No. If I pushed you in any way—"

"You didn't. I wanted to."

"So did I," Hamlin replied, smiling in relief. "I was actually hoping that you did, too."

Edouard hesitated, mulling over something. "Hamlin, I'm really sorry for behaving the way I did—"

"Which moment? There've been several," Hamlin quipped, suppressing a chuckle. He did feel sorry for Edouard, who seemed to struggle so much in his attempts at opening himself up. But he also needed to lighten things up a bit to ease the other prince's obvious discomfort.

It appeared to work. Edouard laughed quietly, blushing. "All of them, I suppose. I've been—I've been a scurvy prick to you."

Hamlin made a face and dropped his gaze to his shoes as he rubbed the back of his neck. "It went both ways," he said. "And I aimed low when I fought back."

"And he'll say he deserved it, and you'll say you deserved it more, and you'll both dissolve into another argument about who deserves to be hated more until the two of you come to blows again, and the past fifteen or so minutes would've been for nothing," Audwin squawked out in a dry monotone. He plumped his feathers this time.

Edouard blinked and turned around to stare at the bird. "Is that creature ill or something?" he asked, genuinely puzzled.

"He doesn't understand what you're saying, Audwin," Hamlin said just as Audwin opened his beak to heap abuses upon Edouard's head.

"You can talk to him?" Edouard blinked, his jaw practically hanging open.

"I can, yes. That's Master Audwin, who's been my guardian and best friend—only friend, really."

Edouard glanced back at Audwin who stared at him, his little eyes narrowing as though in warning. "He shat on me once. The last time I was here, in fact."

Hamlin grimaced. "I know. You'll have to forgive him. He's very protective of me and didn't like what he saw that day—our last quarrel, I mean."

"I still think he's a stiff dandy," Audwin grumbled as he continued to eye Edouard as though preparing to assault him for no other reason than the fact that he existed.

Hamlin quickly rested a hand on Edouard's arm. "Can we walk somewhere?" he stammered. "I just want to enjoy a bit of quiet time with you—unless you're expected to attend to Roderika soon."

"Well, that's my duty for the time being, but as I haven't seen my cousin since I arrived, I assume she's being kept busy by her friends somewhere." Edouard looked a great deal more relaxed by now, and he moved Hamlin's hand down his arm to hold it in his. "I'm not familiar with your father's castle, so you'll have to take the lead."

Hamlin grinned and steered him away from the fountain, throwing one final look of warning behind him, which Audwin understood well enough, and with a long, drawn-out sigh, the raven flapped his wings and flew off, squawking.

"Don't let passion go to your head!" Audwin called out.

How silly was that? Hamlin rolled his eyes. What a fine suggestion that was, coming from a creature that had never known love before.

• • • •

HAMLIN AT FIRST WONDERED if he was in for a lot of intimate, soul-baring talk, but it didn't turn out that way. The two settled themselves on the battlements, watching the celebration and amusing themselves by discussing things they saw in the crowds below them.

Then they walked to the other side, looking outward this time, resting against the crenellations and talking as two good friends would talk. It was all casual and easy, but there was something intensely private about the conversation, though Hamlin couldn't determine what it was that made it so.

Perhaps it was the emotions, still running high, that shaped the tone of their exchange. Perhaps it was their isolation from the rest of the castle despite the very open nature of their retreat. Yes, thank the heavens for peacetime, for the battlements weren't crawling with warriors. Hamlin himself had spent a good deal of quiet time there, strolling the entire length, in fact, of the massive structure.

Now it was their momentary haven, and they'd wander for a bit before pausing and gazing out again, still talking. Hamlin didn't feel the need to rush things. There was time enough for everything, he thought, and for now, it felt good to be lost in quiet talk. Now and then, they'd pause their conversation and lean close for a sweet, tender kiss that lasted a handful of seconds each time.

They were going about things backward, he realized. As with most romantic connections, things usually began in friendship before developing into something deeper. In his and Edouard's case, they had started off falling in love first before becoming friends. Maybe there was an advantage to this method, but whatever it was, Hamlin didn't know—nor did he care.

The sun inched its way across the sky, and at length their stomachs grumbled, forcing them to abandon the battlements in search of food.

"This time, you'll eat with me properly," Edouard said with a grin as he squeezed Hamlin's hand. "No forests and no bribed pages."

"That's a relief. I haven't any coin on me today."

They made their way back down. They might be hungry and a bit delirious for going without food since the ceremony, but they still took their time rejoining the rest of the guests. Hamlin thought they deserved as many idle moments as they could have.

• • • •

A QUIET KNOCK ON HIS bedroom door roused Hamlin from the comfortable haze of pleasant memories. It was a bother to get up, to be sure, but he didn't mind. His spirits were too high still, and he continued to ride the wave despite his exhaustion. He turned to face the door.

"Come in," he called out, and the door swung open. "Mama?"

Queen Elfriede looked through the gap. The corridor behind her was still lit with torches, and Hamlin couldn't see his mother's face with his room already darkened. There was still quite a bit of activity going on all over the castle, though the number of guests had dwindled to about half by now. He expected the celebrations to continue all the way to daybreak, if Otto's wedding was any indication.

Hamlin pushed himself up to lean against his pillows. He rubbed his eyes and watched his mother enter his room, leaving his bedroom door slightly ajar, allowing some torchlight to stream through and break up a little of the darkness. She walked over to his bed and sat down, facing him. Her face and her figure remained in shadows, making it difficult to read her mood before she spoke.

"I didn't see you today," she said, her voice hushed and gentle. "Were you all right? Did you enjoy yourself, darling?"

Hamlin nodded. "I did. I kept myself busy." Thank the heavens for the cover of darkness because he felt himself blush.

"That's good." A brief pause followed. "I thought I saw you with Prince Edouard at one point."

"We were just talking, Mama."

"What, no quarrels?" Queen Elfriede's voice dripped with amusement.

"None. We've gone past those, you know. We're both much older now—and hopefully much wiser as well."

His mother nodded. "I'm happy to hear that, though I'm afraid his mother isn't."

Hamlin frowned. "What do you mean?"

"She saw you two together as well. I don't know when, but she did. She said you two were busy talking and watching the crowds, and she was also in the company of others whom she couldn't leave to—well—go to you. At least that was what she said to me."

"She talked to you about us?"

"Hamlin, you know very well how she feels about you and Edouard being together—or more like being in each other's company, let alone being in the same room or an open courtyard together. She'd complained to me about your hitting Edouard when you were much younger—called me irresponsible and—other things. You were only a little boy then."

Queen Elfriede sighed, bowing her head and taking one of Hamlin's hands in hers. She gave it a gentle squeeze. "You also know how she feels about me personally for marrying your father. I know it isn't fair, but her animosity toward me extends to you as well because you're my son."

"She's always been unfair to you, Mama."

"I don't care what she thinks about me, darling. Not anymore. I do, however, worry about you and whether or not she mistreats you in any way." Queen Elfriede swallowed audibly as she stroked Hamlin's hand. "Did she raise her voice to you today? Threaten you in any way? Made you promise to stay away from Edouard?"

Hamlin blinked. "No, Mama. I never crossed paths with her today, even when I was in Edouard's company."

He inwardly winced at the partial truth. He'd never told her about the real reason why he didn't join her in the banquet hall the last time he was at Queen Franziska's castle. In her own perverse way, Queen Clarimond had kept her word and left his mother alone—at least for that day.

"I'm glad to hear that. She was quite upset when she confronted me earlier about you and her son. One would think that, being the hostess of today's celebrations, I'd be allowed some measure of respect, but..." She paused, sighing heavily again, and shook her head. "I wish I understood people more clearly, darling. I get so tired of these things, you know. And the possibility of your getting hurt through no fault of yours is—it makes me sick. But never mind. I just wanted to know if you were all right."

"I'm fine, Mama. Don't worry about me. I can take care of myself."

Queen Elfriede stood up, walked closer, and bent down to plant a gentle kiss on Hamlin's tousled hair. "I know you can, Hamlin. Good night."

"Good night." Hamlin watched his mother's shadowy figure walk toward the door and slip out without another word. The door shut behind her, and Hamlin's room was plunged into darkness again. He thought about the conversation for a moment, the danger of Queen Clarimond's fury at her discovery of his relationship with Edouard now casting a shadow over what had been a perfect day.

Hamlin didn't have a solution to the problem, though, and fatigue once again overcame him. Reluctantly he slid back under the covers, turning to face his windows, which were open to welcome the fresh night air. The distant sounds of merrymaking soothed him in their own curious way, and before long Hamlin fell asleep, his eyes closing against the moon's light.

Chapter 30

Edouard's twenty-secondth birthday came and went. Hamlin's nineteenth birthday came and went. Aloysia and Clovis's wedding came and went. All were small, quiet affairs, and even his sister had insisted on extremely little fanfare. Now it was all a matter of waiting for that dreadful day.

Two more weeks, Edouard told himself as he stumbled through the brush, sweating and puffing. Two more weeks of chaperoning a cursed princess and coping with the increasing despair of her parents. King Friedrich and Queen Franziska had borne their daughter's destiny with as much dignity as they could muster given the circumstances, though they'd also tipped over to unhappy resignation now and then. Their occasional celebrations for the smallest and silliest things involving Roderika had become the stuff of legend in more ways than one.

With the curse and the unknown future staring them in the eye, his aunt and uncle seemed to have moved on to their next emotional phase, which was numbness and easy distraction. The celebrations tapered, and more modest banquets were held to celebrate the royal family's birthdays.

The number of servants also dwindled, Queen Franziska insisting on giving everyone the freedom of staying with them through the hundred years or leaving, whether to rejoin their families or to establish themselves elsewhere. In fact, every month since the six-month countdown had begun, she ordered the servants to assemble before her, and she put the question to them again.

Many had left, but those who remained were loyal to a fault, with some even bringing family members to replace lost servants. Those who remained for the hundred years' sleep looked upon the future with trepidation and excitement, and there were hushed discussions about new inventions and new laws and so on upon their awakening. Though the ongoing joke was all about being a hundred years behind in fashion.

Ministers and courtiers withdrew or stayed as well, though those who chose to remain made a very small group. There'd been several poignant farewells, and at times Edouard wondered just how many more of these melancholy goodbyes the royal family could endure.

Roderika, the focus of everything, seemed to be unaware of all the scrambling about on her behalf. She continued to sing and dance and entertain and dress herself splendidly, her compulsions not once abating. Edouard wondered whether this was going to continue once the curse was lifted, and for the princess's sake as well as that of her future husband, he hoped so.

Today had been particularly trying. Roderika bubbled with too much restless energy, and the pair had wandered all over the immediate countryside in search of untapped woodlands for Roderika to assault. Unfortunately they found some and, three hours later, the princess was fetched by an army of personal servants. Edouard ordered the group to go ahead, as he was held up by sorting through the collection of sharp things that his cousin had picked up on that day's excursions.

The woods that they'd discovered weren't as pretty as the one that sprawled closest to his aunt and uncle's castle. It was old and crowded with trees, its terrain uneven and dangerous. They'd seen no woodland animal anywhere, though the silence was often broken by the happy chirping of birds that they couldn't see.

Pushing his way through shrubbery and stumbling over massive tree roots with an armload of what he now called "Roderika's relics" was a nightmare. It was an amazing collection, to be sure—tree branches, rocks, twigs, and one item that he couldn't identify but, like the others, was strangely formed. Edouard hoped it wasn't petrified wild boar droppings that happened to take on the shape of a crude spindle as it dried and aged.

At length, he broke through the final line of trees and into sunlight, sighing in relief as he stumbled forward, nearly falling on his face from fatigue and his burden. He walked on, chose an open, grassy area onto which he tossed his load, and groaned as he stretched his arms.

He was about to consider what to do next when the sound of something snapping broke the silence, and he whirled around, startled.

An old woman stood several feet away, watching him in silence. Short and hunched, brown rags covered her entire body, and her old and filthy shawl draped over her head like a hood, throwing her face into shadows.

Edouard frowned as he looked at her and then the woods behind. She must have come out of the trees, he thought. He hadn't noticed anyone when he'd first walked out.

"Good day to you," he called out.

"Good day to you, too, Your Highness," she replied. Her voice was crackling but energetic. "I see you've got quite a collection there."

"Ah—yes. I needed to get them away from my cousin." Edouard paused, suspicious. He narrowed his eyes at the woman, who just stood there, watching him. "Are you one of those wise women?"

"I am, yes. Oh, I've always loved being called that. Wise, I mean. It's so flattering. For someone who was never born a natural beauty, I'll take compliments on my brain any time." She grinned, straightening up a bit. Her face emerged from the shadows, revealing large, keen eyes, a hooked nose that made Edouard wonder if all hags were cursed with hooked noses, and a toothless mouth. Long, stringy white hair fell over her shoulders to her waist.

Edouard nodded. "Don't tell me. You're the one who cursed Princess Roderika on her presentation, and you're here to mock my aunt and uncle's efforts at preventing the curse from taking place. There's no need for you to gloat, though. Uncle and Auntie have long resigned themselves to their fate, and they're just waiting out the days, not resisting."

"Her time's coming, young man, and so is yours."

Edouard froze. "I beg your pardon?"

The old woman just raised a hand, a bony finger pointed at him, and moved it as though indicating something around him. "Destiny," she said. "Hard choices. And—oh, by all the demons—damn it!" She paused for a moment, her hand frozen in the air, and she squinted as she stared hard at Edouard. "I can't do anything where you're concerned. I'll have to decline the commission, I'm afraid."

"What? I'm sorry, what?"

"I was charged to follow you and—oh, what does it matter? Everything's spoiled now." She sighed, dropping her hand and shrugging. "Bugger it. I was hoping to earn some extra money for a special trip south. I heard they've got some of the most remarkable poison mushrooms and bitter roots there—all good for black spells and curses that can turn the demon world upside-down. This commission was supposed to help. Travel is very expensive, you know, and I could've used the money, as the cost is substantial. You must be a pretty special prince to cost my client so much."

"Commission? What commission?"

The hag turned around, waving a hand as she did. "It's all between me and my client, Your Highness. My methods might be questionable, but I still adhere to rules, and confidentiality is one of them. And as far as mocking Friedrich and Franziska—I've been doing that since the princess's presentation. Pride deserves nothing less, you know. Let this be a hard lesson for that pair of royal oafs. Then again, given their grotesque sense of self-importance, I'm sure they've managed to look at their hundred years' sleep as a rare opportunity to be something bigger than they really are. A legend, if you will. Bah!"

Edouard stood in confusion for several moments as he watched the hag strike into the woods and vanish from his sight. Then he turned to regard the pile of "Roderika's relics" he'd just deposited on the grass. Puzzlement slowly gave way to bubbling anxiety as he recalled their brief conversation. What on earth was that all about?

Her mention of a commission and of destiny unnerved him. There it was again, he thought. Fate. The idea of his being a helpless puppet in a string of predetermined events. That bit about the commission also alarmed him, as it boded nothing but ill. That "commission," he now determined, involved him in some capacity, but the old woman's hand was stayed—because of destiny? His destiny, that is?

"She must've seen that ridiculous mystical red string, or whatever it's called," he muttered, frowning, still staring at the pile of bizarre objects lying at his feet. "Then—if so, what would that mean? That red string kept her from doing something?" He guessed that she'd been hired to do *something,* but was immediately discouraged from moving forward.

His mind raced as he tried to put the pieces together—pieces that were nothing more than odds and ends, ideas that were nothing more than guesswork. And by the time he believed himself to be finished with a relatively clear picture of things, his heart dropped.

"Hamlin," he said, horrified. "It's got something to do with Hamlin and me."

Edouard stumbled back from the pile of objects as he tried to remember where he was and thought about what to do next. He turned and ran in the direction of his aunt and uncle's castle, mentally kicking himself for not taking a horse. He made for a pretty unprincely sight, his mother would likely say if she were watching him now. Then again, he'd been painfully unprincely since he'd accepted the temporary role of Roderika's chaperone, with him agreeing to wander behind her without a proper escort or refreshments.

He'd just managed to cover a fourth of the distance when the old woman appeared again, this time standing in his path and forcing him to skid to a halt.

"What do you want now?" he panted, pressing a hand against his side.

"I changed my mind," she replied. "Those poison mushrooms and bitter roots are too precious to ignore. Besides, my joints are killing me, and a trip to warmer climes will do me some good."

"And what about all that talk about destiny and so on?" Edouard considered his own thoughts—his guesswork, that is—and tested them. "I thought there was something about me that you somehow can't affect."

The old hag nodded, sighing and shrugging. "You're right. There is, and things like that shouldn't be tampered with. They can, mind you, but if you want to save yourself the trouble, you're better off avoiding it from the start. That's why I said 'shouldn't', not 'couldn't.'"

"But if my destiny's already set, how on earth can you hope to alter its course? Wouldn't it be nothing more than a bit of a delay? Things still would've fallen back into their predetermined path, am I not correct? Then what you're attempting to do *is* a waste of your time and skill in the dark arts—and all that trouble for poison mushrooms and bitter roots."

"You're a bit of a saucy brat, aren't you? It's no wonder your mother put up so much money to—"

"My mother paid you?" Edouard broke in, outraged. On the other hand, he wouldn't put it past her to pull something absurd like this.

The hag spluttered, slapping a bony, warty hand against her mouth. Then she pointed an accusing finger at Edouard. "You tricked me into betraying my client!"

"I still would've guessed correctly even if you didn't trip the way you did. You should've just let things go after our first meeting."

She let out a string of expletives that burned Edouard's ear, making him wonder if all old people were just as colorful in expressing extreme displeasure. After living for so long, perhaps they'd earned the right to be foul-mouthed. The old woman even resorted to stamping her feet and punching the air with her warty fists before disappearing in a puff of smoke.

"I guess that's that," Edouard muttered, moving forward now. He needed to go back to his father's castle and confront his mother. He and Hamlin had taken care to be discreet about their relationship, their trysts planned in excruciating detail. They also had the protection of Aloysia, Clovis, and Master Audwin, with Aloysia using her own skills in magic to shield the lovers from prying eyes. That is, whenever she was available to do it. With her marriage to Clovis fast approaching, she'd been spending a good deal of time at Clovis's parents' castle, enjoying the company of her future in-laws, all of whom had welcomed her gladly.

If he and Hamlin were caught together somehow, it must've been at an earlier time, perhaps on the day of Baldrick's wedding. That could only be it. Edouard shook his head at the thought, anger still bubbling in him.

"Things shouldn't be this way," he grumbled as he trudged along. "It's no one's business, and no one has the right to ruin things for us. Not even Mama."

"Look, I don't take rare ingredients lightly, Your Highness," a voice piped up suddenly beside him.

Edouard jumped, tripped on a rock, and fell on his rump with a yelp. He gaped at the old hag who'd just appeared next to him, keeping pace. Once he felt his jaw working again, he cried, "Would you mind not doing that? I don't have the advantage of mind-reading, prophecy, clairvoyance, or whatever you call those things, and I can't predict when you decide to engage me in heart-to-heart chatter again!" He'd always hated surprises, and growing up with Aloysia hadn't taught him how to cope.

"I'm simply trying to emphasize just how important this commission is to me as an active magic-wielder."

"A witch, you mean."

"Your mother really should've cleaned your mouth more often," she snapped. She even had the audacity to rest her hands on her hips as she glared at him. "But back to what I'm trying to say. Rare plants for special spells are well worth the effort, and while it's true that trying to alter your destiny means nothing in the end but a momentary delay, I still aim to make it worth your mother's time and money. If you have any mercy in you, you'd feel sorry for me, seeing as how torn I am over this. Back and forth, back and forth, I keep going from one side to the other, and the more I do it, the muddier the issue gets."

"Then don't do it!"

"You forget about the poison mushrooms and bitter roots. At any rate, I'll need to rethink the commission and make a few adjustments—or something. You'll be happy for being left alone, your mother will be happy knowing her money's been well spent, and I'll be enjoying some relief from the grief of old age. Good day, Your Highness."

She disappeared in another puff of smoke. Edouard hoped it was for good as he stumbled to his feet, looking down at his clothes, which were now a right mess. Cursing softly, he carried on toward his aunt and uncle's castle, wondering what that ridiculous old crone had up her sleeve. He needed to confront his mother, to be sure, but he couldn't shake off the nagging feeling that the wise-woman-really-a-witch had done something quite horrible without his realizing it.

Chapter 31

Hamlin awoke with a low groan. His head throbbed. He felt as though his half-brothers had just jumped on him all at once, using his skull for a cushion. He blinked his eyes open, only to see his surroundings swirl around him in a maddening dance. In fact, the bizarre scene made him think of childhood dreams about objects coming alive to chase him down, corner him, and eat him alive. Oddly enough, those monstrosities always started their horrific gorging with his right buttock, and he never did understand the significance of that body part in his nightmares.

His room had grown dark. It was very likely sundown by now. While he couldn't remember what he'd done since the moment he'd felt faint after lunch and had excused himself to go to his room to rest, that wasn't the biggest of his worries. He might have lost six hours, but what concerned him most was the feeling of stiffness all over—a strange tightness in his muscles and even his bones that made moving difficult, though not painful.

Had he fallen ill? Was it something that attacked muscles and bones? Hamlin pushed himself up, and he saw that he was lying on the floor of his room. He'd never made it to his bed. But his head had stopped throbbing, the fog was dissipating and, finally, his vision cleared along with it.

"What on earth happened?" he whispered, rubbing his temples and grimacing. "Was the meat bad? I might have to talk to Mama about the kitchen staff if that's so."

He wanted to have a fire going, he realized. For some reason, he felt quite cold despite the warm evening. He stumbled to his feet, swaying a bit as another wave of dizziness swept over him. He could barely see, and he depended on the murky outlines of his bedroom furniture to guide him.

Hamlin stumbled a few paces and then paused a couple of feet away from his table, frowning as he regarded it. Had the table always been that tall? He squinted, trying to see around him.

"Idiot," he murmured, turning his attention back to his table. Yes, it was much taller. Nose-height, to be precise, not waist-height. The strange tightness of his muscles once again startled him as he reached over the table for a candle. He realized belatedly that he should've stepped outside in order to get a lit torch and use it to light the candles in his room. "What on earth is going on?"

He managed to grab a candle, though it took some doing, because his arm was too short. Hamlin shook his head, pressing his eyes shut, hoping that the sudden rattling of his brain would help set his perceptions to right. Once the dizziness abated, he saw that things hadn't changed, and with a soft curse, he staggered toward the window, where some moonlight shone through. Maybe fresh night air would help clear his head, he thought. Once he stood in the silver light, he took several deep breaths. Then he glanced down.

And promptly froze when he saw his hand.

It was not his own, but a creature's hand. It was small, thin, and bony, the skin blotchy and green, the nails long like claws. Raising it up, he glanced down and found the rest of his body transformed. He'd shrunk, to be sure, to about one half of his full height. His limbs were long, scrawny, and green. His chest was narrow and sunken, and his belly swelled out. He was naked, and when he turned to look for his clothes, he saw them lying on the floor. The candle fell from his hand.

"The mirror," he whispered, barely able to get the words out, and he hurried to where the mirror stood, not too far from the window, and looked at himself.

Hamlin had no hair. His head had expanded sideways till it was disproportionate to his neck and shoulders and slightly wider than his belly. His eyes were huge and protruding, his nose an ugly, wart-covered, and hooked monstrosity, and his mouth was a wide, lipless line that hid rows of sharp and crooked teeth.

"Oh, no," he gasped, feeling his face with his free hand. "Oh, no. Oh, lord, what happened? What—" He hurried to his open window, straining as he rose on tiptoes to peer out.

"Audwin!" he cried. "Audwin! Emergency!"

Nothing but the black night answered him, and he repeated his calls. Below his window, servants continued their daily tasks, and Hamlin was sure that he was going to be summoned for dinner soon. He paced around his room, panic now lancing him, and when he couldn't bear it anymore, he ran back to the window to call for his friend again, repeating the process a few more times before Audwin finally responded.

Hamlin was now pacing and chewing away at his claws, grimacing at the bitterness of those vile things, but he couldn't wring his hands or knot his fingers the way he always did. He barely heard the familiar flapping of wings and the irritated voice of his old friend.

"Your Highness, with all due respect, I was hoping to enjoy a night off from watching over you," Audwin retorted once he'd settled himself on Hamlin's window ledge. "Might I add that you also sound strange. Now what on earth could be so harrowing that you'd—whoa there!"

Hamlin stood before him, still chewing at his claws and hoping that he looked as pitiful as possible. Audwin had given himself up to severe shock and spent the next several moments flapping his wings and squawking shrilly. Black feathers seemed to explode from his body, and they flew about him before drifting to the floor with surreal grace.

"What the devil's filthy bottom happened to you?" Audwin cried. "You're a goblin! You're a royal goblin!"

"I don't know," Hamlin stammered. "I felt faint during lunch, and I went straight to my room. Then—I fainted, I guess. I can't remember anything else. All I know is that I woke up, it's been a few hours since, and I'm—I'm a goblin."

Audwin regarded him in shocked silence for a moment, his beak frozen open. At length he snapped out of his trance and shook his head. "You might be lovely in human form, Your Highness, but as a goblin, you're indescribably foul-looking."

"I don't need your judgment right now, bird!" Hamlin snapped. "I need your help!"

Audwin snorted and flew inside, circling Hamlin a few times and muttering to himself before swooping down and settling down on the bed. "You've obviously been cursed, though I don't know by whom or why. I can find out for you, but it'll take some time."

"But—what did I do? I didn't trespass anywhere or pick forbidden fruit or flowers or desecrate graves. What did I do?"

"It might be a case of doing nothing, I'm afraid. Dark spells are cast for every reason under the sun. Some people are unlucky enough to be targeted only because they exist."

"That doesn't make any sense."

"Human nature never made any sense. Why do you think I've gotten this misanthropic? I've been telling you that since you could understand what 'misanthropic' meant, Your Highness."

Hamlin swallowed as he began to pace again. "What am I going to do in the meantime? I can't let anyone see me like this, and I can't spend my days hiding from everyone, either."

Audwin clucked. "Perhaps you should try to be honest about it. Present yourself to your mother first, as she's the most likely to support you. You'll need an ally in this household, especially in that form."

Hamlin wasn't convinced, but he realized that he didn't have much of a choice. "How long will it take you to find out?" he asked.

"If I set out now, I hope to have the answer by tomorrow noon at most. Birds are a very talkative lot and can't be trusted with secrets, as you know. Someone out there knows what's going on."

"All right, then. I'll try to get Mama to come here."

"Good. I'll return before you know it." With that, Audwin flapped his wings and sailed out, leaving Hamlin still panicking about what a stupid plan he'd just hatched. At the same time, he also couldn't come up with anything better or even more remotely sensible, so he cudgeled his brain for a way to get his mother to come to his room.

The sound of footsteps outside his door halted his thoughts, and he ran to it, pressing his weight against it to keep it from being opened. A knock sounded, and a servant's voice called out to him.

"Your Highness? Dinner is served, sir."

"Thank you," he replied. "Would you mind calling the queen for me? I'm afraid I'm not feeling too well at the moment. I need to see her."

Silence met his words. "Your Highness? Did you just say something? I can't understand you."

"I said that I need the queen here as soon as possible!" Hamlin said, this time raising his voice and speaking more slowly. His mouth was practically pressed against the door. What else could he possibly do to make himself understood?

The servant remained baffled, and when she spoke, she sounded more alarmed. "My Lord? I—I can't understand you! You're talking gibberish! Are you ill?"

"I just said that I'm indisposed! Do I need to spell it out for you?" Oh, for heaven's sake!

"Your Highness, may I come in? I need to see you and report to the queen!" She tried to push the door open, but Hamlin pressed harder against it. She knocked, this time more forcefully. "Please open the door, my Lord!"

The sound of additional voices and footsteps in the corridor beyond made Hamlin's heart drop. He held his breath and tried to listen to the conversation but could only catch the servant's terrified voice. There was more, and a male voice called out.

"Your Highness, are you ill?"

"Just get my confounded mother in here!" Hamlin roared. "How many times must I repeat myself?"

"What's going on? Who's in there?"

Another frightened exchange followed beyond the door and then a brief silence. Hamlin swallowed, wondering if the ridiculous servants had managed to understand him this time.

The door suddenly burst open with violent force as one of the servants kicked it in, throwing Hamlin nearly across the room. Bright, colorful lights exploded behind his eyelids as he flew, then tumbled several feet across the floor before coming to a stop. He groaned at the soreness of his body, and he barely took note of the figures who swarmed inside his room, their frightened voices calling out to him.

"I'm here, you fools!" he cried when he caught his breath, finally rolling over and stumbling to his feet. Before him stood three servants, all staring with their eyes bulging and their mouths hanging open. "Yes, I've been turned into a goblin! Now call the queen!"

The woman let out a horrific scream, then the two men took up her noise, shouting as well. One turned tail and fled the room, calling for armed soldiers—Prince Hamlin had been killed or carried off by a troop of goblins, and one of them was still in his room. The remaining male servant lunged for Hamlin with a fierce yell and tried to grab him by the throat.

"Wait a minute!" Hamlin cried as he scrambled out of the way. "It's me! It's me! Don't you understand what I'm saying?"

"Get it, quick!" the girl continued to wail, pointing at Hamlin and stamping her foot. "That foul thing killed the prince, I know it! I can see his clothes on the floor! Oh, poor Prince Hamlin!"

Could no one understand him? Audwin could, but humans couldn't? Were his words coming out differently? Hamlin didn't know, but that was the least of his worries now. The entire castle would know that a goblin was found in his room, and he was nowhere to be seen. How long would it take before someone would realize that the terrified creature was really him?

A hand grabbing his foot tripped him, and he rolled on the floor, coming to a stop by the girl, who only screamed more loudly, leaping out of the way.

"Oh, bugger this," Hamlin hissed, struggling back to his feet and running to the open door. He'd have to figure out how to communicate his plight to his family. In the meantime, he needed to save his skin. He stumbled out into the corridor and ran as fast as he could in the direction of the less-used areas of the castle.

Chapter 32

When Edouard arrived at his father's castle, the attendants waited as he inspected himself from top to bottom. He felt around his head, his face, his torso and arms, his legs and feet. Nothing seemed to be amiss. All the same, he couldn't dismiss the nagging feeling that something shocking or horrific—perhaps both—had just happened. The old crone's words made him suspect transformation of some kind, though where he got that idea solely based on her babbling about mushrooms and roots, he didn't know. It was a gut feeling, to be sure, but it refused to let him go.

"Your Highness?"

Edouard glanced up to find two pages standing outside the open carriage door, blinking owlishly and waiting for him to get out. "Oh, yes," he stammered. "I'm coming."

He clambered out of the carriage and was about to walk toward the front door when he paused and turned around. "Do either of you see anything strange about me?" he asked.

The two boys exchanged baffled glances at first and then looked him up and down. When he motioned for them to walk around him, they did. Eventually they both stood before him again and shook their heads.

"You look quite normal, Your Highness," the older of the two said.

"Though maybe a bit paler than usual," the other appended, and the pair nodded.

"Very well. Thank you."

Edouard jogged to the door and was soon hurrying through the corridor toward the queen's study. It really wasn't a study in the traditional sense, being a smallish room packed with not only books, but a vast collection of objects that the queen fancied. Odds and ends she'd found in her travels—dolls, small paintings, colorful stones, exquisite silver plates, even discolored bones. That room was her private haven, and she withdrew there for an hour or even two usually after breakfast, claiming that being surrounded by her favorite things was always good for her mood.

"Mama," Edouard said after he'd knocked and been admitted. He stepped inside and shut the door gently behind him.

Queen Clarimond sat on an elegant, throne-like chair, doing needle-work. Her tables and shelves overflowed with her collections, some of her books finding a new home on the floor. She looked at Edouard, surprised.

"Well, what are you doing here, my dear?" she asked, amazement now melting into the usual placid iciness. "As you can see, I'm busy working on that tapestry I want to give your sister for her wedding gift. I'm a touch late, I'm afraid."

The tapestry looked more like a massive blanket that draped her lap and spilled onto the floor, covering whatever items happened to be in its path. Much to her credit, her needlework was quite stunning in scope, and Edouard recognized a garden scene of some kind that was slowly coming to life.

"Mama, I know about the wise woman—witch—you hired to come after me," he said, leveling a hard gaze at his mother.

Queen Clarimond listened, slightly frowning at first. "Ah!" she said, setting her work down. "Yes—Mistress Alyda. A bit of a flighty sort, but she's very impressive where dark magic's concerned. You met her?" When Edouard nodded, a bit shocked at his mother's apparent indifference to his outrage, she continued. "Oh, I admit that I hired her to come after you, but she sent me a message regarding certain difficulties she had that required her to rethink her strategy. Unfortunately she did so after she left the kingdom, so I couldn't demand my money back." She shook her head and clucked, her mood shifting a little as though the gravity of the situation just sank in once she'd given it a little more thought. "She obviously left you alone, but I'm guessing that she at least dealt with—oh, how shall I say it—the source of the problem."

"What are you talking about? What was supposed to happen to me?"

His mother regarded him keenly, her eyes moving up and down in that familiar, critical way of hers. "A spell. One that would alter your feelings for that little wretch. I suppose Mistress Alyda decided to improvise, judging from her halfway sensible message. As to what that alternative might be, I suppose I'll have to trust her judgment, seeing as how I've not much choice in the matter."

"Wait, wait—why did you hire her?"

Queen Clarimond's eyes flashed, and she pressed her mouth into a thin line. "I know about you and that commoner-bastard-prince, Edouard," she replied, her voice steady and calm. "I saw you two together at Reinhard's second son's wedding."

Edouard fell silent, paling, and his mother sighed and shook her head. "Oh, come now, Edouard. You really didn't think that I wouldn't be on my guard when we were in enemy territory, did you? What a thought! I saw you leave immediately after the ceremony, and that little brat followed you."

"And? What of that? I could easily have gone one way, and he'd have gone another. What made you think that we were somehow going to meet?" Edouard knew he was grasping at straws, but being cornered, he needed to do something.

"Ah, but you didn't go your separate ways, did you? I was right and—well, for goodness's sake, all I needed was to see that look in that boy's eyes when he watched you leave to know his intentions. Oh, I felt so sticky from all the sweetness."

Despite his anger and fear, Edouard couldn't help but feel his triumph. Hamlin had said that he'd followed him to the private courtyard, but Edouard hadn't known—or at least he still couldn't manage to believe—that Hamlin was already in love with him before the kiss.

Get off it! a furious voice in his head hissed, and Edouard rallied. "So you followed us?" he demanded.

"I tried, but it was difficult with all the guests and so many people wanting my attention. But I spotted you two on the battlements, and it was very clear that you were both more than friends." She cocked a brow. "As for how long it's been going on, I don't wish to guess, as I'd hate to be insulted by my own son. Any more than you already have insulted me."

Edouard narrowed his eyes at her. "Just from seeing us on the battlements? If I remember correctly, we were watching people in the courtyard and then enjoying the scenery outside the castle walls afterward. I don't see how that translates into something that's more than friendship." He was grasping at straws again.

His mother regarded him in stony silence. "Don't toy with me, young man. Are you and that boy involved? And don't lie."

A moment's thick silence followed before he answered. "We are."

"Let me ask you this, Edouard. Why did you go against my express order to stay away from him?"

"Because we're grown up, and we should be past certain issues, Mama. You really don't expect me to grow old with a childhood grudge," Edouard retorted. There was nothing left in his pitiful arsenal but the truth. "Besides, what I do with my time and the people I want to be friends with are no one else's business but my own."

"There's such a thing as obligation, my dear, and while I must allow young people a bit of space to learn more about life on their own terms, in the end, they *must* see that setting aside childish things for the sake of family or, in your case, the kingdom, is paramount."

Edouard shook his head. "You've already had those obligations met through my older brothers and even through Aloysia. And they were all willing to follow the paths you and Papa laid out for them." Save for Aloysia, perhaps, as she'd sworn to raise her children to be open-minded about magic and even encourage them if they expressed a desire to learn. He paused. "Is this an issue of gender? Do you object to my preference for another man?"

"More like boy, I daresay," his mother replied, rolling her eyes. "And, no, I don't care about his gender. As far as heirs go, we'll have plenty, thanks to your brothers and their—uh—insatiable wives. Your taking another prince isn't an issue. What I object to is the specific boy you've set your cap on."

"You never even tried to get to know him or his mother."

"And neither did you unless you've been doing so behind my back since the beginning." Queen Clarimond paused, regarding him questioningly. "Well? How long have you known about your feelings for this Hamlin creature?"

Edouard squirmed under her gaze, feeling himself revert to a five-year-old again. It was one thing to be coddled and displayed as a paragon of princely virtue, but to have one's doting—blindly doting—mother express severe displeasure and disappointment was another. Edouard had never felt so painfully torn before.

"I don't know when exactly," he said after another moment's pause. "It's all been gradual. But I don't hate him the way you want me to, and I don't think I've really truly hated him as much as I let on." His gaze strayed as a wave of sadness overcame him. "I've been unfair to him and his mother for so many years. It's my fault entirely for provoking him and giving you reason to despise him. I admit it."

"I think you're not feeling too well, Edouard. You should retire and sleep things off."

Queen Clarimond waved him away. Her expression had grown darker, her voice even stiffer.

"Everything will be much better in the morning. Oh, and after Roderika's day of reckoning, I've invited Melisande and her family for a month-long holiday. Well—not her father, mind you, as he's got a kingdom to rule, but his wife and their children will all be present. You haven't seen Melisande in a while, but I can safely say that she's grown up to be a remarkable young lady. Very sober and book-smart, just like you. I think you two will enjoy each other's company. And, yes, despite that disastrous first meeting you had, she's been asking about you."

Edouard pursed his lips as he listened. "I'm sorry, Mama, but I've committed myself to Hamlin."

"Committed? What, are you two married?"

"Well, no, but—"

"Then you're not committed. Only a union that's been sanctified or made official publicly is a real commitment. Now I'm not averse to whatever romantic whims young people have nowadays, but as I said, after a certain point, one's obligation to his family should—"

"But you just said that those obligations aren't necessary anymore," Edouard cut in, exasperated. "Remember my brothers, Mama?"

"You can't be with Elfriede's son! You won't!" Queen Clarimond roared, throwing her needlework down and banging her fists against the chair's armrests. "You're not to soil our good name with the spawn of that money-grubbing whore! Do you hear me? And you'll not fight me on this, Edouard! You'll not! Enough of this talk! We're done!"

"Don't you dare talk to me like I'm a child!"

"Then don't you dare insult me as if I were your inferior! Defy me, Edouard, and you're cut off!"

Edouard listened to his mother in a numb mixture of outrage and fascinated horror. He couldn't manage to talk, and it was all he could do to stare in shock as his mother raged, losing her legendary composure like a spoiled child. Her face was scrunched up and blood-red—a sight that Edouard never thought he'd see. Her jewelry rattled as she pounded her fists again and again to emphasize every word she shouted at her son.

"Yes, we're done," Edouard said after she finished, and she regarded him in breathless anger. Her chest heaved as she gasped for air, her complexion was still as blood-red as before, and her face was still contorted in a grimace. "There's no more to be said about this matter."

He turned around and left the queen's study, slamming the door behind himself. A few servants had stopped in their tracks and now watched him anxiously. He waved them off and they scattered, coloring and murmuring apologies as they fled.

Edouard hurried down the corridor toward the great stairs, his own anger fueling his flight. He needed to communicate with Aloysia as soon as possible. His gut now warned him that it was Hamlin who was marked by Mistress Alyda, and he needed his sister's help in undoing whatever spell had just been cast on Hamlin.

He also needed Master Audwin, though he'd no idea how to summon the cranky old raven. He had a very basic ability to communicate with birds, but Master Audwin was a different story, as it seemed as though only Hamlin could talk to him. Edouard raced up the stairs, down dark corridors, and more stairs that led him to one of the highest tower rooms.

It was old and abandoned—dark and slippery from decades-old damp—and Edouard alternately ran and slid till he reached the window. He could barely breathe and, once he'd managed to calm down a bit, he leaned out and whistled for help. It was always difficult summoning birds, and it took him several attempts to have a bullfinch appear. Then again, it was already evening, and most likely he'd just woken the little thing from its sleep, and it had come just to shut him up.

"I need you to carry a message for me," he panted, and the bullfinch hopped closer once it landed on the window ledge, seeming to listen to his frantic whispers.

Chapter 33

Hamlin thanked the heavens for being goblin-sized, though there was nothing to be thankful for as far as being an actual goblin was concerned. He was small enough to crawl under the thick, protective branches of a bush. There he curled up, panting and sweating from his recent exertions, not knowing what else to do but to wait for Audwin to somehow track him down.

His escape from his parents' castle had been touch and go. Having been transformed into an otherworldly creature that was a great deal smaller than his normal size, he discovered (the hard way) that having short legs didn't promise him much despite his agility. The alarm was raised within seconds, and every corridor thundered under the frantic steps of servants and knights. Hamlin couldn't reach any of the abandoned areas of the castle and was nearly caught a few times. It was nothing short of a miracle that he'd somehow managed to flee the castle and hop on board a wagon on its way out of the courtyard without anyone noticing him. The darkness helped, but perhaps Fortune had decided to take pity on him.

After abandoning the wagon once he was out on open roads, he'd run to the nearest woods and tried to find shelter there.

Once his heart rate and breathing had settled, Hamlin wondered how this had happened. A spell was the obvious answer, but by whom, and what on earth had he done to deserve being singled out in such a way? He thought about his half-brothers, but they'd long moved on to more adult things—women (or, in the case of Otto and Baldrick, their wives) were their biggest distraction nowadays. The last time any of them had raised a fist or had offered his "pretty bum" to a drunk friend for money was about a year ago.

Edouard, then? Was Edouard the connection? Hamlin's heart started racing again. It had to be, he thought. He remembered his mother's concern the night of Baldrick's wedding. They'd been seen then, but since the moment they promised themselves to each other, they'd been discreet—as discreet as they could be, considering Queen Clarimond's insane hatred toward him and his mother.

Even those brilliant, splendid moments making love in secret, protected by Aloysia's magic—he and Edouard had been painfully careful in choosing dates and times for their trysts. They weren't even invited to Aloysia and Clovis's wedding, much to Edouard's dismay, but Hamlin did everything he could to reassure him that he didn't care. He even asked his lover to give the happy couple the wedding gift that Hamlin had taken so much trouble over.

Was Edouard also under a spell right now? "Oh, lord, I hope not," Hamlin breathed, forcing himself not to gnaw his claws this time around. When he'd looked at them, he'd been sickened by how ragged and soiled they appeared, and in such a short time.

He tried to sleep, shifting to find a comfortable spot, and cursing the broken twigs and dried leaves that made up his bed. They cut and itched his bare skin, and the strange nocturnal sounds of the woods did little to soothe him.

By the time he felt comfortable enough, he tried to think of a plan for the morning. He didn't know how long this spell was supposed to last, but he needed to start traveling at daylight.

"Do goblins move around in the day?" he muttered, frowning. All those childhood hours wasted, ignoring illuminated ghost story manuscripts and supernatural learning. Then he sighed. "I'll try, anyway. I just hope I don't burst into flames when the sunlight touches me." What a way to die if that were the case.

$\bullet\ \bullet\ \bullet\ \bullet$

HAMLIN WOKE EXHAUSTED. Considering where he'd hidden himself, it came as no surprise that he barely slept. Dizzy and hungry, he nonetheless forced himself up, blinking the fog away as he crawled through the branches and looked around cautiously.

The woods were quiet, and the sunlight streamed through trees, branches, and leaves, providing him with a welcome feeling of comfort. He heard birds chirping and the occasional sounds of animals skittering and took heart. A glance down showed that he was still in goblin form, and in the daytime hours, his skin looked awful. It was a strange mixture of smooth and coarse—with some areas broken with disgusting gray bumps—and his muscles still felt tight and bunched.

Hamlin scrambled to his feet and went back toward the path. He might be hungry and tired, but his need to find Edouard was much stronger.

The world outside hadn't changed since the evening, but everything felt so foreign—more foreign than the change in height. Looking around him, Hamlin determined his direction and hurried down a path that he knew led to Edouard's castle. Just a way off to the left stood his parents' castle. He tried not to think of what could be happening at that moment within those walls; at the very least, he hoped that his parents were worried and doing what they could to bring him back, but he also knew that there was no way they could help him if he were caught. He had no way to speak to them.

The road toward Edouard's castle was difficult, given its busyness. Wagons, pedestrians, horses, and carriages seemed to come along one after another. Hamlin was continually forced to stop and take shelter behind a rock or tree, or anything, really, to avoid being spotted. A few times he found nothing and was forced to curl up on the road, hoping that those who passed him wouldn't notice him or if, they did, would mistake him for a particularly ugly rock.

The only good thing was knowing that he could survive in daylight, which, he suspected, meant that he wasn't a real goblin.

The distance he needed to cover was great, however, and Hamlin's fatigue and hunger spiraled till he thought he couldn't take another step forward without resting and eating. Unfortunately, he was also quite a distance from the nearest woodland; there were only occasional trees and what appeared to be a brook not too far away.

"I can drink, at least," he said, and he staggered toward the water, tripping over hidden roots and rocks, his dizziness making his vision much worse than before.

Once he reached the brook, he fell to his knees and started drinking the cold, clear water. When he was satisfied, he stared at his reflection, wincing at his transformation. Hamlin wanted to rant, to rage against the unfairness of it all, but only tears came out, and he wept for himself and for his mother.

So many stories had been passed down from generation to generation, all venerating one's One True Love. Judging from the reactions he'd seen at his half-brothers' weddings, many people still believed in it.

So why was his mother's marriage to his father such an issue? Why should she be punished for falling in love with a man who was just as madly in love with her, even if he was well above her station? Shouldn't that be lauded as a real-life example of the One True Love that people swooned over? Why should there be exceptions where love was involved? Why should money be a factor in people's perceptions? Why should children born to such marriages bear the "taint" of their parents' deep and sincere love?

Jealousy among those who couldn't find The Right One despite their connections, perhaps? Hamlin didn't know, and he was too tired to worry about it right now. Gathering his wits and dashing away the rest of his tears, he hardened himself for the remaining distance he'd yet to cover, as he stumbled back to his feet and hurried onward.

Water could only take him so far, unfortunately, and it wasn't long before he was staggering along in a foggy zigzag, his hand pressing against his swollen belly and a groan escaping his monstrous lips. "Egad," he croaked. "I could eat a damned horse!"

"That's not you, Your Highness. Besides, horse meat is revolting—fresh or roasted. Trust me on this."

Hamlin stumbled to a halt with a cry of surprise when a familiar figure swooped down before him to land on the grass. He almost wept for the second time as he reached out and took hold of Audwin, who allowed Hamlin to manhandle him a bit in a show of joy and relief. The raven even bit back a retort when Hamlin kissed his head several times.

"Audwin!" Hamlin cried, laughing, as he held the bird at arm's length. "I'm so glad to see you again!"

"Yes, yes, I know—steady now, steady! Loosen your hold a bit, or you'll crush me to death, and I won't be much help to you anymore!"

Hamlin set the bird down. "What happened last night?" he asked. "I had to escape the castle before I was cut into ribbons."

"I heard. Good thing you managed to do it. As for me, I was able to track down the culprit—though pawn is more like it. Mistress Alyda, the same witch who cursed Roderika. She's on her way to some place in the south, where there are mushrooms and roots and a good climate for aching bones. She was hired by your—uh—not-quite mother-in-law, but you've probably guessed that by now."

Hamlin nodded. "I did. Mama warned me some time ago about her spying on me and Edouard."

"Well, let's just say that the spell she cast on you isn't much more than a delaying tactic—in your case, anyway. I mean, it's really nothing more than an exercise in futility, considering the fact that your future with Edouard's been predetermined. You know—red string and all that." Audwin raised a wing like an arm and gestured with it.

Hamlin nodded again. "I'm guessing that Edouard knows about this," he said, though he meant it to be a question more than a statement. He desperately hoped that Edouard knew by now, anyway.

"Yes. I literally bumped into his messenger last night—but that happens when you've got two birds that shouldn't be flying about at such a hellish hour, off running emergency errands the way we were. Anyway, the bullfinch was on his way to Princess Aloysia, and he told me about Edouard's request to undo the spell."

"Can you?"

"I'm no magician, Your Highness, but the princess is. I expect her to arrive soon enough and set things to right."

"But I can't even communicate with humans right now—only animals, it seems. How can I talk to her like this?"

"You don't need to. I'll take care of it. I'm also hoping that Edouard would appear with her, but as you know, they don't live in the same castle anymore."

Hamlin swallowed, looking around. The road appeared to be deserted for the moment. "All right. What do we do now?"

"Follow me, Your Highness. All we need to do is to keep walking toward Edouard's castle, and she'll find us along the way."

With that, Audwin spread his wings and flew up, circling Hamlin for a moment before moving off, with the little goblin in tow. If he weren't so overcome with emotion at the moment, Hamlin would've realized what an odd pair they made—certainly a picture that could only be found in nursery stories.

Audwin led him down a smaller path that took him away from the main road and from the possibility of being caught by passersby or searchers sent by his parents. Hunger continued to gnaw away at his belly, but he soldiered on. Spell-breaking first, he reminded himself with gritted teeth, then feasting afterward.

The sun was almost directly above them, showing that it was near noon, when hoofbeats broke the silence. Hamlin stopped and looked around in a panic, searching for a rock or tree to hide behind. The horse had left the main road, judging from the increasing loudness of its movements, and Hamlin held his breath, hoping that it was help.

"Steady, Your Highness!" Audwin called as he sailed past Hamlin to vanish through the trees and in the direction of the horse. Then he started squawking wildly, and the horse stopped, neighing. There were other noises that followed, which all seemed to melt into each other in Hamlin's sleep-and-food-deprived brain.

Eventually he recognized hurrying footsteps, and through the shadows of trees, a figure burst through, calling out for him.

"Oh, heavens!" Aloysia cried, skidding to a halt, and she gaped at him. "Hamlin?"

Hamlin shrank back, and he nodded. "Yes, it's me," he said, and he realized too late that what he was saying wasn't doing him any good.

Aloysia blinked as she stared at him. Then she turned to look at Audwin, who hovered nearby. With a sigh, Aloysia walked forward and knelt before Hamlin, shaking her head and clucking.

"The things people do for love. And here I thought the world was too cynical for its own good," she muttered, raising her hands and closing her eyes. As Hamlin watched, her hands seemed to vanish into a soft mist that grew and grew till it seemed to swallow the whole world, leaving Hamlin standing alone.

Chapter 34

Edouard stood before his parents, watching and waiting with forced calm. Acceptance of that morning's outcome had sunk in—at around midnight, in fact, when he'd made his choice following an evening of cold silence between him and his mother and his refusal to appear at dinner.

He'd hardly slept, knowing that Hamlin was in trouble, and he wasn't there to help him, but Edouard had needed to be in the castle for a few hours more before taking that final, irrevocable step. He needed to face his parents one last time, to show them that he was not only capable of making hard decisions on his own but also willing to suffer any consequences that came with them.

He hadn't eaten breakfast, either. Though his choice had long been made, his stomach was still in knots when the cock crowed, and he didn't dare ingest even so much as a spoonful.

"And that's your decision?" King Rikard asked, his voice quiet and cold. He regarded his son across the table—the same library table at which Edouard had spent so many happy hours lost in books and manuscripts, much to his parents' delight. Now it was completely bare save for one book, which lay open before the king. A quill and a pot of ink stood next to it, within the king's reach.

"It is, Papa. I'm sorry for the pain it costs you, but I can't reconcile myself to your demands."

"The demands, as you know, Edouard, are simple. We don't care what gender you fancy. What we do care about is your lover's connections—if any. You're a prince, not a merchant, with a different set of obligations."

"I know, and I have to disagree with you. Respectfully, that is."

He watched his father exchange looks with his mother, who sat next to King Rikard without once uttering a word. She'd said all she wanted the previous day. There was nothing more for her to say to her son, it appeared. If only both of them could see Edouard well enough to realize just how much this decision had broken his heart, they wouldn't sit in icy judgment of their youngest boy.

Edouard had already let loose his emotions the previous night once he came to terms with the repercussions of his decision. It took him some doing, but he managed to convince himself that things would work out in the end. All he needed to do was to stick with his resolution, be true to himself, and honor his bond with Hamlin with a bravery that he'd never before expected of himself. He was so tired of rules. He'd lived within so many of them for so long, and all of them at his expense.

He wished that Hamlin were with him, helping him through the mind-numbing difficulty of being forced to choose by his own parents. As it were, he was completely alone—no friend, no confidante, no one to talk to or simply be with through the most awful moment of his life so far.

His decision could easily turn out to be the biggest mistake of his life, but he had no way of knowing. What would it matter if someone were with him, then? Who had the ability to look well into the future in order to learn how things worked out?

It wouldn't have mattered. Edouard realized that now: with or without a confidante, no one had the power to reassure him of the wisdom of his choice. All he could depend on was his heart and mind.

"Is there anything you wish to say, Clarimond?"

The queen shook her head, turning her gaze elsewhere and pointedly ignoring Edouard, who felt as though he were dying inside. King Rikard took the quill and dipped it in the ink pot. He read through the open page until he reached a particular line, on which he rested the quill.

He looked at Edouard again, this time his face nothing more than a blank, his voice its perfect match. "I strike your name from the family," he said, and he drew a line across the text. "I no longer recognize you as my son, Master Edouard. You're free to go where you wish, and the best of luck to you and your endeavors. The rest of the family will be informed of your disgrace, and none of their doors will be open to you."

Save for the doors of the cursed castle, Edouard thought. What choice did his aunt and uncle have at this point in time, after all?

He replayed his father's words in his head. Why even bother wishing him luck? Edouard swallowed and turned to his mother, who only watched him in the same cold silence as before. No recognition, no pity, no mercy—and all for what? There was time enough for Edouard to ponder the more difficult questions.

For now, he needed to leave the castle. He bowed and turned around, glad that he wasn't required to speak. He couldn't bear the thought of breaking down in front of his parents, and even as he fumbled for the library doors, he could barely see with the tears rapidly filling his eyes. The corridor was empty, thank the heavens, and he took advantage of that privacy to wipe the tears against his sleeve.

It would be embarrassing, yes—wasn't he known for his aloofness and intellect? He'd always had great mastery of his emotions, but now, he wasn't sure if that were true any more. Perhaps he was simply a master of choking his heart into suppressed numbness. Now, when grief overwhelmed him, he didn't quite know how to handle it, and he felt ashamed of his vulnerability.

Before long he was back in his room, collecting the things he was allowed to take, then it felt as though he'd only blinked twice before realizing that he was leading his horse out of the stables. He mounted, turning once to say goodbye to his servants, who stood in speechless shock. Word was spreading rapidly through the castle about his being disowned; he had no wish to stay long enough to be gawked at.

With one final glance, Edouard bade his home goodbye and galloped out of the courtyard and into the open road beyond the battlements. He'd get used to the freedom eventually, he realized, but first he needed to find Hamlin.

He turned in the direction of Queen Elfriede's castle, hoping that the message he'd sent the previous night had reached its intended recipient. The main road was quiet, and he slowed his horse, sometimes stopping him here and there as he strained his ears to listen. He heard nothing of significance for the first ten miles until he reached a bend on the road, which wound around the base of a low hill. Once he cleared that, he stopped his horse again and he strained his eyes to see what was going on up ahead.

There were figures in the shadows of some trees not too far from the road. One was dressed in white and probably gold, judging from the way the clothing glinted in the sunlight. The figure in white was kneeling or squatting before the second figure, which appeared to be curled up.

"Hamlin?" Edouard breathed, and leaned forward in the saddle, straining to see.

The faint squawking of a bird made his heart jump, and sure enough, above the two figures, a black bird flew in circles.

"Hamlin!" he cried. Edouard spurred the horse on. "Hamlin!"

The bird stopped and instantly flew toward him, and Edouard laughed as Master Audwin circled him this time before descending to rest on his shoulder. "It's good to see you, too, Master Audwin," he said, earning himself a soft peck against the side of his head. "Thank you for looking after Hamlin."

He spotted his sister's horse tethered to a small tree, and Edouard pulled his horse into a skid, then jumped off to run up to Aloysia and Hamlin. His sister was talking in soft, soothing tones, though she didn't touch him as he lay curled up on the grass—stark naked. Aloysia didn't seem to care; Hamlin's health and safety were obviously paramount in her mind. She was weaving spells around him, it appeared, because she moved her hands in gentle patterns around Hamlin's figure while dropping her voice to a whisper.

Edouard thought better than to interrupt, and he stood at a respectful distance, concern darkening his face, as he watched. He unclasped his long cape, draping it over one arm. At length Aloysia finished, and she sat back, resting her hands on her lap and sighing. When Edouard took a step forward, she glanced up and smiled.

"He's all right, Edouard," she said. "It was just a temporary spell—very easy to undo. Then again, I think it was nothing more than a half-hearted attempt at fulfilling a commission. Mistress Alyda didn't really try too hard."

Edouard nodded, falling on his knees once he reached Hamlin's side and throwing his cape over the pale, shivering figure. He gently placed his hands on his lover's shoulders and shook him. "I'm here, Hamlin. Everything's back to normal now. For you, that is," he said, the final bit appended hastily.

"Edouard?" Hamlin opened one eye and then the other. A wild flurry of emotions played across his face for a moment as he raised himself up and allowed himself to be pulled into an embrace. "I was on my way to your home when Aloysia found me."

A quick exchange of stories followed, though Edouard waited to be last to share his. He learned about Hamlin's fainting and the chaos when he woke, and he also head of Aloysia's quiet evening being shattered by the wild screeching of a little bird that wouldn't go away, no matter how many arrows Clovis threatened it with.

"I'd have gone out to look for Hamlin last night," she appended, "had it not been for the fact that I had to review the spell I needed to use. I've never done that before—undo someone else's spell, that is. Not knowing what kind of spell it was and how complicated it was going to be didn't help me one bit." She smiled at Edouard. "We're lucky Mistress Alyda didn't really seem to be interested in it."

"No, she was a great deal more concerned about keeping the money and traveling south," Edouard said, still holding Hamlin tightly against himself.

"And how did you manage to get out of Mama's sight?"

He hesitated, dropping his gaze to Hamlin's as he fought to come up with the right words. "I've been struck out. Disowned."

Hamlin's head snapped up, and Edouard suddenly saw his bright blue eyes wide in mute horror. Calmly, he recounted his experiences the previous night and that morning, leading up to his appearance there. Aloysia, Hamlin, and Master Audwin all listened in shock.

"What will you do now?" Aloysia asked in a hoarse whisper, her eyes swimming. "This isn't fair, Edouard. Where are you going? How will you survive?"

Edouard smiled, feeling tired. "I'm going to our aunt's. I—I decided to join them. I want to start over even though it means leaving so much of myself behind." He didn't realize till then just how monumental his decision was. It was one thing going over possibilities in his mind; it was another thing completely when he was sharing it with people—real, live people who cared deeply for him. And for one mad moment, Edouard wished that he weren't there, breaking their hearts, that he'd just gone off to Queen Franziska and settled down quietly, waiting for the first day of their hundred years' sleep. But that would also be the coward's way out, he told himself.

"Oh, Edouard," Aloysia said, shaking her head. "Are you sure about this? I mean, you can stay with us, you know, and plan your future with Hamlin there. You've got so much freedom now—so much independence."

"I don't think I can."

Edouard struggled for the right words, and when he spoke them, somehow they still didn't feel adequate enough—or precise enough—for what he needed to express. How could one satisfactorily say that the present didn't have a place for him? That he looked to the future with a good deal of hope, with the changes that a hundred years would bring? He had too much baggage to manage the present, Edouard thought, especially now that he'd been disowned and turned out of his parents' castle.

Word would have started spreading by now, and wherever he turned, he'd be the center of gossip and sordid stories. What was worse, he'd be dragging Hamlin and Queen Elfriede down with him. Edouard wouldn't be surprised if they were to be blamed for his defiance, and the heavens only knew what repercussions that would have. He was sure that people were simply waiting for the right scandal to create even more ammunition to use against Queen Elfriede.

And Aloysia? For all her good intentions, she'd be ordered not to welcome her disgraced brother or suffer something similar; it wouldn't be long before she'd be receiving her parents' directives. She'd be dragged down as well as poor Clovis, who'd done nothing wrong but attach himself to Edouard's family through marriage. And what of Clovis's family?

No, it was far better to start over with his aunt's family a hundred years from now.

"What about us?"

Edouard's thoughts scattered at the quiet question, and he blinked away the haze and looked down at Hamlin. How many times did he need to hurt people that day, he wondered? It was all Edouard could do to offer Hamlin a faint smile.

"You have to let me go, love," he whispered.

Chapter 35

Hamlin felt vulnerable—literally and figuratively—standing under the trees, naked but for Edouard's cape. He shivered, but not from the cold, as he waited for Edouard and Aloysia. They had gone a little way off to talk some more, and Hamlin was obliged to stay behind. It was a good thing in the end. At least he had time to consider, take several deep breaths, and regain his composure.

"Your Highness, I can wait for you."

Hamlin looked up to find Audwin perched on the lowest branch of the tree he stood under. "No, it's all right," he said. "Go along now and rest. I'm sorry for all the trouble I've been causing you, Audwin."

"It's no trouble at all, despite my usual complaints," the raven said, his voice gentle. It was a rare tone for Audwin, and when he used it, every word meant a great deal more to Hamlin. "I'm here for you, as you know."

"I do know, and I appreciate it. But I need time alone with Edouard."

"Very well. I'll wait for you at your father's castle."

Audwin flew off, leaving Hamlin feeling even colder and more dejected. He pulled Edouard's cape more tightly around himself, savored the feeling of the material against his bare skin, and tried not to think of what the future held for him.

At length he heard the sounds of a horse and rider, and Edouard appeared from the line of trees. As he neared, the shadows cast by the thick canopy of leaves revealed a pale, sunken-eyed young man who, Hamlin suddenly realized, was far different from the figure of pride and confidence he'd cut in his earlier years.

"It took Aloysia a while to accept my decision," Edouard said once he'd explained it all. He smiled, looking wan and lifeless, and if Hamlin knew of a magic spell that could change the course of Edouard's life, he'd be using it without a second's thought. "But she's willing to help me and, especially, you."

"I don't understand why you're doing this," Hamlin replied. "We could just as easily run away together if you'd like, and I wouldn't care. I've got nothing here, anyway."

"Yes, you do. You've got your mother, and she needs you."

Hamlin wished Edouard hadn't reminded him, but it was inevitable. His mother was foremost in his mind since his lover made that horrible announcement. "Papa's with her. She can cope, I'm sure."

Edouard kept his eyes on him, his face unreadable beyond the obvious fatigue. "Hamlin, you know very well that your father can't be at her side all the time. Think about his duties. He's also been busy grooming your half-brothers for the throne."

That much was true. King Reinhard wasn't a young man, and age had been taking its toll on him. He'd been preparing his sons for the inevitable and he'd been keeping Hamlin's half-brothers busy with different diplomatic trips as well as the usual inspection—as Hamlin always called it—of the kingdom, its borders, and all the towns and villages it contained. Meetings with counselors and ministers were also more frequent, and many tedious hours were being spent reviewing laws. Hamlin enjoyed the idlest time, and he'd taken care to remove himself from everyone's company in order to avoid distracting them.

With Edouard's insane scheme staring him in the face, Hamlin felt his uselessness bearing down on him in one asphyxiating wave. What would he do once Edouard was gone? What about his father and mother? The king, being a good deal older than the queen, was already marking his remaining years, and Queen Elfriede had yet to reveal her plans once Otto ascended the throne.

"Then you can stay with me and Mama," Hamlin said. "Why would it be any trouble for her? She's never had anything against you—or even your mama, despite her insults. Think about it, Edouard, we can travel together if you'd like, do everything we've talked of, with Mama's blessing. We can settle down in another country if you'd like."

"Hamlin, the times aren't as friendly elsewhere. England and France are at each other's throats. Granted, they've always been at each other's throats, but it doesn't look as though things are going to get better any time soon."

"Elsewhere in the continent, then?" Hamlin prodded, a little desperate now. "Those aren't the only countries we can travel to, you know."

"Love, please." Edouard kissed him.

He pulled back only slightly, and it was a trick that already Hamlin knew too well. Edouard wished not to be seen completely, preferring to hide his face in the shadows by leaning too close for Hamlin to see him fully.

"I've done enough damage here. I've torn my family apart, made myself unwelcome to my brothers and sister, and I've dragged you and your mother down with me. You know very well how much the aristocracy despises Queen Elfriede. Choosing you and my independence over my obligations has given them more reason to shun her. Your father's old, and he won't be around for too long. Your mother will be alone in a court lorded by a new king who hates her as much as everyone else does. Do you really want her to put up with that alone?"

Hamlin shook his head. "No, but I still don't understand why you have to take such a drastic step."

"I want—I *need* a new beginning. It's selfish of me, perhaps, but I refuse to add to the wreckage I've already caused." Edouard paused, a forced smile on his face, and he held Hamlin's face between his hands. "I'm a scholar, and I intend to continue what I do best. I'd like to make myself useful in my aunt and uncle's court after the hundred years are up. Perhaps I'll manage to be useful outside the court. Who knows? At least no one will know me, wherever I go, and I can settle down to a quiet and private life somewhere."

"Without me, of course," Hamlin cut in bitterly. He grasped Edouard's hands then gently but firmly pushed them away, stepping back. "I need to go home. I'm sure my parents are worried sick."

It took Edouard several seconds of awful silence before he could speak again. "We need to dress you first," he said, his voice unrecognizably thick.

* * * *

AS EXPECTED, HAMLIN became the inevitable butt of jokes on his return home—or at least of jokes among Mallory's idle group of friends. Not that Mallory tried hard to squelch the insults. In fact, the older prince had taken care to emphasize Hamlin's status as "half-brother" and "commoner-prince," working every devastating little detail regarding Hamlin's embarrassment into the conversation well before the rescued prince returned home.

Along with expressions of shocked relief from servants and a few courtiers came snide remarks and tittering that shadowed Hamlin's steps as he retired to his room. He barely managed it with his head held high. The humiliation was overpowering, and he dreaded having to show his face at dinner, let alone walk around the castle without blushing and pretending deafness.

The fact that he'd also just lost Edouard to the prince's mad scheme only served to make Hamlin's grief so, so painful.

Sleep helped, and Hamlin rested for much of the day, half-wishing that there was such a thing as a perpetual dream state, where he could lose himself and not face the world. But he was summoned to dinner, and his hunger forced him downstairs.

To his horror, Mallory and three visitors had already seated themselves, while the king and queen had yet to appear. They all sniggered, elbowed each other, and whispered when Hamlin made his appearance and hesitated at the door.

"Come on, Hamlin, don't just stand there," Mallory called out, his tone mocking, as he waved his younger half-brother over. "Time to eat!"

The sniggering continued as Hamlin took his place in apathetic silence. He was forced to face Mallory and the others, who'd taken up all the chairs on one side of the table. It was quite obvious that they'd done so on purpose, just as they'd gathered—on purpose—before King Reinhard and Queen Elfriede had arrived.

"So sorry to hear about your ordeal last night," one of the guests said, smirking. "It must've been terrible, being a goblin for several hours."

"Yes, all that trouble, having your life turned upside-down and the court turned inside-out," another piped up, nudging Mallory with his arm. "And for what?"

"Being Edouard's personal bum boy is apparently hazardous to your health," Mallory added, his eyes narrowing at Hamlin, who felt his blood drain away. News of Edouard's disgrace and its cause had already spread. "You might have good taste in men, but you're not very bright about other things. Like, oh, whose family he belongs to. You do realize how much Queen Clarimond hates your mother. In fact, we've all had great fun with the ban she'd placed on her family interacting with you."

"My sisters would think it rather romantic, actually," the third guest said. "They'd go on and on about forbidden love and some such. You really shouldn't be so harsh on little Hamlin."

"Well, I suppose he does his mother proud in this case. Is this sort of thing infectious? It does appear to be something inherited," Mallory replied, his voice taking on a harsher edge now, though his friends' tone remained mocking and light.

"You know, I've never met anyone who's managed to destroy a family like this. I suppose some congratulations are in order. There's a first time for everything."

"Edouard shouldn't be blameless. Hamlin's got good taste in men, but Edouard really could've done better; otherwise, he wouldn't be out there, shunned by everyone he knows, am I not right?"

"Strange things happen when you let your hanging bits do the talking."

Hamlin's first urge was to leave the room, but he held firm, biting his tongue and helping himself to food as abuse after abuse was heaped on him. If he was going to remain with his mother, he needed to learn how to endure the worst insults. His physical and emotional fatigue also didn't help, anchoring him to his chair like an awful weight and keeping him from fleeing.

Edouard was right about how people would be using his disgrace against him and his mother. In his father's castle, the levels of vitriol had shot up, disdain shifting from whispered remarks to open insults. What more outside the kingdom, where the aristocracy gossiped non-stop and added fuel to the fire? His mother wouldn't be welcome anywhere, and while Hamlin didn't care a jot as to where he'd be allowed to mingle, the thought of Queen Elfriede's total isolation from her peers cut him deeply.

She needed him more than ever, and Hamlin was glad that he wasn't so weak as to abandon his mother to the heartlessness of courts all over the land. When his parents finally appeared, the conversation had already shifted to other things, and Hamlin, feeling sick and utterly wretched, could only manage a nod in greeting before turning his attention back to his food, which he vomited once he was in the safety of his bedroom.

Chapter 36

The first task that Edouard took on after entering his aunt and uncle's castle was to sit Roderika down and help divert her by making her read book after book. The princess, feeling bored, didn't put up a fight and soon lost herself between pages of illuminated romantic manuscripts.

"Well—better than nothing, I suppose," Edouard muttered when he caught sight of his cousin's literary choices. He sat down across the table from her, opening a book on philosophy. The library was clean, neat, and sublime in its calm; it almost felt spiritual, and Edouard looked forward to reading as much as he could.

There were only three days left before Roderika's day of reckoning, and the castle was beginning to take on a grim and anxious feel. Edouard overheard servants suddenly questioning their decisions to stay. Some left with many emotional apologies to their monarchs, but most overcame their doubts and remained.

With that, servants immediately busied themselves to preparing the castle for the next century, but they also worked at the monumental task of easing their nerves. Edouard felt ambivalent toward their methods. On one hand, he appreciated the bustle and the noise, and on the other hand, their bubbling anxiety was palpable, and sometimes walking past them set his teeth on edge.

His guilt had been eating away at him. Since his arrival, he hadn't been sleeping much, his mind filling itself with images of Hamlin and Aloysia, his parents, and other acquaintances.

For the first few days, he'd fallen ill but, as it happened, rest and food were all he needed, with his aunt offering him a much-needed ear. After a good deal of cajoling, she'd convinced him to open up about his troubles, and once he started talking, he couldn't stop. She'd listened more than she'd advised, stroking his damp hair and hot forehead and nearly making him break down in tears.

He'd never had anything like a comforting touch from his mother. Through the years, when he'd fallen ill, he'd had nothing but visits from the physician, accompanied by an occasional viewing by his mother, though there's been no real emotional connection between them—just an in-scrutable, assessing look with a few words of congratulations for being a strong child before she left the nursery or his room.

When Edouard finally recovered and was up and about again, he was a mere shadow of his former self. He conversed easily enough, spent time with his cousin and entertained her, explored the castle, and did everything he'd always enjoyed while visiting his aunt and uncle, but those moments felt awfully hollow. Edouard spent his days in a numbed daze until a voice in the back of his head chided him for his mood and ordered him to help poor Roderika, who was very much a victim in her own story. So he took on the task of being his cousin's informal tutor and introduced her to books—lots of them.

"You know, cousin, I envy you."

Edouard blinked and glanced up, his concentration gone. "What?"

"I hope I find someone who'll love me the way you and Hamlin love each other," Roderika said, her face clouded as she rested her chin on her arms, which she folded on the book that lay open before her.

"Of course you will," Edouard stammered, blushing. His aunt had been talking? Good grief, but aristocrats are so mind-numbingly idle! "You shouldn't doubt that."

"I don't know. I've known plenty of people whom I thought were my friends, but no one wanted to stay with us."

"You really shouldn't blame them, Roderika. It's a difficult decision for anyone to make. I'm sure they'll miss you just as much as you miss them."

The princess sighed, pursing her lips as she stared at the table. "I don't know about that. Some of them didn't even bother saying goodbye." She paused. "It isn't fair, you know. I never asked for this."

Edouard listened to her, touched. "A lot of things in life aren't fair, and that's the way of things, unfortunately. There's a purpose for them, I'm sure, and we never find out what it is right away. Sometimes it takes years—in our case, a hundred."

"Like you leaving Hamlin behind like this. There's a purpose for it?"

"It's complicated, Roderika. Sometimes I'm convinced that I know what I'm doing, and sometimes I wonder if I'm going mad."

Roderika sat up, turning the page of her book. "That's a big sacrifice you're making, cousin. Leaving the person you love the most for his own good? That must be dreadful."

"It is, yes. I wouldn't wish it on anyone, trust me."

The princess finally glanced up and met his gaze, her eyes darkened and thoughtful, her air quite melancholy. "I wonder if people will laugh at me when I wake up. A hundred years would've passed by, and I'd be a century behind in what I know."

"We're all wondering about the future. It'll be quite a jolt, but we've surrounded ourselves with people who'll stick with us through everything."

"I don't know if I could that I understand why Mama and Papa did this. I mean, you know." Roderika paused and waved a hand to indicate something more encompassing than the library. "I suppose it would've been easy to hate them for making me and everyone else go through with the curse, but I can't find it in myself to resent them. They did what they did out of love, I think."

"Parents do some of the most maddening things out of love for their children, yes." Could he say the same for his? Edouard sighed. Then he frowned at his cousin. "Why are you philosophizing over this all of a sudden? It never used to bother you."

Roderika shrugged, offering him a sheepish little smile. "I don't know, really. I think it's got everything to do with the fact that I'm running out of time, and I can't stop it."

"We're all in this, cousin. We'll see each other through this." Edouard nodded at Roderika's book. "Now go on and read. Fretting over something we can't control won't do us any good."

Roderika smiled, visibly relaxing, and went back to reading. Edouard, for his part, couldn't get himself to focus as he had before. His thoughts kept drifting to Hamlin, and he found himself going back and forth about whether to contact the younger prince to give him a choice to join him at the enchanted castle. He kept recalling the stricken look on Hamlin's face during their last conversation, his lover's desperate suggestions, and his bitter farewell.

What he'd do to erase that memory, make things better for both of them. But he believed that this was his best option and that leaving Hamlin to look after his mother was the best thing he'd ever done in his life.

"Take good care of yourself, love," he whispered, a faint, fond smile lighting his face, though his eyes took nothing in even as they were fixed on the pages of his book.

• • • •

CLOVIS AND ALOYSIA visited him the following morning, and their meeting, surprisingly, didn't suffer under the cloud of immense grief, though there was palpable sadness. They'd all gone through the process in their own separate ways, and though Edouard still found it difficult to say goodbye all over again, he was grateful to be given one more chance to talk to them.

For the most part, their visit was all about Edouard's final requests involving them as well as Hamlin and Queen Elfriede.

"I'd really appreciate it if you could spend some time with them, even if it's only once a year," he said, to which Aloysia rolled her eyes. "I'm serious, Aloysia."

"I know you are, and you know very well that it'd be incredibly stupid of either of us to avoid them the way everyone is now. I've started writing to Her Majesty, you know, and she's written me back. I hope to teach her how to communicate with animals as I've a feeling that Master Audwin still has a role to play in this affair."

Edouard chuckled. "Oh, do you now? All right, then. I'm content."

"You know, you'll never be forgotten," Clovis spoke up, glancing at his wife, who gave his hand a squeeze. "I've been writing—documenting, I suppose—your story. Even if your family refuses to acknowledge you, you'll be the stuff of legend in ours." He grinned.

"And your children and their children's children and so on and so forth can enjoy my sordid adventures. Am I right?"

"Pretty much." Clovis's smile faded, and when he spoke, the edge of sadness was back. "We hope to raise our children correctly—the right way. Maybe it's a silly dream, but when you wake up after a hundred years, I'd like our descendants to welcome you into the family, knowing full well what your story is."

Perhaps the final judgment would be made by Time itself. Edouard quite liked that idea, though it was uncomfortably romantic and sentimental.

Hamlin must have rubbed off on him. He certainly wouldn't have gotten that from his parents.

"You can't guarantee anything, I'm afraid," he said with a rueful little smile.

"We'll try our damnedest, then."

Edouard nodded, swallowing the lump that formed in his throat. "Thank you. Both of you. I wish I knew how to give blessings, but you have them, anyway."

Before long, Aloysia and Clovis bade the cursed court farewell; Edouard enjoyed the longest and tightest embrace he'd ever had from his sister. Even Clovis swept him up in his arms despite Edouard's height, and Clovis pulled away, his eyes reddening.

"Be well, you two," Edouard said as he stood by their waiting coach while they boarded.

"Edouard," Aloysia said, leaning out the window after the door was shut. She reached out, and he gave her his hand. "Have faith."

"I'm trying." He gave her hand a kiss, but she didn't let go. There was an odd light in her eyes as she regarded him.

She opened her mouth as though to counter him, but then seemed to change her mind as she closed her mouth again, this time to smile at her brother fondly. "Goodbye, Edouard."

"Goodbye."

Edouard stepped away, and the coach jerked into motion, slowly rumbling out of the main courtyard. Aloysia and Clovis both stuck their heads out of the coach, and they waved. He waved back, his heart overcome by the realization that he wasn't going to see them again. Their words offered him some comfort, and while he wasn't sure if their plan of preparing their descendants for his awakening would work, he was still grateful for their concern and their efforts at ensuring that he wasn't going to be alone or forever cut off from family.

He glanced at the sky and blinked away the gathering tears. "Bless you," he whispered, hoping that the wind would somehow carry his words. Strange how life worked, he thought. It wasn't too long ago when he'd have scoffed at such a ridiculous notion of wind and messages. But not anymore. Not anymore.

Chapter 37

Hamlin watched the sky overhead, wondering what time it was—or, rather, what day it was. He was curious, and he wanted to care, but he still couldn't find it in himself to do so. He'd been seeking shelter from the world in his favorite childhood retreat, lying on the grass the way he used to, wondering why the carefree innocence of the past was gone and gone forever. Was there such a thing as a spell that would bring it all back?

One True Love—what utter shit it was. Nothing but stupid stories made by stupid storytellers in hopes of teaching stupid lessons to stupid listeners. Hamlin wanted nothing more to do with it, though it pained him if his mind simply grazed the surface of any subject involving romantic love.

How did separating oneself from the person he purported to love be a mark of devotion? Especially if that separation meant "forever," with no hope of communicating in any way?

"What utter shit," he muttered.

"It's Roderika's fifteenth birthday today, Your Highness."

"Go away, Audwin. I don't want to hear it."

"I just wanted to share."

"What for? Do you think that I could convince him to get over his insanity? You're better off telling him that directly."

Audwin snorted from his hiding place somewhere in the private garden. Hamlin didn't bother looking for his friend. In fact, for the past two weeks, he hadn't bothered doing much of anything. "I thought I'd clear up the nature of the day in case you're wondering, and I'm quite sure that you are. It's mid-morning, and the sun sets at five-thirty today. That's when poor Roderika's curse will take effect."

Hamlin's chest tightened. "I hate you," he snapped, turning to his side and closing his eyes against the world. "I didn't want to know."

"You do know, and you still have a chance to do something about it."

"I can't leave my mother, Audwin! You know that! She'll be alone!"

"Darling, who're you talking to?"

Hamlin gasped and sat up, turning around to find his mother standing at the entrance to the private garden, looking around her in confusion. "No one, Mama. I was—I was just having a conversation with myself. It helps clear my head sometimes."

Queen Elfriede looked doubtful, eyeing him with narrowed eyes. After all these years, he'd never convinced her that Audwin really did exist. But when he blushed, she sighed and smiled, walking up to him and taking a seat on the nearest bench. She patted the space beside her, and Hamlin scrambled to his feet and obediently sat down. His mother took one of his hands in hers and stared at it in silence for a moment, clearly considering what she was going to say next.

"Hamlin," she said at length, giving his hand a gentle squeeze. "Time's running out. You need to get ready and go."

"Go where?"

"Why, to Franziska's castle, of course!"

Hamlin stared at her, shocked. "You can't be serious, Mama," he stammered. "I don't want to leave you alone."

"Are you my protector now?" she replied, bemused. "I never asked for one, though I thank you all the same—my brave knight."

"Mama, I'm serious. I can't follow him. You can't order me." He shook his head. "Don't make me regret pouring my heart out to you over this. Besides, you forced it out of me."

"You were making yourself ill from all that pent-up grief. I needed to force it out of you, or you would've died of a broken heart. And, yes, I really do believe that a person can die from a broken heart, even though you've always scoffed at it."

Hamlin stayed quiet, looking elsewhere.

"I love you more than life itself, but I'll wring your neck if you insist on being stubborn."

Her smiled softened when Hamlin sighed heavily and rolled his eyes.

"Darling, there's no greater joy in this world than to love and be loved—unconditionally. I've been extremely lucky with your father, and I'm doubly blessed to have you. And for all the trouble I've put up with because of other people's ignorance—willful ignorance, at that—every moment that I'm alive and in your father's company, all the gossip and insults mean nothing in the end. They might weigh me down sometimes, but they make me regret nothing. And you'll understand just how true that is when you yourself experience what I have."

Hamlin had to stare at the grass, not daring to speak.

"And any mother worth her salt wants nothing more than to see her child happy, regardless of her biases, her opinions, or whatever anyone else thinks. Do you understand?"

"I'll be losing so much if I go, Mama."

"Every choice we make comes at a price. Edouard's already living with it. He's risked everything for you and for his happiness."

"You won't have anyone to confide in when others trouble you."

"Hamlin, I'm a grown woman. I'm a queen, for heaven's sake," Queen El-friede replied, laughing gently. "I can protect myself well enough, and when your father eventually dies, well, I have my own private retreat elsewhere, and I'll withdraw there when Otto and Hedda take over. I'll be away from the court for good, and in that great house I hope to live the rest of my days with only my trusted servants to look after my needs. Besides, I also have a friend who'll be left behind when the curse takes effect. I won't be completely alone."

Hamlin looked up at her, and she was still smiling.

"Aloysia, dearest. She and I've been corresponding ever since Edouard was cut off. She's a lovely young lady—a bit odd in some ways, but a devoted sister who's also willing to give up much for her brother's happiness. And she's teaching me how to communicate with animals, though she won't explain why. I think she said that certain birds require a special language—or something. I've no idea what she's talking about."

"I don't want to leave you," Hamlin said. He lost his fight for control, and he wept.

"You never will, love. I'll never leave you, either. It won't be obvious right now, but it will be in time. Hamlin, listen to me. If you wish to honor your father and me—or what your father and I have—you have to go to your Edouard. Stay with him. Brave everything that tries to make a mockery of your love for him. He's worth the pain and the trouble, and so are you."

Hamlin barely heard the rest of what his mother said. Overcome with grief, he held her in a desperate bid for comfort, and she murmured a steady stream of reassurances and affection as she embraced him. He admitted to himself that he was terrified of the future—of how his decision would affect his parents' lives forever.

Would he wake up after a hundred years to learn how broken-hearted his mother had been and how her loneliness and grief drove her to an early grave? What about his father? They might not be close, considering King Reinhard's duties, which assured his absence from Hamlin's life almost every day, but the man still doted on his youngest son and never faltered in his expressions of pride over Hamlin's accomplishments.

This was going to take a bit of getting used to, Hamlin told himself in a vain attempt at levity. Eventually he gave up and simply hung on to his mother in silence, his sobs dissipating as she gently stroked his back.

"Take this with you, darling," she said after another moment of silence, and Hamlin pulled away to find her pressing something in his hand.

It was a lock of braided hair whose ends were tied together with a red ribbon, forming a circle. He looked closely and found both gray and blonde strands woven into each other, and he glanced at his mother, who regarded the braided circle of hair with a soft smile of fondness.

"My hair and your father's," she said. "Take that with you and remember us. If you find yourself faltering or doubting your sacrifice, or if others try to undermine your and Edouard's love, take it out of your pocket and remind yourself. Believe me, Hamlin—you're the son of two of the most stubborn people in the world. I daresay you've enough courage for the both of you." Queen Elfriede met his gaze. "I spoke those same words to the most remarkable boy some years ago, and I hope he believes them."

• • • •

HAMLIN HESITATED BEFORE the gates, and he raised his eyes to take in the imposing structure of Queen Franziska's castle. Behind the battlements, a quieter and more sober celebration was taking place.

It was Roderika's fifteenth birthday, and within a few hours, she was set to prick her finger on a spindle—though no one knew how such a thing would appear, but magic was real and it would have its way, so it was useless fretting over details. It was going to happen in one of the tower rooms, he was told. Hamlin also knew that around four o'clock, the gates would be closed to the world, not to be opened for a hundred years.

"And this is where we say goodbye, Your Highness," Audwin said as he flew down to rest on Hamlin's arm. "For now, that is."

Hamlin regarded his old friend with a fond smile. "At least I'll be too busy sleeping to miss you."

"I'll keep myself busy. This old body needs to rest, finally, and I'll have to find new forms to take until the hundred years are up. I'll keep an eye on the king and queen for you—as promised. I just hope they don't notice me and try to shoot me down."

"Mama's learning how to talk to animals. I think I see Aloysia's purpose now."

"That's a relief. I must admit that I look forward to being her new confidante. Huh. I must've eaten something bad to feel something so uncharacteristically pleasant. And, yes, I promise to tell you everything about your parents' remaining years when you wake up. I'm sure they'll want me to give you countless messages as well."

Hamlin laughed, touched. "You've always been my best friend, Audwin. Thank you."

"It's a pleasure. It'll be interesting to see your response to a century's worth of changes when you wake up."

"I'm glad you'll still be with me—though in a different form."

"I'm your guardian. I'm mystically bound to you. I'll leave this earth only when you die, which, I hope, won't be for at least another fifty years after the century's up."

Hamlin shrugged, chuckling. "Let's hope we all wake up to peacetime." Something in his gut assured him that they would.

"And more advanced and progressive thinking—well, that goes without saying." With that, Audwin bowed his head, flapped his wings, and flew away. Hamlin watched his friend soar, his own heart soaring with him, till Audwin vanished from view.

Hamlin patted his horse, murmuring gentle words to the creature, which he'd also be taking with him to the next century. They were soon trotting down the road and through the gates, receiving a few scattered greetings from people. Eventually Hamlin stopped and dismounted while a man took his horse and Hamlin gave orders regarding his bags. They were to be brought to a guest room somewhere, and he didn't worry too much about finding it. For now, with the sun nearing the horizon, he needed to find Edouard.

King Friedrich and Queen Franziska were entertaining the few ministers and courtiers who wished to stay with them, so Hamlin raced off to where he knew Edouard would be. It was the same room where he'd had his first real fight with the other prince all those years ago. It took a bit of effort to find it again, with his mind jumbled from the emotional day, and he had to stop a couple of servants for directions.

At length he found it and, after breathing several times to calm himself, he knocked and was ordered to enter.

"Edouard?" he said as he stepped in.

Edouard was sitting at a table, reading, and at the sound of Hamlin's voice, he quickly turned and stood, nearly knocking over his chair. They stared at each other in silence at first. "Hamlin? What—you're here to join me?"

Hamlin nodded, closing the door behind him. Edouard continued to stare in amazement, and Hamlin started to knot his fingers as doubt began to cloud the moment. "I am," he said. "I can't think of any other place I want to be. I hope I'm not spoiling your plans or anything of the sort."

Was he supposed to give a long speech about his feelings and destiny and the hundred years' sleep? Just as he started to fumble mentally, he was swept up in a tight embrace and kissed senseless. Well—he'd have plenty of time now to ponder all kinds of subjects. For the time being, he wanted nothing more than to make good his recent promise to the most remarkable woman he knew, and he gave back as well as he took, holding Edouard and kissing him back with equal energy.

There was time enough for so many things.

In fact, when Roderika's fateful moment finally came, both princes had taken care to be back in Edouard's room, their shoes kicked off, and they lay under blankets in his bed, holding each other and talking idly as they waited.

They felt the moment when Roderika pricked her finger in one of the castle's tower rooms, and what a strange experience it was. The room seemed to spin, colors and shapes seeming to melt into each other. Hamlin felt a pressure against his chest, but it only lasted a few seconds before he was able to breathe again. The air felt warm and heavy, and from some indeterminate distance, he could hear people crying out in surprise or alarm or running about.

The drowsiness gradually came, and Hamlin turned to kiss Edouard, his eyes feeling heavier. "Enough talk. I suppose I'll see you in a hundred years."

"Will you still love me when you see that I'm a hundred years behind in fashion?"

"That's easy enough to fix." When Hamlin sensed a shadow of wavering nervousness in Edouard, he grinned, kissing him again. "Don't fret over us. I'm not going anywhere. I'll be the first thing you'll see when you open your eyes." He fumbled around his pockets, drew out the braided lock of hair, and pressed it against his heart.

"I love you," Edouard whispered, awed joy lacing his words even as his eyes drooped. "I *love* you."

"I love you, too—more than I can say."

Edouard smiled sleepily and moved his head to let it rest against Hamlin's. Silence fell with the fading of the sun, the smell of fresh roses permeated the air, and all was still in the enchanted castle.

Don't miss out!

Visit the website below and you can sign up to receive emails whenever Hayden Thorne publishes a new book. There's no charge and no obligation.

https://books2read.com/r/B-A-LFQC-VYDV

BOOKS 2 READ

Connecting independent readers to independent writers.

About the Author

I've lived most of my life in the San Francisco Bay Area though I wasn't born there (or, indeed, the USA). I'm married with no kids and three cats.

I started off as a writer of gay young adult fiction, specializing in contemporary fantasy, historical fantasy, and historical genres. My books ranged from a superhero fantasy series to reworked and original folktales to Victorian ghost fiction.

I've since expanded to gay New Adult fiction, which reflects similar themes as my YA books and varies considerably in terms of romantic and sexual content.

While I've published with a small press in the past, I now self-publish my books. Please visit my site for exclusive sales and publishing updates.

Read more at https://haydenthorne.com.